Coffee
& THE
Contingency
PLAN

JESSICA COSTELLO

Cover Design: Sam at Ink and Laurel www.inkandlaurel.com

Editor: Stella at stellawilkinson.com/editing

For anyone foolish enough to have that one special daydream. The one you can't stop thinking about no matter how many people try to tell you it's impossible. Don't listen. Chase that daydream, and don't stop until it's reality.

Chapter One

VAL

Behind every morning person is an addiction to coffee. What, you thought I made it through the last three years of college merely out of spite and ambition? I tried that routine as a naive freshman, but the moment I discovered the masterpiece that is a white chocolate mocha from Give 'er the Beans, my favorite coffee shop located a stone's throw from campus, my life changed.

It took some time to get here. My first mistake was trying to slug a cup of their dark roast in desperation the morning after an all night bender—of studying, obviously. Turns out black coffee was too rich for my blood there at the beginning. My handwriting for the essay I wrote later that morning had been comparable to an inflatable tube man trying to make his way through a windstorm. After swearing off it for months afterward, my best friend here at college, Breegan McCormick, talked me into trying again. She ordered for me —a blended drink that was ninety-five percent sugar and a little caffeine. My order has changed multiple times since then, but I always come back to my beloved white chocolate mocha.

Which is why I'm here at Beans on the last Friday before classes, shuffling into my favorite booth by the window with a large latte in hand. The name of this place made me giggle the first time I found it, but the owners are a husband and wife duo, and the husband had a stint in racing before he got injured in a terrible wreck. The name made more sense, along with the switch to a safer profession.

It's a cozy little spot, only steps from campus with plenty of windows and natural light. I fell in love with space immediately. There are green plants in all the nooks and crannies, and the place is covered from floor to ceiling in wood. The walls are filled with farmhouse-style knick knacks, interesting car parts, and art by local artists. The large counter toward the back of the space is covered in pallet wood, and I'm obsessed with it.

It's a toss up between here and the campus library where I spend more time during the school year. But I only come here early in the morning. With its proximity to campus, it's easy to finish homework before heading to class.

Before I knew better, I stopped in at all times of the day for a change in scenery when I'd spent too many hours in the library. The coffee smell itself helps me focus, and their cinnamon brown sugar scones are my favorite carb—and that's saying something, because I love my carbs. But now I know that these hours before the rest of the world wakes up are their own kind of magic.

I look around at the scattered patrons as I pop the top off my cup to get the liquid to perfect sipping temperature. Everyone is minding their own business. And the best part? Everyone is *quiet*. It's like we all have this unspoken agreement to leave each other alone.

I pull everything I need from my backpack, organizing it all in front of me, including my favorite writing utensils. I've been called an office supply junkie a few times in my life, and I can't even be mad—it's an accurate assessment. Back-to-school is my favorite time of year, not only because I'm eager to graduate and get out of here, but because the sales are a great excuse to stock up on all my favorite things while they're cheap.

I unzip my pencil pouch and pull out my new Lilac Haze Stabilo highlighter to mark up the academic schedule I printed from the North Iowa University website. I still can't believe the number of months I have left here on campus is down to single digits. My senior year begins next week and if all goes to plan, I'll be on the first plane out of this state as soon as I've tossed my cap in the air. I'm still not sure about the destination, but the bigger the city, the better.

I'm not sure how long I've been bent over my DIY planner I made out of a journal over the summer when the bell above the door chimes, but judging by the way my spine cracks and pops as I sit up, it's been a while.

Squeak, squeak, squeak.

The sound of wet shoes on the tile floor has me sending a glare in the direction of the coffee shop's newest patron. But my glare loses its spark as soon as I recognize the unruly brown curls and black-rimmed glasses.

I set my highlighter down, wiping my hands on my shorts. My heart beats overtime watching him move toward the counter, unaware the entire female population is watching him. The pretty blonde barista's mouth splits into a smile as he arrives, as if this isn't his first time here. If that's true, how have I never seen him here before?

I haven't seen him since a chance sighting on campus last semester. We walked right past each other, but where my focus had been on him, his was on the pretty brunette tucked under his arm as they flirted, walking the main stretch through campus.

Brody Ryan.

The guy I've had a ridiculous crush on since high school is standing right in front of me.

He was a student athlete at our rival school. My high school best friend, Hannah, was lead photographer for the yearbook staff, so I frequented all sporting events by her side. She usually had to drag me along, but for baseball games against the Freeport Falcons, I was a willing spectator. Two words: baseball pants.

My eyes lower to his ass, purely out of habit. Although he's wearing a pair of black athletic shorts instead of white baseball pants, it still looks as good as I remember.

We've never met, Brody doesn't have a clue who I am. And I've harbored a crush on the guy for years. That thought mixed with the sight of the barista leaning over the counter, ample cleavage on display, I shake my head to clear him from my thoughts, annoyed with myself. Nope, not desperate enough for his attention, nor do I have the same—assets with my barely-B cups.

When I found out we were attending the same college freshman year (and I spotted him with a different, but also beautiful girl—*I'm sensing a theme here*), I was excited. For about a millisecond.

But back then I was still working through everything I'd been through those last two years of high school. Those thoughts always have a way of bringing me back down to earth.

So instead of shooting my shot with him, I put on my blinders and got to work instead. I haven't thought of him much since. By now it's too late for young and naïve Valerie Boyd's daydreams to come true.

And I won't even be around here a year from now, I remind myself.

I resume my work, but look up just as Brody turns for the door, coffee in-hand. His brown curls are still damp, like he came here fresh from the shower. Before I can tear my eyes away, his land on mine, catching me staring. I feel my cheeks flush when he flashes me a smirk, his free hand raising in a wave.

I drop my highlighter to wave back. Except in my excitement, my clumsy hands catch on the rim of my nearly full cup, which I'd forgotten to recap.

It happens in slow motion. I want to stop the cup from overturning, but before I can force my body to move, there's coffee everywhere—including the spread I'd been working on in my planner.

I stand up, but my shorts have already been saturated. My only saving grace is the temperature cooled enough to save me from third-degree burns.

"Oh my god," someone murmurs. A few people gasp. I look up in time to see Brody retrieving a rag from the hipster-bearded barista, who's eyeing my table with pity. Great, who *didn't* see me make a fool of myself?

Hipster barista smiles and nods in answer to whatever Brody's saying to him across the counter. I turn away, afraid to look.

I grab for napkins from the holder at my table, but there are only three left. I do what I can with them, but it's not nearly enough for the mess I've made, and they're saturated in seconds.

Footsteps approach my table, and I know it's him before lifting my gaze.

This is so not how I envisioned meeting him someday.

"Looks like you could use a little help," Brody says, an amiable smile on his face. He gets straight to work sopping up the mess in front of me. "You didn't burn yourself, did you?"

"No, but this is so embarrassing," I say, letting my hair fall like a curtain of curls so he can't see my pink cheeks. "Thanks for your help."

"Can't say I've ever seen someone so excited to say hi

before—except maybe my three-year-old niece. She spills things all the time and I still adore her, so don't feel bad."

He flashes me a lopsided grin when I turn to him, heart stuck in my throat.

I huff out a laugh that sounds more like a snort. "You know," I say, reaching for the towel, my fingertips brushing his hand. Electricity crackles up my arm in the wake of the innocent touch.

"Uh," I say, trying to unscramble my brain. "Let me take that. I'm sure you've got somewhere to be. But thank—"

"Order for Brody," Hipster Barista calls across the quiet space.

Brody turns toward his name, letting go of the rag. "Be right back," he smiles, turning toward the counter. I watch him go, his sandalwood scent wafting straight toward me as he moves.

I make eye contact with the smiling Hipster Barista over his shoulder, and look away, embarrassed. As I do inventory on my soggy belongings, I sigh in relief at seeing my leather-bound journal holding all my favorite quotes is untouched by the mess I made.

Its pages are full of quotes I've collected. I started the tradition back in high school, per my mom's recommendation, when she started finding scraps of paper with my scribbles all over the house. She bought me my first journal, and I've continued collecting them on pages ever since, adding anything from book quotes and lyrics to poetry and powerful lines I hear or see. I set the journal in my bag, thinking of my mom, until I hear two paper coffee cups land on the table.

"Think you can refrain from throwing this one at me?" Brody asks, sliding a cup my way.

"What's this?"

"A new coffee for your trouble." His smile has the butterflies in my belly living their best life.

My eyebrows scrunch. "You didn't have to do that," I say even as I grab it. "How'd you know my order?"

He tosses a thumb toward the counter, "You come here enough, Otis the barista remembered your order—white chocolate mocha, right?"

His green eyes sparkle under thick-rimmed glasses as I meet them and nod.

He leans a hip against the back of the booth across from me, somehow making it look effortless. "Mind if I join you for a bit?"

I look at my belongings lying out to dry and shrug. "It's not like I can get much accomplished at the moment, so why not?" I try to smile, but it feels more like a grimace. Ugh, why am I so awkward?

He chuckles, settling in across from me. Our bare knees brush with his movements. "Yeah, my bad."

"It's not your fault I'm a klutz."

"You're right," his gaze drops to his hands clutching his coffee, then returns to mine. "If I could do it all over again, I wouldn't change a thing."

"You wouldn't even save me the embarrassment of throwing my morning caffeine across the table for all to see?" He shakes his head. "Why not?"

"Because your embarrassed blush is adorable."

At his words, I feel my cheeks heat all over again and look down to try to hide it.

"Have we had a class together or something? You look familiar."

I nearly choke on a sip of coffee. "I don't think so."

"My name is Brody," he says, holding his hand out across the table.

"Nice to meet you, Brody," I say, reaching out to shake his hand, which engulfs mine. My skin tingles as I pull away.

I sip my coffee for something to do. *Why does he make me feel so damn nervous?*

He laughs, watching me. His own cheeks take on a pink hue, and it makes me feel less awkward. "That was my way of trying to get your name, but let me just come out and ask—what's your name?"

I run my fingernail along a groove in the table, contemplating how terrible an idea it is to let him get to know me. Or how embarrassing it is that I already know his name, but he had to ask for mine.

"What do you think it is?" I ask, making a game of it.

He sits back in his seat, finger and thumb at his chin in contemplation as he leans his head this way and that. "Rachael."

I smile and shake my head.

"Nicole, Rebecca," I continue to shake my head, so he keeps trying. "Hannah," he tries next and I laugh, which gets him excited. "Did I get it?" His eyes are alight with humor, and it hits me—I can't believe he's sitting across from me and we're having an actual conversation.

"No, but it's my high school best friend's name."

His eyes turn to slits. "Really? So you're V—"

My ears perk since he's got the right letter, and he notices, if that cocky smile is any indication.

"Vanessa?"

I sigh, "Still no, but I thought you had it there for a second."

"So it starts with a V?"

I shrug, unsure if I want him to get it right.

"Vivian? Veronica? Viola? Violet!" He points across the table, sure of himself. I continue shaking my head before he says, "Valerie!"

The smug look drops off my face, and he notices before I can recover.

"Did I get it right, Valerie? Val, maybe?"

I pull at the four-leaf clover pendant hanging from my neck, nerves settling as the pad of my finger rubs across the

8

cool surface. My dad gave it to me after my mom passed. He said it was the first piece of jewelry he ever bought her, and I wear it every day. "You got me. I'm Valerie, but most people call me Val."

"Val," he says, soft and slow, like he's trying it on for size. It's only three letters, but it sounds far too good on his lips. "It suits you. Nice to meet you, Val."

"Nice to meet you too," I say, self-conscious under the weight of his gaze. I rattle my new cup side to side between us. "And thanks for the coffee."

"Of course." He nods to my pile of coffee-soaked crap on the table. "What were you working on before the incident?"

I laugh nervously, desperately trying to come up with an explanation that makes me look like less of a dork. "I was transferring the NIU academic calendar into my planner," I say, patting the damp pages at the end of the table.

He laughs, shaking his head. "What? Last time I checked, we've still got a few days before the semester starts. Why are you trying to rush it?"

I shrug. "It's an important year, and I don't want anything to jeopardize my chances of getting my dream job after graduation."

"Ahh," he says, leaning in closer, holding his chin up with his palm. "Will you be out celebrating the new semester with the rest of the student body this weekend?"

My eyes flick to the table, "No, I don't think I will be."

"Why's that?"

I meet his eyes over my cup as I take a sip. "I'm not much of a partier, I guess."

"Well, that's a shame."

"Why?"

His eyes rove over every inch of my face like he's contemplating something. "I was going to invite you to my place. There's about a ninety-seven percent chance my roommates will have a party this weekend."

9

I shrug. "There's a ninety-seven percent chance I wouldn't have shown up, anyway."

He leans back, bringing his hands to his chest like my words were a physical blow. "Damn, Val. You could at least lie to me."

I laugh when I realize how I just sounded. "Nothing against you. It's just not my scene."

He nods, looking at me like he's trying to figure me out. Good luck, buddy. You'll cross the mote, slay the dragon, and climb the tower, only to find the door to *that* chamber locked.

Oh great, now even my thoughts are taking on the language of my current read.

"So, what *is* your scene?"

I grin. "A good book and a quiet room. Maybe a glass of wine."

"A bookworm, huh?"

I dig through my school bag, coming up with a paperback, wiggling it in the air before I place it back inside. "You could say that."

"What about food?" He asks, tracing circles on the lid of his cup. "You have to eat every once in a while, right?"

A nervous laugh escapes me then. "I see where you're trying to take this, and you should really quit while you're ahead."

His answering smile has me second-guessing my stance on the matter. "Why's that?"

I shake my head. "I'm not looking for a boyfriend."

"Whoa," he says, holding his hands up between us. "I never asked for a date. I only asked about food."

My cheeks heat, realizing he's right. My mind jumped over so many conclusions, landing on the assumption that he wanted to date me. I cover my face with my hands, laughing at myself.

His husky laugh joins in across the table before he says, "Just kidding. You were right about my intentions."

I drop my hands, looking at him with so many questions bouncing around in my head. The loudest one being—*did my high school crush just imply he wants to take me on a date?*

"I'm flattered, really," I say, my mouth opening and closing as my brain searches for words that aren't incriminating, "but I can't."

Really, Val? That's all you can come up with?

He snaps his fingers in that *aw shucks* way, "I knew you'd have a boyfriend."

"Oh no," I say, wishing I could take the words back as soon as they're out of my mouth. Why didn't I just let him believe I had a boyfriend and let him go on his merry way?

"No boyfriend?"

"Uh, no?"

He slides his glasses back on his nose. "Why'd that come out as a question?"

"I'm not sure," I say, bringing my latte to my mouth to stop it from making me look like even more of a fool.

He chuckles. "What's your majo—"

"You know, I've really got to go." I say before he can get another question out of his mouth. It's a blatant lie. I planned to spend half my day here, but he doesn't need to know that.

I start tossing my damp belongings into my bag, ignoring the confused look I'm getting from across the table.

"Where are you going? We were just getting to know each other."

Exactly.

I turn to him, zipping up my bag. "You don't want to know me, Brody."

"How could you possibly know what I want?"

I huff out a humorless laugh. "I don't. But I know what *I* need, and it's not some cute boy with dimples trying to flatter me all semester."

"So you think I'm cute too, then?"

It's the *too*—implying he finds me cute as well—that

11

almost gets me. But I square my shoulders and say, "Thanks again for replacing my coffee. Have a nice day, Brody."

"Wait, how do I know if I'll ever see you again?"

"You don't," I say under my breath.

"So give me your number. I'll invite you to my next party. I'd practically be doing you a favor, getting your nose out of your books."

"Not gonna happen," I smile, grabbing my phone from the table.

Before I can pull away, Brody's fingertips brush the back of my hand as he holds me in place. The tingles dance through my skin again. I look up to find his searching gaze.

"Val, where can I find you?"

I shrug, pulling my hand out from under his with the movement, and toss my backpack over my shoulder. "Around, if you're lucky."

"Oh, I'm lucky," he says as I push open the door. "See you around," are the last words I hear as I walk out of his life.

Chapter Two

"What the hell are you smiling about?" My best friend, Wes, asks as I walk into the house later that morning. "I thought you said you were just grabbing coffee?"

Wes and I had been at the gym before I went to grab a coffee. It was meant to be a quick pit stop before picking up my books for the semester. It's been two hours, so of course he has questions. It's not my fault a freckle-faced girl with piercing amber eyes and blonde curls threw a wrench—or more accurately, a coffee—into my plans.

I wipe a hand down my face, schooling my expression before he starts firing off a million questions. "I told you I needed to go to the bookstore too. Don't get your panties in a twist."

"You know me—I'm free ballin' it, man," he says, swaying his hips.

"Too much info," I say, thumping my bag of overpriced textbooks on the countertop and crying a little on the inside when I think about all the tough classes I'll be taking this semester. Last year I went against my academic advisor's recommendation of splitting up my hardest classes. I took a couple then, but left most of them for this year and if I could, I'd go back and punch my past self in the face for his stupid decision.

Add the pushback I get from my dad at every turn, and I'm dreading what will inevitably happen this year. Failing grades, a dad who refuses to listen to my input about my own life, and a future career I'll hate if I can't get my shit together and actually graduate.

I may have teased Val earlier about being overly prepared for the semester, but part of me is envious of her ambition. I've spent my last three years on campus, focusing on everything but my studies.

Intramural sports? Check.

Getting Drunk? Check.

Girls? Check—but nothing resembling an actual relationship after what happened freshman year.

Figuring out what to do with my major in Exercise Science? Not until last year when I worked an internship at the Hudson Fieldhouse. But contrary to popular belief—namely my father's—figuring out my future did not magically make me a better student.

"Earth to Brody," Wes says, waving his hand in front of my face. "Okay, now you've really got to tell me what happened. And don't tell me it was nothing. I know you."

His ice-blue eyes pin me to the spot and I know I won't be able to get away without giving him something. I take a deep breath, "I don't know. I met a girl."

"Oh, ladies' man Brody found himself a girl. What's new?"

"Shut up."

"Well, the good news is, you can invite her over tonight because Isaiah already bought a keg."

Tried that.

Isaiah is another roommate. Like me, he's always down for a party.

"I didn't get her number."

I busy myself by removing my books from the yellow sack from the bookstore to avoid Wes' annoying, fatherly concern.

"Ahh, I get it."

I send a glare in his direction. "What the hell is that supposed to mean?"

He shrugs. "I mean, it all makes sense now. You're smitten, asked for her number, but she didn't give it to you. So now you're even more hung up on her than you would be if you were already texting her."

He laughs when my silence fills the room.

"Oh, you've got it bad, don't you?"

"Pft, no," I lie, but it's no use. I can't deny this girl is stuck in my head.

That evening, after we've set the keg on ice and placed the tap, people trickle through the back door of our humble abode. There's a set of concrete stairs leading into the basement. We try to keep all shenanigans corralled here so we can at least try to get our deposit back once we move out at the end of the year. Despite our efforts, people still disrespect the house. One, because they're drunk, and two, it's not their home, so what's there to care about, right? I can't tell you how many times we've kicked people out for broken light bulbs and full bottles of liquor exploding on the concrete floor. Once, a guy was clearly trying to do drunk parkour down the steps and he broke the wood railing. He never got invited back.

"There's my favorite guy," a sultry voice halts my progress as I put together a last-minute party playlist at the stereo in the corner.

I turn, a smile already playing at my lips. "Ivy, how was your summer?"

She smirks, "It was good. Missed you though," she says, running a long, manicured fingernail across my collarbone and down my chest with clear intent.

Ivy and I hooked up periodically last year after meeting through my roommate, Isaiah, and his girlfriend, Steph, but we were both adamant about it not turning into more.

Her touch does nothing for me. Instead of entertaining her flirtatiousness, I gently pull her hand from my chest and steer the conversation into more innocent territory. "I'm sure you did just fine without me. Keg's in the other room if you're thirsty. Have fun tonight."

Her shoulders slump and the smile drops off her face as she registers my rejection, but I can't find it in me to feel bad. For a reason I can't explain, my skin is crawling with unease in an environment that used to feel like home.

It's time to stop screwing around, Brody, the words my dad drilled into my brain over the summer echo in my mind despite the music blasting right next to my ear.

My phone buzzes in my back pocket before I can let my mind drift off in the direction of those thoughts for too long.

I find a notification from the Minor League Baseball app on my phone.

Nashville Salamanders' Center Fielder Malakai Moore with a Three-Run Walk off.

Oh, fuck yes!

Malakai Moore has been my best friend since grade school, who's busy chasing his dreams in the Minor Leagues. He's still one of my best friends, even though our lives are headed in separate directions. His other best friend (and the little sister I never had), Lainey, spent the last week of summer in Nashville with me to visit and catch a couple of his games. It was nice, just the three of us like old times.

I fire off a text to congratulate him.

· · ·

Brody: A Walk Off?? You'll be in the MLB forgetting all about me in no time. Proud of you, buddy.

"You good?" Isaiah appears at my side, holding a beer out for me to take. "Saw your hands were empty. It's unlike you at a time like this."

I pocket my phone and accept his offering. Then I look around the room full of people I barely know and nod. This is unlike me, and I'm not sure how to feel about it.

————

The next morning, I'm woken up, not by a knock at my door, but to Wes barging through it like he owns the place.

I pop my head up, and through one bleary eye, I find him in the minimal light from the hallway. "Up and at 'em, buddy. We're heading to the gym."

"Ugh." I lie back and close my eyes.

I hear the rustling of a pillow just before the soft puff smacks me right in the face. I jump onto my knees on the mattress, bringing the pillow I'd been sleeping on with me. I wind up, channeling my old baseball days with the round-house smack I lay on Wes' face once, twice, three times until he shoves me backward. Since my body is barely functioning yet, I flop against the mattress so hard, I nearly bounce right off the bed.

"Alright, I'm up, you jackass. Give me a second to blink the sleep from my eyes."

He gives me a stern look on his way out the door, turning on the overhead light for good measure.

I feel bad for this guy's future children. He's ruthless. He'll have them scrubbing tile floors with a toothbrush by five-thirty am.

Did I mention it's Saturday morning?

I get ready and am in the kitchen ten minutes later where Wes tosses me a blender bottle with pre workout already mixed inside.

"Thanks, Dad."

We both chug, and we're out the door.

My love for the gym stems from two things, habit from high school sports, and my passion for training. The latter was what made figuring out my major so easy.

When I was in high school, I was an athlete—a good one, at that—but I knew I'd never make a career out of it. Exercise Science as a major was a no-brainer from the beginning. But my baseball coach was a stickler for protecting yourself on and off the field and he firmly believed it all started in the weight room.

Now that I'm entering my fourth year learning about the inner workings of our bodies, I understand why he felt that way. Last year, I got my first taste of helping others understand the importance, and now I crave that feeling of watching it click for someone.

But what seemed like a future occupation to me and everyone who knows me, looked a lot different to my dad. He's an investment banker and comes home with well over six figures yearly, so he's always looking for ways I can use my passion to make more money.

Why not become a physician? He asked, immediately following my announcement about becoming a strength and training coach or physical trainer after I graduate.

Not only do I not have the patience to spend so many years chained to a desk in college, but I'm a terrible student. College is not my thing.

If I could pay one lump sum and start working with real people who could use my help, I'd pay it and start on Monday.

The last thing I need is more schooling, but my dad doesn't agree. His never-ending lectures about hard work and putting in the time go in one ear and out the other at this point. I know he's never going to understand me—I've known it for years.

My big brother, Luke, is his star child and always has been. Rightfully so. He took my dad's advice and is quickly climbing the ladder at a firm identical to dad's. But he was smart enough to get away, and lives in the suburbs of Des Moines, where his wife, Kait, grew up. They have the cutest little three-year-old, Mia, who has me wrapped around her finger.

Would my life have been easier if I'd listened to my dad every step of the way? Possibly. He'd be on my ass about things less, that's for sure. But I want to do my own thing. I don't need to live in his footsteps.

"Whoa, man. Where ya going?" Wes asks, as I press the weights above my chest again.

He was spotting me as my mind went off on a tangent. "What?" I ask, out of breath as he takes control of the bar and weights, setting them back in their cradle above my head.

"I lost you there. I thought we were doing reps of fifteen? You were at seventeen."

"Oh," I say, finally sitting up, arms burning.

"Is this about that girl again?" He asks, switching me spots. "Because I saw Ivy shooting you seductive looks all night last night. Maybe you should've let her help you blow off some steam."

I'm shaking my head before he finishes the sentence. "Ivy and I were never an item, and never will be. I don't want to use her like that, either. We had an understanding before, but I'm not interested in that anymore."

"So you're what—interested in a relationship now?"

That thought terrifies me. "Not really. But I wouldn't mind something a little less superficial."

"Well if that's the case," his voice strained as he makes his first press, "I say you go back and try to find that girl at the coffee shop again."

I nod, perfectly happy with his assumption I'd been daydreaming of Val. Better than having to talk about my dad, my least favorite conversation topic.

"Yeah, maybe you're right. You wanna grab some coffee after we're done here?"

He screws up his face. "You know coffee isn't my thing."

I roll my eyes, "Right, but how many times have I been your wingman in the three years we've known each other?"

He falters in his press and I help until he gets his control back. "Point taken."

The ding of the bell above the door greets us as we enter the coffee shop. My eyes immediately flick to the table Val was at yesterday morning, but it's vacant.

"Damn," I mutter under my breath.

"What?" Wes asks, surveying the place. He's so used to being the person behind the bar in an establishment like this, he's fidgety being a paying customer and follows my every move like a lost puppy.

I continue scanning faces and tables, and although a blonde smiles at me when our eyes meet, she's not the one I'm looking for. "She's not here."

It's a bummer, especially given the fact Otis, the barista told me she's here almost daily. Maybe it's because today's Saturday?

He looks around one last time as if he could find her without knowing what she looks like, then pats my shoulder. "Sorry, buddy."

We step up to the counter and the girl from yesterday is behind it again. She gives me a secret smile. Afraid to come off as an asshole, I give her a closed-mouth smile, but nothing else.

"Hi, can I get a large salted caramel latte, please?"

"Of course," she says, punching my order into the cash register.

"And I'll take a large strawberry banana smoothie," Wes cuts in.

She smiles at him, then looks at me to make sure I'm okay with that. I nod, rolling my eyes as I pass her my card.

"If I didn't know better, I'd say she was the chick you met yesterday," Wes says as we step away from the counter to wait for our drinks.

"Who?" I say, looking around the space frantically, just in case I missed someone.

He nods his head back to the counter, a dubious jet black brow mocking me.

I follow his gesture to find the girl behind the cash register still looking at me even though there's a customer giving their order right in front of her.

"She flirts shamelessly with me every time I'm here."

Wes huffs out a laugh. "Pot meet kettle."

I can't help but laugh, because he's not wrong. I usually am a shameless flirt. Hell, I've even flirted with coffee shop girl more than once. But it's harmless. And my mind is otherwise occupied with a quick-witted, firecracker of a girl with springy, blonde curls, freckles splattered across her nose, and an obsession with office supplies.

Shit, I was really hoping she'd be here again today.

But she left in quite a hurry yesterday. I stared at my ceiling well into the middle of the night, wondering whether I made her feel uncomfortable enough to split before she had the chance to finish her little journal she'd been scribbling in—and spilled coffee on. There was enough coffee spilled for it to be a fresh cup, too. She said it wasn't my fault, but I still feel terrible about it.

21

Shit.

When my name is called from the barista working the machines, I grab both our drinks. Handing Wes his, I walk out wondering if she's avoiding this place because of me.

And if she is, how the hell else will I find her?

"Do you think I creeped her out?" I ask before I think it through.

"Who, the barista?"

"No, Val." I give him more context, telling him about our encounter as we round the car and get in. "Do you think she left because she thought I was a creep?"

"Probably," Wes laughs.

I glare at him. "You're not helping."

"Since when do you care so much about the first impression you give a girl? I've seen you flirt with hundreds of girls, many of which turned you down. So what's so different about this girl?"

What is so different about her? I ponder his question as I prepare to drive us home.

"This is delicious," Wes says, breaking me from my thoughts. "And I think I ended up with the wrong cup," he turns it until I can see the number scrawled across it with the name Clara written above a heart.

I groan, "Finders, keepers," I say, smacking him on the shoulder before turning the key in the ignition.

Chapter Three

VAL

If there's one thing my best friend from back home, Hannah, is known for, it's delayed responses to my messages. Her answers either come immediately or a week later. There's no in between. So I'm not even surprised the morning of the first day of school, when her reply to last week's frantic text about Brody finally comes through.

Val (last week): You will never guess who I just ran into at the campus coffee shop!!!

Hannah (this morning): Santa Claus?!

Oh, look! Hannah, the smart ass, is out to play already this morning.

Val: You're alive! And no, Brody Ryan! Do you remember him?

This time she decides it's urgent enough to reply immediately.

Hannah: Holy shit, no way. The guy from Freeport? You never told me he goes there. I expect a full debriefing tonight after work!

Closing out of our conversation, I open Instagram, typing his name into the search bar. Not that I'd ever admit it to him, but I've followed him since a night back in high school when Hannah and I were tipsy in her parents' basement and she influenced my decision to do it.

He's got so many followers, it'd be nearly impossible to find me in the mix, even if he wanted to.

He posted his last photo just over a week ago of him, his best friend Mal, and a girl who is lucky enough to be sandwiched between the two of them. Their arms are around each other, laughing candidly. It appears to be in a bar setting, geotagged in Nashville, Tennessee.

"Hey, whatcha doing?" A sleepy Bree asks, coming up behind me with a coffee in her hand. I stare at it like a salivating dog. I've already had two cups today, but it didn't feel the same. I usually treat myself to a large latte from Give 'er the Beans on my first day of school. I get there early enough to sit in my favorite booth and go over my notes for the semester, check my planner, and even begin flipping through my text books if I have enough time.

It's my favorite first day ritual, but I skipped it this year, as I try my best to remove temptation by avoiding the cute boy who was far too interested in my life last week.

But I've walked around like a zombie the past several days, living on Folgers and bland vanilla creamer. Needless to say, I'm jonesing for a white chocolate mocha from my favorite place.

And I know there are other places I could go around town, but Beans is so convenient for me, it's a block away from campus, located one block west of my walking route to class. Not to mention the coffee tastes far better than the overpriced bean water you find at the bigger chain coffee shops.

"Nothing," I say, flipping my phone upside down in my lap, making it obvious I'm up to no good.

Bree sits on the couch cushion next to me and sets her coffee on the table in front of us while squinting at my odd behavior. "I don't believe you," she says and before I see it coming, she snatches my phone from my lap.

"Oh my, who's this hottie?" She says, turning back to me with hearts in her eyes.

"Don't you dare. I saw him first." Her charisma and beauty is a lethal combo, and I know she could snatch a guy right out from under my nose, not that she would. She's gorgeous with her short, black hair with natural loose curls, light brown skin, and a smattering of freckles across her nose —and she knows it. She walks around with a confidence I wish I could muster even half of. I watch men practically flock to her on the rare occasion she gets me to leave the house.

She rolls her eyes. "Like you have the balls to make a move. You forget I know you. Who is he?"

I never told her about the other day. One, because she was working when I returned, and two, by the time she was, I'd been sitting in my mortification for too long. I didn't *want* to tell her.

I take a deep breath, taking the phone from her. "His name is Brody Ryan. I had a huge crush on him in high school. He had the best butt on our rival's baseball team."

She pops a dubious brow. "And you just sit at home looking at his profile when you're bored?"

"Um, no," I say, scrolling through his pictures as she looks over my shoulder. "Remember when I went to the coffee shop last Friday?"

"Yes."

"Well, I ran into him. Actually, there's more to the story, but he actually sat down at my booth and talked to me."

"Okay, tell me everything," she says, so I do. When I'm finished, she's looking at me like I admitted turning down a million dollar cash prize. "And you didn't stay to see where things went? You should have gone out with him!"

I roll my eyes. "You know why. I just can't, Bree."

She gives me what I call her mama bear look. "You know

25

my stance on this, Val. You deserve to get out there even if you find a job a thousand miles away next year. The shit you went through before I met you was terrible, and I can't imagine having lived through it. But you know your parents would want you to be happy, right? They'd want you to squeeze the hell out of what you have left of your time in college. To wring out every little drop. It's not meant to be a race to get to your cap and gown. It's meant to be experienced."

The mention of my parents is a shot to the heart, especially on such a big day. If they were still here, I would have woken to a call from them both to wish me a happy first day of my senior year. Hell, if they were still here, I'm not even sure I'd be planning to move halfway across the country at the end of the year.

"I've been experiencing plenty, thank you very much," I say, forcing myself to put that thought to bed.

"Oh, really? What was the last thing you experienced that wasn't for extra credit, or a class project, huh?"

I look away, pretending to calculate, but coming up empty-handed. "Okay, so you're right, but a lot of them were actually fun."

"And who's to say you wouldn't have fun at the things you always turn down? We need to enjoy our last year together. It makes me fucking sad thinking in a year, we won't be together anymore. I'll be back in the suburbs of Chicago with some boring job, and you'll be...wherever you'll be. Let's not waste our last months of living together sitting right here on this couch, okay? I want to get out of this tiny little house we call home and *live*. I want *you* to live."

"Okay, okay. Fine, I'll start saying yes more when you're going out or whatever. But can we also do things I enjoy too? I don't need to go to a bar every weekend to have fun."

"Fine, yes. We'll compromise. Now jump in that boy's DMs and tell him you changed your mind. He's fine, and I have a good feeling he could teach you a few things, if you know what I mean."

I contemplate that thought for longer than I should. "You're right, he probably could. But it's still not happening."

She scoffs, returning to her coffee cup.

She's been trying to get me to date since we met my freshman year of high school. We met when the college paired us with two horrible people in the dorms. Thankfully, we lived across the hall from each other, so it wasn't all bad. We've lived together ever since.

Objectively, I know she's right about me putting myself out there this year, but that doesn't mean I'm ready to. I've dated in the past. I lost my virginity in high school to a boy who had no clue what he was doing. I went through a brief phase freshman year where I was drowning my past hurts in hookups and booze. But a letter from the college stating I was on academic probation after my first semester was the kick in the ass I needed.

Against my better judgment, I continue to scroll his profile until I'm all the way back to his high school years. My eyes catch on a photo of a shirtless Brody in a backyard pool with a dog in his arms. I click it to get a closer look at his abs. He's got a baby face and braces compared to the guy I met the other day, but it's the version of him I remember most. When I scroll to read the caption, I do something incredibly dumb— I ACCIDENTALLY LIKE THE POST.

You have *got* to be kidding me.

"Oh shit, oh shit, oh shit."

"What?" Bree asks around the rim of her coffee.

"I liked his post from," I squint at the timestamp below the photo, "Four years ago!"

"What?" she asks, more frantic this time.

"What do I do? Should I unlike it?"

"No! He'll get a notification either way, so you might as well own up to it. Makes it look like an accident that way—or you could send him a message that says, 'Oops! I guess now you know I was sitting here stalking your profile, wishing I'd made a move last Friday. Give me another chance?'"

"You know you're not helping, right?"

She squints at my screen. "And didn't you say your first class started at 8:10?"

"Yes," I whine, still hung up on my mistake.

"Well, you're about to be late, go!"

I look at the time in the top left corner of my phone and realize she's right. "Shit, how is this happening?"

I lunge for my bag and run for the door, giving a quick goodbye on my way.

My walk to campus is spent thinking about my parents, thanks to the topic Bree pushed on me this morning.

My parents weren't perfect by any means, but they made my childhood feel like they were. Being their only child, it was the three of us against the world. Thanks to them, I'd grown up with the picture perfect idea of the love I wanted to have someday. They never hid their affection toward each other from me. I still remember the way they used to look at each other with so much love in their eyes. That and the love stories I'd been reading since I was eleven years old had me living life in rose-colored glasses back then.

Things seemed so perfect while I was too busy with high school activities to realize my mom wasn't quite herself my junior year. I had pictures of junior prom dancing in my head when my parents sat me down to tell me about my mom's cancer diagnosis.

Looking back, although I'd only been seventeen, that was the moment I grew up.

It was almost exactly six months of watching her health deteriorate and holding onto her desperately—as if that was enough to make her stay—before she was gone.

When that day came, I no longer cared about anything. I didn't attend prom, I could barely finish my homework. My relationship with my dad basically collapsed after she was gone. With our perfect little unit broken, we were never the same.

There were days we tried to bring things back to normal, going on little day trips that Mom used to always talk us into. But we'd get home, just the two of us, and melancholy would set in yet again.

I knew life was hard for dad after he lost his soulmate, but I was too lost in my sorrow to realize his own health was declining. They said it was a heart attack that took him almost nine months to the day after we lost my mom, but I know he died of a broken heart.

After losing both of them, I was just…numb. It's hard not to fall back into those feelings every time I think too hard about losing them. But there's a part of me that is at peace knowing they're finally together again.

I finished my senior year a shell of a person. I checked out of life entirely until my best friend's mom helped me find grief counseling. Hannah and her family took me in after my dad's funeral. And they took my bad days in stride, giving me grace with each step of the process. I still wasn't myself when I moved off to college. But ultimately, it was Hannah and Bree who helped me see that was no way to live.

I've still had a hard time letting new people in the past few years, but I've made some progress.

———

I'm so lost in my thoughts of them, I don't notice a biker approaching on my left until he's finding the gap that barely exists between me and an oncoming pedestrian. It forces both of us to jump out of his way and I try to sidestep the puddle left over from last night's storm that rolled through. My foot splashes right in, soaking my entire sock.

"I hope your day sucks too, asshole!" I yell at the cyclist who's moving so fast he's already a block away.

"Oh no, are you okay?" A sweet girl whose appearance screams freshman asks, looking me up and down. She seems to have made it out of the incident unscathed. At least that makes one of us.

"Shit." I say, looking myself over, then turning back to her. "Thanks, I'm fine," I say, trying to smile, but I'm sure I look deranged.

"Well, that guy was a dick. Hope your day gets better."

"Thanks, yours too," I say, then book it the rest of the way to class, walking in five minutes late.

Accelerated heart rate, too-tight, itchy skin—this feeling right here is the reason I'm early to everything. I hate knowing all eyes in the room are turning to get a look at the sorry schmuck who showed up tardy.

I drop into the first empty seat I can find, focused on settling my erratic breathing. Putting on a brave face, I look up when I realize the professor hasn't said a word since I sat down.

"Nice of you to join us. I've already taken attendance, which means your tardiness will, in fact, count against your grade. You and everyone else in the room will do well to take that as a reminder to make sure it doesn't happen again."

If I could self-destruct into a pile of ash, nothing would stop me from flipping the switch. I can feel eyes on me all around the room—which is one of those large auditoriums— as my cheeks heat.

Starting the year off right, Val. You dumb ass.

The person sitting to the left of me, who has, stayed quiet through my side show slides their syllabus between us where we can both read along. I'd ask for my own, but the professor has already moved on. In my first two minutes in his class, it's clear he's one of *those* professors. You know, the ones who get off on watching people fail. The kind who pinpoint a student on the first day they're sworn to hate the rest of the semester. Lucky me!

I lean over to read what he's covered so far, and as I do, a familiar scent wafts toward my nose—sandalwood and coffee.

"Hey, at least you didn't have a coffee to spill this time," says a familiar voice, I look up and nearly choke on an inhale, spluttering until his hand pounds on my back in a life-saving maneuver. *No, please! Just let me die!*

As if once wasn't enough to embarrass myself in front of Brody Ryan, I plopped down at the same table on the worst— and last—first day of school I've ever had.

I finally manage to snap my jaw shut and tune back into what the professor is saying in time to hear, "I hope you're all comfy where you're at, because the person you're seated with today is your partner for the rest of the semester, no exceptions!"

"Guess I'm luckier than I realized," he says, referencing our conversation at the coffee shop last week.

I just have one question to ask the universe in this moment —What. The. Fuck?

Chapter Four

BRODY

"Holy shit, you found her?" Wes asks as I sit across from him while he works at The Saloon, a bar only a few blocks from our place, telling him what happened yesterday.

I've been visiting him at work ever since he got the job our sophomore year. If it wasn't syllabus week, I'd have my homework spread across the bar while sipping on a beer. Having me here makes work go faster for him and makes homework more tolerable for me. It's a win-win situation. And if I'm lucky, I get distracted by something happening around me and don't even have to do my homework.

"Technically, *she* found *me*, but yes," I confirm before sipping my beer. I rake my teeth against my bottom lip and add, "I can't get this sense of familiarity out of my head, like I should know who she is, but can't quite place her."

"Maybe she was a past fling of yours and she's pissed you don't remember her."

My mouth unhinges at the idea. I think about her unruly blond curls that smell like a cupcake—I caught a whiff when she flopped them over to the other side of her head in frustration during class—then her plump bottom lip comes to mind. Nope, I'd remember kissing those lips. "Yeah, not possible. I wouldn't forget her."

Wes' eyebrows do a high jump on his forehead. "If I didn't know you better, I'd assume you're already half in love with her."

I scoff, "Of course I'm not."

I've told exactly one girl in my life I loved her. Even after almost three years, I'm still in no rush to jump back into such a relationship. She tricked me into believing she was my best friend—that I could trust her. Then the first moment she saw a way out, she took it.

Wes rolls his eyes. "I know Mel did a number on you freshman year, but you can't miss out on love because of the actions of a girl who didn't even deserve you."

"We were together for three years and she acted like I was it for her. Then we started college, and she ran off the moment she saw something more shiny. She was only dating me because my family has money."

He gives me a look on his way to serve drinks to the small group at the corner of the bar. When he gets back, he leans in and says, "She was as shallow as they come, Brody. Not every girl is going to get heart eyes when they see your parents' house, at least not in the same way she did—like she was getting a glimpse into her future if she stayed with you. Plus, you two dated in high school. She saw firsthand where you came from. Someday, a girl is going to see you for who you are deep down, and they'll love every piece of you, no matter how much money you've got in your pockets."

"I never carry cash, so I hope you're right," I joke, trying to lighten the mood.

Wes rolls his eyes, knowing I'm deflecting. He takes drink orders for a small group who walked in, so I pull my phone out and open Instagram. I haven't been on since the last time

I posted a photo from Nashville when Lainey and I visited Mal.

It loads to a ton of notifications, and my Nashville post is where most of them come from.

All but one, which has a different thumbnail.

@vboyd23 liked your post.

I click on the notification to find a happy birthday post I made years ago for our family dog who has since passed—from my senior year of high school.

Random.

I click through to @vboyd23's profile, my smile turning devious when I find the name Valerie Boyd—one that matches my new partner in class. And if I'd still been questioning whether it was her, the blonde curls in her profile picture answer them all.

"Interesting," I mutter to myself, clicking the follow button.

When a new notification rolls in, I smile.

@vboyd23 accepted your follow request.

I immediately click through to send her a message, because how could I resist?

@brodyryan15: You stalking me, ma'am?

According to the time stamp, she liked my post before we even had class together, and since my account is private, she'd been following me without me knowing.

I cannot wait to give her endless shit about this.

But first, how does she know who I am?

. . .

@vboyd23: I don't know what you're talking about. You're the one who sent a friend request. Sounds like you're the stalker.

@brodyryan15: Says the girl who was already following me.

She leaves the message on read for long enough to make me think she won't answer.

@vboyd23: Guess my finger slipped.

@brodyryan15: We've met before, haven't we? I knew you looked familiar.

@vboyd23: I follow random people all the time. Don't flatter yourself.

I shake my head at her evasiveness. There's got to be an explanation, but if she's not forthcoming yet, that's fine. I've got all semester to wear her down.

@brodyryan15: Evading the question...you're cute, Val. I'll give you that.

@vboyd23: You know telling a grown woman she's cute is a backhanded compliment, right?

. . .

@brodyryan15: Oh, Val. You're gorgeous as far as looks. I was referring to your character. But it's cute that you're fishing for compliments.

@vboyd23: Don't you have something better to do than to stalk me on social media? It's not becoming of you.

@brodyryan15: I've got all night, actually.

@vboyd23: Well, I don't. See you tomorrow. Don't be late.

@brodyryan15: Wouldn't dream of it—but I'll be dreaming of you tonight.

That last line is cheesy as fuck, but I don't care. Watching her squirm has become my favorite pastime. If only I could see her face when she reads my message.

@vboyd23: I can't deal with you right now. Good night, Brody.

@brodyryan15: Good night, Val.

I'd feel bad about driving her to close out of our conversation, but in the short time I've known her, I've learned she's quick to run away when she gets the tiniest bit uncomfortable. If I have anything to do with it, I'll be helping pop the protective bubble she seems to live inside. And I think I'm going to enjoy every moment.

Chapter Five

VAL

By the time four-thirty rolls around, I'm already exhausted from a day full of classes and I'm regretting my decision to schedule a study session with Brody on a day that was already packed full of other commitments. If luck was on my side, he'd stand me up today.

Especially after last night's surprise messages on Instagram.

I still can't believe Brody caught me cyber-stalking him last night. It would have been a harmless slip of the finger if he'd turned out to be a guy I embarrassed myself in front of once. End of story. But no, in true Valerie Boyd fashion, I had to crush on—and embarrass myself in front of—my grade-determining project partner. There's no way this is going to end well.

For a girl who rarely relinquishes control of anything, I can already feel his careless attitude becoming an insatiable itch in a spot I can't quite reach.

I'm surprised to find him already sitting at a table in our

predetermined meeting spot near the YA section of the library. He's here, and early. Maybe this semester won't be as terrible as I thought.

He's facing me, but his head is bent toward his laptop. His preoccupation gives me an extra moment to take in the sight of him without all the charm running on overdrive. His brown curls are barely peeking out from under a navy blue Chicago Cubs baseball cap, which hides his face. But the gray shirt sporting his high school mascot—the Freeport High Falcons— is a dead giveaway. His muscular forearms flex and twitch as he taps at the keys on the keyboard.

I'm so transfixed, I don't realize he's aware of my presence until he swings his laptop shut.

I tear my gaze away from his arms to find his smirk, indication enough he caught me staring. Why does he have to have this effect on me?

"Val, how's your day been?" He asks, standing to pull out a chair right next to him.

I set my bag on the ground and sit, extremely aware of the closeness of our clunky wooden chairs, but trying not to show it. "Decent, yours?"

"Good," he says, sliding a white paper bag with the Give 'er the Beans logo toward me. I salivate at the sight like I'm Pavlov's dog. "I was hungry, so I brought us snacks."

Brownie points for Brody.

"Thanks, I'm starving," I say, unraveling the bag to find my favorite. I reach inside for a cinnamon brown sugar scone, taking an unladylike bite once it's in my hands.

"These are my favorite," I say around a mouthful.

When I look up, Brody is chuckling. I wipe my mouth and my hand comes away with crumbs.

We both laugh as he says, "Really? Never would've guessed."

I finish in record time, washing down the remnants of dough with water. Then I pick up my planner, uncapping my favorite black Paper Mate Flair Pen and scanning the monthly spread in front of me.

"Holy shit, that looks awesome," Brody says, leaning in. "Is this the same journal you dumped your coffee on?"

My cheeks heat. "Yeah, don't remind me."

He pulls it closer to himself, inspecting my work. "Seriously, you're talented, Val. How'd you do this?"

"Well, these," I say, pointing to the real coffee stains, "are from clumsiness." He chuckles as I continue to the other side of the spread, "And these, I made with watercolor. My August spread ended up taking on an accidental coffee theme," I say, laughing at my misfortune.

"The only thing it's missing is a cinnamon brown sugar scone."

I lift my eyebrows, "Yeah, well, I'd need drawing skills for that."

He reaches over me to a pencil sticking out of my pencil pouch. "May I?"

I squint at him, trying to figure out where he's going with this. Against my moral code, I nod, "I usually guard my writing utensils with my life, but since you brought scones, I'll overlook it. Just this once."

He plucks it from my bag, his arm brushing against mine. Then he slides my planner closer until he's bent over it. He hovers the tip of the pencil over a blank space in the corner of the page.

Finally remembering myself, I lean up, throwing my hand at the spot he'd been looking at. "Wait, what are you doing?"

"Do you trust me?" he asks with a smirk.

I laugh, "Not in the slightest."

"Will you trust me? I promise I won't ruin it."

I release the tension in my shoulders, letting my hand slide from the paper. "Fine."

His grin grows into a full-blown smile. "Good choice."

Finally, the pencil touches down onto the page, and I

watch in awe as it scrawls across it with practiced precision. Slowly but surely, a replica of the scone I just scarfed appears on the page.

When he finishes, he sets the borrowed pencil into the gutter of my planner and slides them both back in my direction. "There, you can add color when you get home."

His eyes lift to mine and he smiles when he realizes I'm still staring. "Where'd you learn to draw like that?"

He shrugs it off. "Art class, I guess?"

I lift my eyebrows at his nonchalance. "Brody, you're talented."

He shrugs. "Drawing was something I always loved to do when I was young. Then I got caught up in sports and kind of forgot about how much I loved it. It wasn't until high school I started drawing again, at the instruction of my art teacher. He was great at helping me reign in my skills. I still enjoy it, but don't spend a lot of time doing it, you know?"

I look down at the sketch, then back to him. "I think maybe you should, though."

His cheeks flush as he looks away. "Thanks."

He shuffles his belongings around, and I have a feeling he's not used to accepting compliments.

Maybe there's more to this guy, after all. And there's a part of me who can't wait to see more of what he hides behind the facade.

He rifles through his backpack but gives up on whatever he'd been looking for, muttering something to himself as he throws open his laptop instead.

"You good over there?"

His fingers crunch the keys, eyes scanning back and forth across the screen.

"Trying to pretend I didn't just realize I don't have a pen in my bag, so I won't get yelled at." His eyes move to mine, a sheepish smile playing on his lips.

I swivel my gaze to my overstuffed pencil pouch that still

lies wide open between us. I pick through, finding him one of my least favorite pens.

He smiles when I hold it out to him, his fingers brushing mine as he accepts it. "Thanks, Val."

"Don't mention it. And don't expect this kind of treatment every day. Start bringing your own shit. You've got me breaking my own rules over here and I don't like it."

He leans in, "Look at you, only a few days into the semester, and you're already under my influence, cupcake."

Yeah, in more ways than one. Wait, what did he just call me?

"Cupcake? Yeah, you're not calling me that."

His smile widens. "Guess we'll see."

"And, Val?" He asks, leaning in even closer.

"Yes?"

"You smell good."

With a palm to his forehead, I push him away. "Okay, get to work, playboy."

"Brody?" We break apart, turning toward the girl who just materialized at our table. She's gorgeous, with long brown hair, effortless beach waves, and a full face of makeup. "Oh my god, it is you. The library is one place I never expected to find you."

"Oh, hey, Bianca. It's been a while. I know," he says, pointing a thumb behind him at me. "This girl here has got me changing my ways this semester."

She finally turns to me, her smile falling flat, but I'm as surprised by his words as she is. I stare down at my hands, desperate to hide the smile creeping across my lips.

"Cool!" she replies, sounding overeager. "You and the boys planning any parties soon? You better invite me. We had so much fun last time!"

Brody gives me an apologetic look before turning back to Bianca. "We don't invite people over anymore because they don't respect the house when we do, you know?"

I turn back to my notebook, tuning out the rest of their

conversation because every time Brody tries to exit the conversation, Bianca just keeps talking. It's hilarious.

When they say their goodbyes, I'm assaulted by Bianca's floral perfume, as she leans over Brody to give him a hug.

"We *have* to get together before graduation," she says.

Brody gives her a noncommittal answer and waves as she walks away.

"She seems fun," I say with a smirk, still looking at my notebook as I answer the questions our professor gave us yesterday in class.

"Would've been nice if someone had been a pal and saved me somewhere about halfway through the conversation," he accuses, leaning lower as he tries to catch my gaze.

"But you looked like you were having a great time! And I wasn't aware we were friends."

"Would people who aren't friends meet at the library and sit this close?" He places his arm on the back of my chair for emphasis.

I try my best to look unfazed. "Hate to break it to you, Brody, but people do this all the time."

I look up to find him nodding like he just realized how right I am. "I guess I'm more of the divvy-it-up-and-finish-in-the-nick-of-time type."

I bark out a laugh. "Then it's a good thing I'm here to help you change that."

He tosses his arm over the back of the chair, and as he opens his mouth to say something, someone calls his name from across the room. This time it's a guy.

He hangs his head, and although I'm annoyed, I can't hide my smile as he approaches our table.

"It might not hurt for us to get a study room next time. Okay, Val Pal?"

Chapter Six

"You know, I was thinking, wouldn't life be easier for both of us if we swapped phone numbers?"

Professor Rhode turned us loose, pronounced Roadie, AKA road head. Yes, I'm twelve years old and laugh at the name when I think too hard about it, usually earning a smack from Val. Since we're ahead of everyone, thanks to my studious partner, we've been talking about everything but class for the past five minutes.

"I'm not giving you my phone number, Brody. You already send me memes on Instagram daily because 'they remind you of me,' no matter how insulting I find them. Trust me, you don't need another way to get in contact with me. We're already far too connected."

"Not in the way I'd like to be," I mutter, but the glare she's giving me tells me she heard me loud and clear.

"I don't think I need to remind you this is strictly an academic acquaintance. We're both working toward the same end

43

goal—passing this class at the end of the semester. There is nothing else happening here," she says.

"Keep telling yourself that, cupcake. I have no problem waiting you out. I'm patient."

"Enough with the cupcake. Now, I'm available in the late afternoon next week on Monday, Thursday, or Friday. Which day would you prefer?"

That snags my attention. "Did you just ask if I wanted to meet you in the library late next Friday afternoon?"

She turns to me with a deadpan expression, "Yes, I did. Is that a problem, party boy?"

My eyes turn to slits. "Who says I'm a party boy?"

She turns back to what she'd been writing in her notebook. "It wasn't hard to figure out. You practically told me as much."

When I don't answer, she leans down to get a better look at my face. "What, did I hit a nerve there?" She doesn't say it unkindly, although she's adopted a teasing tone.

I laugh it off. "No, just sounded a lot like my dad."

She grimaces. "Okay, I don't know your dad, but your face when you said that? I apologize."

I laugh, opening my mouth to explain further, but Professor Roadie brings us back into a class discussion, halting our conversation for the moment. I tune in and out of what he's saying, slumped in my seat and leaning to the side where I have a perfect view of Val. She's got her blonde curls tossed over her right shoulder, writing a million words a minute—something I should probably write down too, but I'm content where I'm at.

I know she's not wearing any makeup this morning because her freckles are out to play across the slope of her nose and apples of her cheeks. She's got her bottom lip between her teeth, completely unaware of what the sight does to me.

"Why are you staring at my notes if you're not writing anything down?" She whispers, making me jump to attention.

"Yeah, sorry," I say, clicking the end of my pen and writing random words in my notebook that the professor is saying at the front of the room, although they make no sense jumbled together. The act doesn't last long, though. When her writing hand is on the page furthest from me, I reach across the space between us and draw a star in the margin before she slaps my hand away, somehow still writing perfect letters on the opposite page.

A few minutes later, when Professor Roadie has lost my attention with his monotonous lecture, I reach across again, this time writing VB + BR inside a heart because I know it'll annoy her. I try to draw it on the trunk of a tree, but she notices what I'm up to when she's about to flip the page, sending a glare in my direction, but when she sees my doodle, she laughs, smacking me in the arm before she starts writing again.

I have to hold myself back from cheering out loud when our professor finally announces the end of class. Val and I have been walking out together after each lecture—not because she wants to, but having less to carry has its perks, and I can pack my bag faster than her and wait until she's ready.

The last time we walked out together, she practically ignored me, so I nearly fall over in surprise when she waits at the end of our aisle to walk with me instead of making me chase her out the door.

"Give me your phone," she says, her hand held out to me.

"What?"

She waves her fingers in a *gimme* motion, and I pull my phone from my pocket, unlocking it before she changes her mind. I watch over her shoulder as she opens a new message, types her number into the recipient box, then in the message box: *Brody-Special Events Management class. He knows this contact information is for school purposes only.*

She turns to me with a searching look when she has it typed out, asking me if I understand. I put my hands up in a sign of innocence, which she doesn't believe for a second, I'm sure. She's too smart for that.

She presses send, then holds my phone out to me. After grabbing her phone from the back pocket of her shorts and opening the message she sent herself, she adds me as a contact under Brody Ryan-SEM Partner.

So professional. "How many Brody Ryans do you have in your phone that you have to categorize me like that?" I lean in close enough she can hear my whisper in the busy stairwell, "Besides, you spelled *sex* wrong."

Her eyes grow large, looking back at what she typed. "Omigosh, it says SEM, an acronym for our class. Knock it off," she says, bumping into the railing with her hip, making a show of walking faster.

She can pretend I annoy her all she wants, but I don't miss the smile she's trying to hide.

On Saturday night, I'm lying in bed feeling a little buzzed after returning from The Saloon, where I spent the evening with Isaiah.

We stumbled home a little bit ago after I let him peer pressure me into too many two-dollar beers and twofer shots supplied by Wes behind the bar.

All day I've been opening my phone, staring at Val's name inside it.

I pull up our text conversation.

. . .

Brody: Brody-Special Events Management class. He knows this contact information is for school purposes only.

Later that day, I sent her another text.

Brody: Howdy Partner.

Val: School purposes only, Brody

I replied with a GIF of Jack Black saluting. She never answered.

I smile down at my phone, my fingers typing of their own accord.

Brody: How's my Val Pal today?

Val: As flattered as I am, no booty calls allowed.

I laugh out loud in the silence of my room, the space lit by nothing but my bedside lamp. Her comebacks always have such blunt delivery. I don't know why I like that so much. Maybe because she's the exact opposite of the girls I usually encounter, their intentions almost too clear. Val makes me work for every smile, every damn eye roll.

. . .

Brody: Booty call? It's not even 11pm. Booty calls start much later than this. Not that I'd know, just what I've been told. Stick with me and you'll learn these things.

Val: Right, I'll pretend I believe you, if only for my sanity. Did you need something?

Brody: Just sitting here pondering the question: What does a workaholic like you do with her weekends?

Val: I'm reading. What does a fun-seeker like you do?

Brody: Please tell me you're not reading your textbooks again. Don't think I didn't notice the stack you brought with you to the coffee shop the day we met. I just got back from the bar down the street where my buddy bartends. Moral support and all that.

Val: So you're drunk-texting me? And no, this is reading for pleasure. I'd tell you what it is, but I wouldn't want to bore your cute little party boy brain.

Seeing Val use the word pleasure causes a twinge deep in my core. It's such an intimate word compared to the careful conversations we've had so far. Also, did she call me cute?

Brody: The buzz has worn off pretty quickly. Nothing you could say would bore me, just so we're clear.

. . .

Val: The book is a romantic comedy. A love story with some laughs mixed in. AKA the best combo.

Brody: Wait, does this book have sex scenes in it?

Val: I'm not answering that question. I don't see it ending well.

That means yes. No doubt about it.

Brody: Valerie Boyd, I had you pegged all wrong. You sit at home reading sex books, don't you?

Val: This conversation is over.

Brody: Took it too far, noted. I'll quit while I'm ahead. Good night, Val. No coffee Monday morning, I'm bringing Beans for both of us. Enjoy the rest of your weekend.

Well, that may have been a fail, but I go to sleep with visions of Val reading romantic comedies in my head, which quickly turns into us acting out scenes together. I can't help where my mind goes when I'm unconscious. Don't judge me.

Monday morning, strolling through campus with two coffees in-hand, I smile. In a matter of weeks, I think I've of worn Val down a bit. She's still cautious of my intentions. But I'm growing on her. She's made that clear.

It's in the lingering looks she sends my way when she thinks I'm not paying attention. Little does she know I'm attuned to her presence. She even texted me back Saturday night, although reluctantly. It makes me wonder if she might enjoy my badgering more than I realized.

I know I'm laying it on pretty thick every time I flirt with her. I enjoy making people laugh, it's in my nature. But the things girls usually laugh at make her roll her eyes. With her, I'm still finding my footing, and I like that she doesn't make it easy.

As hard as I'm trying to change her mind about me, I don't know what I'd do if she actually gave me the time of day. Possibly pass out, or suffer a case of whiplash from the sudden change. I can't get past the feeling there's something blocking her from letting her guard down around me. I can only hope she'll let me in on it, eventually.

I step into our classroom ten minutes early to find only a handful of people, including Val, who's bent over her notebooks jotting something wildly across the pages, her planner.

Rarely have I seen her without it. We're completely different in that regard. I buy the bare minimum for college— notebooks, textbooks, and I still use the same backpack I had in high school. I find a pen or pencil from whatever source I can. I got through three years of college by taking my notes on a laptop—even then, spending more time scrolling social media than taking notes. When I needed a writing utensil, there was usually a person within arm's reach willing to let me borrow one.

But that's not Val at all. I had to smile when she first warned me to bring my own shit to our study dates. First, because she clearly had me pegged, and second, because she was that defensive of some measly pens and pencils. Then I looked up the markers I always see her using, and damn, those things aren't cheap.

As I approach the table, I can practically see the wheels turning inside her mind. She's using the black pen I've noticed is her favorite.

One wayward curl hangs in her face, obstructing her view from the intricate letters she's writing. My fingers itch to brush it behind her ear.

I step up to the table, careful not to startle her and ruin her handwriting. I set her coffee down next to her, unable to stop myself from adding, "Make sure you don't spill it this time."

She finishes writing and I laugh, watching her head move in my direction as her eyes stay on the task at hand, ensuring her penmanship is consistently perfect across the page.

Seriously, it's perfect.

It looks like she printed it from a computer, rather than created by a human hand.

When her eyes snap up, they bounce between my face and her coffee. "Whoa, you did bring it. I almost didn't skip coffee this morning, afraid you wouldn't deliver."

"I always deliver on my promises, Val."

The smug smile she'd been wearing drops. "Good to know."

Chapter Seven

VAL

It's Thursday evening and Bree's birthday, so we're sipping drinks in our living room with a handful of her friends. She's roped me into a drinking game called ring of fire. The *lucky* winner (sense the sarcasm) chugs the drink in the middle once the can tab pops from us stuffing as many cards as we can underneath it. Thankfully, the drink in the center is a white claw and not a beer, so I might not actually puke if it ends up being me.

That's right, I'm drinking on a weekday. I'm positive Brody would be proud if he knew—not that I'll be telling him.

Last round I became thumb master, so I set my thumb on the edge of the table discreetly before opening our text conversation on my phone—something I do far more than I'd like to admit.

I swear, ever since Brody started texting me, I've suddenly got phantom buzzing syndrome. Even when he's not sending me messages, I think I feel my phone going off, only to check it and find nothing. I stare at the dreadful device until Bree's friend, Missy, elbows me to get my attention. I look up to find everyone's hands in the circle for a cheers and join before we all take a sip.

I've been trying to keep Brody at arm's length, but I can't contain my excitement whenever his name pops up on my phone screen. He sends me the most random, corny messages, but I look forward to them.

He told me last Saturday night he'd bring me coffee on Monday morning. I spent the next day and a half fully expecting him not to deliver on his promise. I had a line fully prepared and everything. When he set a coffee cup down in front of me, I realized I've been grossly underestimating him.

We haven't talked since class yesterday, but that's my fault. I've been letting him carry the conversation, pretending it will be enough to keep me from getting attached. The way I had to talk myself out of seeing what he was up to last night, and my itch to text him now is saying otherwise.

Thankfully, I'm saved by my next turn. And with the attention back on me, thumbs pummel the edge of the table like a hailstorm as the girls remember I'm thumb master. Unfortunately for Bree, she's leaned in, telling her friend, Ari, a story animated in a way only she knows how to be. She doesn't notice what's happening until we all point and shout at her to take a drink.

Speaking of noticing things, something I missed while daydreaming about a certain bespectacled boy was how much further the can tab lifted during the last round. I stare at the card I drew like it's an eviction notice. "Come on, Val. Let's see it!" Bree calls from across the table, slamming her drink on the table after her chug, laughing because she knows I'm screwed.

I take a deep breath, wiggling the card into what tiny bit of free space there is left under the tab. You could hear a pin drop with the way everyone falls silent. Which is why, when the can makes an audible *tsssss* noise as the tab opens, I'm the only one in the room who isn't laughing.

"NOOOO!" I yell at the can.

Bree does the honors, removing the cards and finishing clicking the tab with a smug smile. "Drink up, bitch."

So much for staying sober tonight.

"How's Brody?" Bree asks as we stand in line at the bar she chose for the night.

"I haven't talked to him since class yesterday, but he's still as flirtatious as ever."

Bree teeters on her heels and leans into me as the line moves forward, a telltale sign she's feeling tipsy. Since she's got such a petite frame, keeping her upright is easy. I lean in, throwing my arm around her.

"Happy birthday, Bree." I say, resting my head against hers, fully aware I'm changing the subject, but I'm hoping she's too tipsy to notice. "I'm glad you threatened my life in order to get me out here with you tonight."

She laughs, "Whatever it takes. I'm glad you're here, roomie."

We make it past the bouncer and head straight for the bar where I get a round of lemon drops for the group as everyone else orders their drink of choice.

"To Bree!" We all sing-song before we throw them back.

I've barely stacked my glass back on the bar before Bree nearly rips my arm from its socket. Though she be but little, she is fucking *strong*.

"To the dance floor!" She yells over the intro of a new rap song she's been playing on repeat in our apartment since she returned from summer break.

Reluctantly, I follow. I've always loved dancing, but that doesn't mean I'm good at it. And since I'm in my head far too often, I tend to care too much about what people think to let loose in public. Bree knows this about me and holds her drink out to me in the middle of the dance floor.

"You're dancing tonight. I don't care how much alcohol I have to pour down your throat."

I take a big chug to quiet her, realizing a bit too late how tipsy I already am. As the song picks up tempo, she takes hold of my hips, moving them back and forth manually until instinct takes over and I finally find my rhythm.

Some of the girls have paired off, and I'm watching Bree flirt with a cute guy who complimented her *birthday bitch* sash. So I don't notice someone sidling up next to me until a familiar voice far too close to my ear says, "It turns out the *Vale*dictorian *does* know how to party. On a weeknight, no less."

Chapter Eight

BRODY

I notice Val the moment she walks up to the bar with her friends. I'm not about to spew some bullshit about the air shifting with her presence or anything like that. It's her laugh that catches my attention. It rang out like a siren song in the lull between two songs playing on the dance floor.

Christ, I sound like those books she reads.

Knowing her aversion to nightlife, I'm not actually expecting it to be her on the other end of the sound. But there she is, leaning against the bar. What a pleasant surprise. Her eyes are bright with laughter as she waits for drinks with her friend. I have to resist the urge to go to her, especially when Wes leans in, turning his ear to hear her, but I don't. The resulting twinge in my chest at their proximity surprises me.

I can't hold back my smile, watching her obvious reluctance as her friend drags her to the dance floor.

"Who is that?" Isaiah asks, catching me watching, and making me realize I've been staring too long.

"No one," I try, but he tips his head back, giving me a long look.

"Doesn't seem that way from where I'm sitting."

I turn back to find her, but she's already disappeared into the throng. "We have a class together."

"The girl Wes has been giving you endless shit about, perhaps?"

I take a slow sip of my drink, laughing as I drop the straw back into the glass. "Yep, that's the one."

He turns toward the dance floor. "You gonna go after her?"

"Nah."

Even as I say it, my legs itch to do just that.

He clicks his tongue, "I dunno man, Steph was telling me you let Ivy down easy a couple weeks ago. Thought maybe this girl had you in a chokehold."

I laugh, only to realize he's not far off. Val hasn't been far from my mind lately, but I've been holding myself back from texting her the past few days. I don't want to come on too strong. To be some creep she has to avoid for the rest of the semester.

"Brody's girl is here," Isaiah says as soon as Wes walks up to our end of the bar.

"What? Where?" He asks, looking around like he even knows what she looks like.

"Dance floor," Isaiah tosses his thumb over his shoulder in the general direction.

"What are you doing still sitting here, then?"

I shrug, "Well, first of all," I turn to Isaiah, "She's not my girl. Second," I say, turning to Wes, "I'm trying not to appear overeager, okay?"

"But you're still gonna go out there, right?"

"Yes!" I say, my mouth writing a check my ass wasn't ready to cash. But before I can talk myself out of it, I'm on my feet saluting the guys before I turn on my heel and book it toward the dance floor.

I spot her easily once I get closer. She and her friend are standing in the middle of a sea of people, her friend moving her hips back and forth as if Val's the Tin Man and her friend is Dorothy, who just greased her up to help her walk again.

Val looks gorgeous in some complicated black romper that shows more cleavage than I would have ever expected. If I had to guess, her outgoing sidekick probably talked her into wearing it. Not that I'm complaining. Her long legs look endless in tiny shorts and heels, enticing me from several feet away.

I walk toward her as if pulled by an invisible string, leaning in close and say, "It turns out the *Val*edictorian *does* know how to party. On a weeknight, no less."

She whips around, the picture of shock when she finds me standing there.

"Brody!" she says, clutching her chest, looking down when she remembers the lack of material covering her there. When her eyes meet mine again, there's a pink tinge to her cheeks, like I've caught her doing something she shouldn't. It's fucking adorable. "What are you doing here?" She asks, as if I'm the bookworm who's out of place on a weeknight,

I nibble the end of the straw in my cup, relishing each moment her gaze hangs on my mouth.

"I think the real question is, what are *you* doing here?"

She points to her friend, who's now got a dance partner. But her friend doesn't pay any mind to him, opting to look between Val and I like she's writing our love story in her head instead.

"It's my roommate, Bree's birthday."

"Happy Birthday!" I yell over the music, tossing in a wave for good measure.

"Thank you," she says, leaning away from her dance partner to ask, "And who might you be?"

I look between Val and her roommate before saying, "I'm Brody," and holding my hand out for her to shake.

Instead of taking it, her jaw drops, making me wonder if Val might have mentioned me.

"You're even hotter in person," Bree says, confirming that not only has she heard of me, but has also seen a picture somewhere.

I laugh, about to comment further when Bree's dance partner chooses that moment to whisk her away as if he's had enough of our chit chat.

Val's still staring in disbelief after her friend as I lean in to be heard over the thump of the music, "Wanna dance?"

What I thought had been a good idea quickly turns south when instead of accepting my outstretched hand, she's eyeing it like it's a dead fish.

Normally I'd be worried about what my friends think, undoubtedly watching this entire exchange, and the endless shit they'll give me when I return to the bar after she lets me down easy. Instead, I'm searching the scrambled remains of my brain for something funny to say. A joke to ease the awkward tension of the moment—to make it look like I hadn't been hoping for a good outcome in this situation.

But I'm coming up short, so I stand there as her gaze drops to her feet, my fingers itching to brush her hair behind her ear and demand to know what's holding her back.

I step away to set my empty cup on a nearby table, but Val catches my hand to stop me, surprising the hell out of me. I turn back and smile, shaking the empty cup before I set it down and let her pull me in.

We're still standing feet apart until she's shoved from behind. Her face and hands land on my chest with an oof. I see Bree's head buried in her dance partner's chest, acting like nothing happened.

"You okay?" I take Val by the shoulders, pushing her back just enough to look her in the eye, brushing a few strands of her hair behind her ear. A puff of vanilla wafts straight to my nose with the movement.

"Sorry about her," she says with a wave of her hand. "Her one rule for tonight was to have fun. Apparently, she's trying to point me in the right direction."

Her hands lace around the back of my neck and she's forced to step even closer because of our height difference.

I discreetly wipe my clammy hands on my shirt before settling them on the thin material at her hips. "Sounds like Bree is a smart girl."

She rolls her eyes. "Don't let her hear you say that. We'll never hear the end of it."

I laugh. "Is this the one and only time I'll see you out and about like this?"

Her nose scrunches adorably, "Might happen a time or two more before we graduate, but on a weekday? Yeah. Bree used the friendship card to get me here tonight."

I move a hand to my chest in mock seriousness. "I'm honored I could witness such a rare event."

She laughs, landing a light smack on my chest, "Good, you should be," her head swivels around, looking for something. "Who were you here with, anyway?"

I point up to the bar. "I came with my roommate Isaiah, but my best friend, Wes, is a bartender here. I was sitting at the bar when I spotted you."

"It's like kismet."

"Kiss what? If you want to kiss me, Val, just go for it. I will happily oblige."

I'm rewarded with an eye roll. "No, kismet. You know, fate —destiny?"

"It's all those books you read that get you thinking like this, isn't it? The girl is always gorgeous behind her glasses. The boy always gets the girl. The sun always shines, and there's never any rain."

She shakes her head, looking away like I've truly offended

her with my rant, and I instantly regret making light of something she likes. "It's called romance, but way to be the stereotypical hetero male who thinks it's nonsense. They're stories with an actual plot and believable main characters who overcome real-life problems. I think if you actually tried reading them, you'd enjoy them."

I put a finger under her chin and lightly lift her gaze back to mine. "I haven't figured out why, but I constantly take it too far with you. That was meant to be a lighthearted joke." We sway together to the music for a moment before I lean in to whisper in her ear, "Of all the bars, in all the towns, in all the world, she walks into mine…" I drift off, recreating a Casablanca quote, and tailoring it to our story. I look down to find her smiling at me like I invented pizza. Does she like pizza? Not sure, I've never asked.

"Do you like pizza?" I ask, before I can think better of it.

"Love pizza. Who doesn't?" She's not even the slightest bit thrown off by my randomness.

"Lame people, that's who. What else do you like? And don't make it some boring answer like number two pencils."

She rolls her eyes. "If I were to pick a favorite pencil, it would be a PaperMate ClearPoint. Everybody knows that."

Everyone but me, apparently. "I should've known you'd have a favorite pencil."

She waves away my reply. "As for something I like, I'd have to say, collecting quotes."

I squint down at her. "Does that mean like, a running collection of stupid shit the people around you say so you can make it into a book someday? Or better yet, use it as blackmail—wait, you don't have anything *I've* said written in this collection, do you? If so, you're gonna need to tell me. I can't have our friendship ruining my reputation."

"Well shoot, I already had it published. I could let you cash in on a percentage of the royalties."

I bark out a laugh. Seeing Val uninhibited like this is a

treat. But I don't dare tell her that, because her guard would be up faster than I could blink.

"So what are these quotes you speak of then?"

"I pull them from books, movies, social media. Anything that resonates, I write it down in a leather-bound journal."

"The words leather-bound journal sound so good coming from your mouth."

She rolls her eyes, shaking her head at me, but I don't miss her smile before she leans on my shoulder to hide it. She leans up, whispering in my ear, "What about you, Brody? What's something you like? And don't make it something boring like calculating the stats of MLB players." She says the words in a hilariously deep voice like she's trying to mock me and I'd laugh if I couldn't feel her whole body pressing against mine.

"If my best friend makes it to the big leagues, you can bet I'll be calculating stats like it's my job."

"And now I look like an ass."

"Yeah, but it's a nice ass," I say, squeezing her hips. Her sweet little intake of breath in my ear causes a tingling sensation to shoot straight to my groin.

She smacks my arm, bringing me back down to earth. "You did *not* just say that."

"I did. You didn't come here looking like *that*, thinking no one would notice, did you?"

She looks back over my shoulder before I can watch the blush I know is painting its way across her cheeks.

I lift her chin with a finger. "Don't hide that adorable blush from me."

The music drowns out her uncomfortable laugh and she repositions her arms around my neck, accidentally bumping her groin against mine. Sweet Jesus, I'd been trying to avoid thinking about our proximity, but she gave me a stark reminder.

"So, are you gonna answer?" She asks, like what just happened didn't affect her.

"What?" I ask, suddenly forgetting where we were at in our conversation because I was too attuned to the one our bodies were having.

"What do you like?"

The feel of you brushing up against me.

"Uh, I enjoy going on road trips."

She smiles. "Tell me about your favorite one."

I look behind her shoulder, recalling the memory, taking a deep breath before I answer. "Our senior year, my friends and I all applied to different colleges, so as one last hurrah, the three of us spent a week going on campus visits together and touring each other's campuses. We overloaded on snacks, and I curated the perfect road trip playlist, complete with school songs to play as we reached each college's campus. It was epic. I'm still not sure how any of our parents let us do it, but it's one of my favorite memories."

"I'm jealous."

"Have you ever gone on a road trip?"

She gets a far-off look, and the corners of her mouth turn down like I've kicked up a terrible memory in her mind. "I have, with my parents," she says. And just like that, a simple question has sucked all the life out of our conversation. I wish I could take it back.

The music changes, and as people pick up the beat of a new song, I realize we're not even moving—just standing in the middle of the dance floor, leaning in close to hear each other. Val must realize it at the same time because we pull apart the slightest bit like we rehearsed it. I catch Val's hand before she can get too far. "Can I buy you a drink? You can meet my friends too."

She looks up at me through long lashes, making me think she's going to turn me down this time. But my saving grace, Bree comes up behind her, looping an arm in hers. "Did someone say drinks?"

Before I know what's happening, she's linking an arm in mine, pulling us both toward the bar.

"Looks like Bree has the hots for Wes," I whisper in Val's ear.

She turns to her friend, who's balanced on her knees on her bar stool, leaning over the bar to flirt with Wes, who's clearly enjoying himself.

"She's a shameless flirt, especially when she's drunk. Don't read too much into it."

Isaiah was here long enough to meet Val and Bree, then took off to meet up with his girlfriend. The rest of Bree's friends are still tearing up the dance floor, so it's just the three of us and Wes when he's not flitting around behind the bar.

"What about you? Any competition I should be aware of?"

Val's sipping water, much to Bree's disappointment. But I'm sure she knows as well as I do. If she gives Val a hard time about not drinking, she may not show up at all next time.

She lifts a brow. "Do you think I'd have been dancing with you if I had someone? And you can't have any competition if there's no tournament. I'm not dating anyone this year."

I laugh, but it falls flat when I realize she's serious. "Why not?"

She shrugs, "Because I'm out of here as soon as I have my degree."

My stomach tightens. "Where to?"

"California? Maybe Chicago. Anywhere but here." Her nose turns up like she smells something terrible.

"That's a shame. Any reason behind it?" I take a sip of beer so she can't see how invested I am in her answer.

She takes a deep breath before smiling up at me. It doesn't reach her eyes. "I uh—I lost both of my parents before I graduated high school. Nothing keeping me in Iowa anymore."

"Wow, Val. I'm so sorry you went through that."

Her lips curve in a sad smile. "Thanks. It's been a while, but..." her voice breaks, and I don't hesitate before pulling her into a comforting embrace. She goes rigid at first, but curls into me after a moment. "Gosh, I'm sorry. This is ridiculous." she says against my t-shirt, inhaling deep to get her breathing back to normal. "Whoa, you smell good." As soon as the words are out of her mouth, she laughs, palming her forehead. "Gosh, forget I said that. This is why I never drink in public. I cry and the filter between my brain and mouth disappears."

I laugh too, leaning my cheek on the top of her head. "All jokes aside, you okay?"

She straightens, and I miss her warmth immediately. "Yeah, I'm okay. Just get sad sometimes."

"Well, I'm here for you if you ever need a shoulder. I'm a pretty good listener."

She tries to hide her smile behind her water as she brings it to her mouth. "Thanks, Brody. And I'm sorry for bringing the mood down."

I place my hand on her knee and squeeze, bringing her attention back to me. "Don't apologize."

Her eyes move over my face for a moment before she says the last thing I expect, "Wanna get pizza?"

Twenty minutes—and after promising Wes I'd bring some slices home for him—I'm standing arm-in-arm with Val and Bree at a pizza place down the road that sells slices as big as your face. I only had two drinks in the past several hours, so I'm practically sober at this point. The girls are both swaying with each step we take. Val keeps smiling up at me, which is doing things to my chest, and Bree is passed out on my shoulder.

We move up a couple steps and Bree suddenly revives, her deep awakening breath scaring the shit out of me.

"So are you going to give Wes my number?" She asks.

"Weren't you asleep? How are you thinking about him right now?" Val asks, mirroring my thoughts.

Bree peeks around me to say, "Because I was dreaming about what he's capable of. If my dreams are even close to reality, I want him to get my number. If you were smart, you'd do the same," she says, looking at me like I'm a piece of meat, then sending Val an admonishing look. "But that's none of my business," she adds before passing out on my chest again.

"She has a point," I joke.

Val squeezes my arm. "Stop it," she says with a laugh.

When we're in a booth stuffing our faces, Val turns to me.

"I'm glad we ran into each other tonight."

"Is it because I paid for your slices?" I say shoveling a piece of pepperoni in my mouth and making a joke out of things, since I never know how to react in these situations.

She shifts under Bree's head, which is a dead weight on her shoulder. "Thanks for that, but no. It's because," she takes a bite, chewing as she thinks over her answer. "It made you more of a person in my eyes."

I laugh, "What was I before? A robot?"

She shrugs, causing Bree to startle and revive long enough for a bite of pizza. "That didn't come out right. I mean, I got to see you in a different light. I like you, Brody. You're good shit, and I now see you as a friend. I don't take friendships lightly, either."

Being stuck in Val's friend zone isn't ideal, but I'll take what I can get. "I'm glad you feel that way. Told you I'd show you how to have a good time." Since I need to get off the subject, I add, "Speaking of friends, we should get yours home before she starts snoring."

Val searches my expression—for what, I'm unsure. Apparently not finding it, she nudges Bree. It takes both of us to get her up and out of the booth. With Wes' promised slices in-hand, I somehow lead both girls out and into a cab.

I let Val, who's been quiet since thanking me for help getting her friend into the back seat, give him directions to her place.

When we arrive at a tiny, but put-together home a handful of blocks from campus, Bree proves to be impossible to revive after the car ride, and I end up carrying her into the house.

The first thing I notice when we walk in is how good their house smells—like coffee, but fall at the same time. Val turns on lights as we go, illuminating little bits and pieces of her life as we go. Photos of both girls all over the place, a small, albeit overstuffed bookshelf in an alcove off the living room, and wall decor that says Let's Stay Home with a bright pink post-it note stuck to it that says no, let's go out! Showing both their personalities.

Val tosses a door open at the end of a hallway that I assume is Bree's and turns on the light. There are clothes all over her bed like she couldn't decide what to wear when she was in here last. Val sweeps them to the floor, and I set her on the bed.

"Need help with anything else?"

She waves both hands, leading the way back to the front of the house. "I'll get her all settled in a second. Thanks for carrying her in. I won't let her live it down, I promise."

"Good. Listen, thanks for tonight. I'm glad we ran into each other. Hopefully, we can do it again sometime, but like, actually on purpose."

She smiles, stopping in front of the door. "I'm glad we did too. Guess I'll see you bright and early," she says, leaning in to wrap me in a hug before her body realizes what's happening. I can tell, because as soon as her head lands on my chest, she pops right back up and says, "Whoa, sorry. I'm not sure where that came from."

I smile in answer, palming the back of her head and

pulling her back into my chest, enveloping her in an embrace, which she melts into.

When we pull apart, she's still so close. My gaze flicks to her mouth, where her teeth are sunken into her bottom lip. She leans in with a hand against my chest. We both move in closer, but a honk from outside breaks the spell and we shoot apart.

"Good night then," I say, scratching the back of my head as she stares down at our feet.

A second honk. "Okay, yeah good night," she says, pulling the door open, watching my every movement as I walk out of her house. With every step closer to the cab, I feel like more of a coward. When the door is open, I turn to wave, but find the front door already shut.

"Started thinking you weren't coming back," the driver says when I fold into the backseat.

"Thought about it," I mutter.

When we're a block down the road, I notice a small handbag on the seat I remember seeing slung across Val's shoulder earlier. I open my mouth to tell the driver to turn around, but think better of it as a plan forms.

Chapter Nine

VAL

The next morning, I wake to the sound of knocking. My eyes blink open, heavy with sleep. With a deep breath, I turn to find my phone on my nightstand. The one eye I have open tells me it's seven forty-five and I pop out of bed like a spring. I haven't slept in so late in ages. When my head pounds with the movement, I remember the reason I'd been dead to the world—and why I'd forgotten to set my alarm.

The knocking starts again, and this time I realize it's coming from the front door.

"Val!" Bree moans down the hall, "You've gotta get that. I'm soooo hungover. And tell whoever it is to shut the hell up!"

I laugh, starting when my phone goes off with a new text message. A smile creeps across my lips when I see who it is.

Brody: Rise and shine, Val Pal. I have something I think you're going to want :)

. . .

Val: Just woke up! Give me a second!

I throw the first sweatshirt I can find over the oversized t-shirt I slept in last night, along with the yoga pants I wore yesterday, then dash to the bathroom across the hall to pee and brush my teeth in record time.

When I finally unlock the front door, there's a smiling Brody waiting on the other side with my purse tossed over his shoulder, posing like a fashion model as he also juggles a drink carrier with three cups, and a bakery bag in his hands.

"Good morning!" He says, far more chipper than I'd expect him to be.

My gaze zones in on his lips and the memory of wanting to kiss him in this exact spot last night comes back.

"Brody," I say, jumping to attention, stepping out of the way to let him in. "Didn't expect to see you until class later. Come on in. Did I forget my purse?"

He walks straight to the kitchen island to set down his coffee shop loot.

"For you." he holds a large cup out to me as I walk up behind him. "I have to admit, I'm surprised you slept in so late. I figured your internal clock would wake you up at five am on the dot."

I take the coffee, rolling my eyes. "Yeah, maybe if I hadn't been out so late last night. Color me surprised that you're awake and moving around already."

He gives me an incredulous look, a hand to his chest. "Excuse me, ma'am, but I've already been to the gym with Wes this morning. And out of the kindness of my heart, I picked up two extra coffees and some bakery items for the two drunk girls I saw home safely last night. Decided a wellness check was necessary."

I take a sip of said coffee, grinning at Brody over my cup. "My hungover ass thanks you. And thanks for getting us home too," I say, skirting right over the fact that I almost kissed him. Did he know that was my intention? "Getting Bree home in that condition on my own would've been a struggle." I point at the purse around his neck. "After seeing you with my bag, I might have to give it to you. It just—" I fling my hand in an all-encompassing circle, "works for you."

He smiles, striking another ridiculous pose before taking it off. When he's got the strap halfway over my head, he halts his movements.

"*Wait a minute,*" he pulls my purse back into his grasp. I look up to find him frozen in place, staring at my chest—wait, no, my sweatshirt.

I look down, thinking maybe I spilled coffee or something, but it's just an old sweatshirt from high school. "What—" I ask, but then it clicks.

Oh shit.

In my haste to answer the door, I didn't pay any mind to what I was throwing over my head, just that it would cover up my state of bralessness.

"Where did you get this sweatshirt?"

"Um," I say, looking down at the yellow sweatshirt with the Wolves mascot pasted across the front. "I went to Wellford."

Brody's mouth hangs open.

"Don't make this weird," I say with a grimace, knowing how bad this must look in his eyes.

He holds up his hands, the strap of my purse flinging in the air with the power of his movement. "This makes you the enemy, because I went to Freeport."

"I know."

His eyebrows pop into his hairline. "How long have you known?"

I back up a step, predicting his reaction. "The whole time."

"Valerie! Why didn't you tell me?" My chest pangs. His

expression is more hurt than mad.

I shrug, looking away. How do I explain I never planned on telling him because I didn't expect us to become friends? That the true reason is embarrassing—I knew who he was, but he didn't have a clue I existed. Who wants to admit that? Instead of admitting either, I say, "I guess I didn't realize it was that big of a deal."

He sets my purse on the counter, eyes never leaving mine. His hands fall to my shoulders as he leans closer. "Of course it's a big deal, Val. We have something in common, and you weren't even planning on telling me."

I take another sip to keep myself busy. "Sorry. I tend to ignore anything that makes me think of home. But I know I should've told you when we became friends."

His face softens, and I remember crying on his shoulder at the bar last night. At least I won't have to explain that part. He pulls me into a hug. "I wish I would've known you in high school."

Me too.

The next Monday afternoon, my phone rings when I'm almost to the library for a study date with Brody. Half expecting it to be him calling, there's a flutter of excitement in my belly as I reach for it. It's not his name on the screen, but I still smile as I answer. "Hannah!"

"Hey, bestie! Do you have a second?"

"I'm on my way to the library, but I can talk for a second. What's up?"

She takes a deep breath. "Well, I put in my two-weeks-notice today!"

"What?!" I shout, drawing the attention of many passersby, but I don't care. "Hannah, I'm so proud of you! Things must be going better than I realized?"

She's had a camera in her hand for as long as I can remember, and it's always been her dream to go full time with her photography business. She earned an associate's degree at the community college back home over a year ago and has worked a dead-end job that pays well, and lived with her parents ever since to help her save up for this moment.

"Yes. I've booked enough weddings for next year to keep me afloat. Then there are engagement and family sessions too, so it should be a kick-ass year. It was time, because I can hardly stand my boss for these next two weeks as it is. I'm still freaking out though, which is why I called. I needed my cheerleader and smart choices advocate to tell me I'm not crazy for taking this step."

"Of course you're not crazy. You'll be so busy documenting beautiful memories for people, you won't even remember being this scared a year from now. I'm so excited for you." I say, kicking a rock on the sidewalk. "You know, this is cause for celebration!"

She squeals. "That's the other reason I'm calling." I've known her for long enough to get nervous during the pregnant pause that follows. She's planning something, and her silence tells me I'm not going to like it.

"Come home for Thanksgiving. You can spend the week with my family. We'll celebrate then."

That familiar pang hits me straight in the heart, like it always does at the thought of going home. The memories lingering there still haunt me.

Despite my reservations, I say, "I could probably make that work."

"Good, because I'm going to lose you at the end of this school year, and I want to make the most of it before I can't. I don't think you realize how many people back here would love to see you, too. My family is part of said group."

I force out a breath. "Okay, fine. I'll be there, I promise."

"Anyway, how's having Brody in class going?"

My mouth slips into a smile at the mention of him before I can catch myself. "A lot has happened." I spot him walking toward me looking like the cool guy in a chick flick, his backpack draped carelessly over one shoulder nodding at people he knows. "Shit, he's heading my way. I'll fill you in later."

"Oh my god, are you two hanging out?" She asks, reminding me just how far behind I am on filling her in.

"We're studying together. It's a thing. I'll tell you later," I whisper as he eliminates the space between us with his large stride.

"Okay, don't do anything I wouldn't do! Love you!"

"Love you too, bye." I say, rolling my eyes at her comment as Brody reaches my side.

When I turn to him, he's got his smile at the ready. "Did you just say those three little words to me?" He asks, tossing an arm over my shoulders.

"That was my best friend, Hannah."

He squints like he's wracking his brain for the name now that he knows where I grew up. "What's her last name?"

"Hawkins."

He nods, "I remember a Holt Hawkins from baseball. Any relation?"

"Her big brother. His best friend is Miles O'Harrow."

He snaps his finger, pointing at me. "I almost caught one of his home runs my freshman year. Went right off the tip of my glove. It still haunts me to this day, if I'm honest."

"Leave it to a macho male to still be salty about something that happened in sports almost eight years prior."

He scratches the back of his neck looking sheepish, "Well, when you put it like that…"

I smile and pat his arm. "It's okay. I was already judging you, anyway. Should we head in before they get rid of our study room?"

I look away from his dimples before they can ruin me from the inside out. "Sure, let's get this study date started."

I roll my eyes, although I've given up trying to explain to him that this is, in fact, not a date.

Chapter Ten

BRODY

Since class this afternoon, I've been preoccupied with my thoughts. We're a month into the semester and despite the time I've spent here in the library with Val, I knew I wasn't off to a great start with my grades. That thought was proven true when I received feedback on a paper I turned in last week.

After seeing my grade was well below average, I braved a look at my classes on the college website and my stomach bottomed out.

"You're pretty quiet today," Val says, while filling out her planner. "If you don't start talking pretty soon, I might start believing something's wrong."

I palm the back of my neck, but I must not answer quickly enough, because she halts her favorite marker to look up at me.

"Is something wrong?"

I shrug. "My grades are shit."

She caps her marker and drops it onto the table, giving me her full attention. "What happened?"

"I haven't done that well on any of my quizzes or papers this far, and it's showing. I'm not sure how to fix it though. The only class I'm doing well in is the one we have together."

"And why do you think that is?"

I push my glasses back on my nose. "Because of you."

She shakes her head. "No, it's because you're taking the time to put in the work. Can you honestly say you're doing that for all your classes?"

I think of the minimal preparation I did for a quiz in my class last Thursday. "No, not even close."

She opens her hands in front of her. "Well, there's your problem."

"Where do you find the time for that? I already stay up too late and wake up too early."

"I'm sure you do, but it's all about what you put into those hours that matters." She holds her marker in one hand while she caps and uncaps it with two fingers, the clicking noise something that would drive her nuts if I were the one doing it. "Do you see any moments in your daily life you could spend differently?"

I watch several hours of mindless television every night. I guess that doesn't need to happen. "Yeah, I guess there are. But I don't have a clue what I'd actually do if I were to spend them differently. Studying isn't my forte."

"It all starts with actually taking notes during lecture, rather than doodling in the margins of your table mate's notebook."

I smile. "I only do that with you, Val."

I think her cheeks turn pink, but it's hard to tell when she hides her face behind her hair. "The next tip is to read the chapters you're assigned, which I know you don't do."

My cheeks heat as she crosses her arms, looking at me with her eyebrows raised. She's not wrong.

"Can I study with you? Maybe I'll actually sit down to do

my work if I have a companion." I'm finding it so hard to look her in the eye, and this is why I rarely ask for help.

"When would that happen? We already have a hard enough time getting together for these study dates."

I smile after hearing her call it a date. "I'll be more flexible, I promise." I say, meaning it more than I realized. "This year is my last chance to prove I'm not the piece of shit my dad assumes I am. That I have a say in my own damn future. I need to do this, even if it sucks sometimes."

"Jeez, guilt me into it, why don't you?" She jokes, but I hate she sees it that way.

I shake my head. "No, I don't want to guilt you into it. I'm sorry. The tutoring center should have some advice, I'll go there instead." I return to my notes, but can feel Val's gaze on me.

"Brody," she says, tossing her favorite marker at me to get my attention.

I catch it, uncap it, and hold it over my notebook like I'm about to use it, raising a brow at her. "Yes?"

"Give that back," she says, leaning across the table, but she doesn't have a chance of reaching it with her short arms.

"You threw it to me, I'd say this goes against your usual rule of me not using your precious markers," I slowly bring the tip closer to my notebook, but before I have a chance to even think of what I'd write, she's rounded the table and reaches across my body for it. Toying with her, I use my large wingspan to make it even harder for her to reach.

The vanilla scent of her hair wafts into my nose as she loses her footing, landing in my lap.

"If you wanted to sit with me, all you had to do was ask," I say, capping the marker and letting my arms wrap around her loosely.

She tries to stand and fails.

I'm smiling when she turns around, murder in her eyes as she pries the marker from my hands. "I'll help you on one condition," she leans in nice and close, my breath catching in my throat.

"Oh yeah? What's that?" I ask, leaning closer and pretending her proximity hasn't knocked me off-kilter.

"Bring your own shit. Mine is off limits." She lifts from my lap, then turns in afterthought. "Make that two conditions. The flirting," she says, moving back into my space, "Stops. Now."

———

"You're the most ridiculous person I've ever known," Val says the next morning as I sit across from her at the same coffee shop booth as the day we met. I've been trying to keep a straight face since she spotted me walking in the door.

She took my promise to be more flexible seriously, texting me last night with orders to show up here at six-thirty am. I pissed Wes off when I told him I had to move our gym session back by a few hours, but he'll have to deal. At some point, my grades are going to have to be more important than my six-pack, and I think yesterday was the wake up call I needed.

"Harsh, don't you think? Cutest, funniest, most charming —any of those will do. But ridiculous? Never," I say with a teasing smile as she watches me shuffle my things around and grab the steaming coffee cup in front of me. "Is this for me?"

She shrugs. "I figured it was my turn to buy."

"But you're doing this as a huge favor to me. I'm supposed to be the one providing caffeine."

She waves off my worries, going back to those pretty letters she's always writing.

The ridiculousness she was referring to is the art kit I ran to the craft store for last night as soon as I agreed to meet her this morning. Will I use it? Maybe. But I mostly bought it to get a rise out of her. Her reaction was worth the investment.

It's one of those art kits kids always ask for on Christmas

and contains every medium imaginable. I unzip the black bag it came in. The one I walked in the coffee shop with swinging at my hip like a CEO's briefcase.

I set it on the table in front of me, nearly pulling a Val move and knocking over my coffee. Thankfully, my reflexes are fast and I practically lie on the table to keep it upright, realizing too late how wobbly it is.

As expected, Val halts her pen, glaring at me. "You're doing a great job of reminding me why I usually study alone, you know."

I grimace, "Sorry. Give me one second," I say, bending to look for the culprit of all the shaking. I wobble the table and find the leg closest to the window is missing its bottom pad. I find an extra piece of cardboard in my kit and fold it until it's about the same size as the gap under the leg and shove it under.

"Now try," I say, coming back up to find Val shaking her head but smiling.

She humors me by attempting to shake the table, but it stays put.

"Well, aren't you a regular MacGyver?"

I smile, going back to my art kit and picking out a few skinny markers I can use.

"If I'd known you were buying one, I would have let you borrow mine from first grade." Val pipes up from the other side of the booth as I continue exploring my new supplies.

"Thought you said your markers are off limits?" I raise my eyebrows in challenge.

She laughs, shaking her head. "Ready to get started?"

I hold up a finger. "One more thing," I pull my backpack onto my lap, unzipping the largest compartment. I pull out a large pack of expensive chunky pastel highlighters that the store attendant helped me pick out last night. "These are for you," I say, setting them down on her notebook.

When I brave a look, Val's mouth is hanging wide open, staring at my gift.

"Val? You good?" I ask, a little nervous.

"Uh, yeah," she finally says, picking up her new high-lighters gingerly between two fingers. "Brody, do you have any idea how much these things cost?"

I laugh. "Yes, you have an expensive hobby, Val. But it's okay, because you're worth it. I've seen you with a couple, but figured you needed all the colors. It's my way of saying thank you for this."

I look down at my notebook, uncomfortable with the way she's looking at me. Out of nowhere, she lands on my side of the booth, throwing her arms around me. I barely have time to reciprocate before a kiss lands on my cheek. "Thank you, Brody. Really," she waits for me to look at her before adding, "I've been saving up to buy a few colors when they went on sale, and you went and got me the whole rainbow." She stares at me like she's seeing me for the first time, hugging me again before she's up and back on her own side of the booth, like it never happened.

"Alright," she says all easy breezy, as if I can't still feel the press of her lips on my cheek—although there is a brand new smile I've never seen before, lifting her freckled cheeks. "Should we start with some study strategies?"

Chapter Eleven

VAL

The next few weeks pass in similar fashion—Brody and I spending even more time together outside of studying, getting to know each other in a way I never expected. We realize our favorite restaurant is the same little hole-in-the-wall Italian restaurant off campus. He drove us there after a late night at the library and we shared two entrées.

Then there was the night he talked me into being a stand-in with his roommate's intramural kickball team. I've never been the most coordinated, so I was nothing more than a warm body to make the team eligible to play that week. That was until I started getting the hang of things and caught the other team's best offensive player's kick. I still think he kicked it at me, knowing I was the weakest link. Joke was on him though, because I turned around and kicked a double for the game-winning run.

Brody even surprised me one Friday morning to tell me he'd earned a higher grade in his worst class after studying and acing his last test. All the extra time we've been spending studying has paid off for him. Hell, I even find *myself* getting more work done.

Lecturing Brody about screwing around during our study dates makes me feel like a hypocrite if I scroll social media or reading a book on my phone. Oddly enough, letting someone in on what used to be my sacred study time has even been beneficial for me.

All the extra activities have helped take my mind off the stress of going home for Thanksgiving. Hannah's checked in on me a handful of times the past few weeks to make sure my plans haven't changed. They haven't, and as much as I'm looking forward to seeing the Hawkins family, I always feel a little uneasy at the thought of going home.

The most obvious reason is that my parents are gone, and I no longer have any living family members. And everyone looks at me when I return to town, like I might break down in tears if they wait long enough. The best part about being at college is that no one knows me, and no one knows my back-story like the people in my small hometown do.

There's also the fact that, since my father's funeral, I've been avoiding stepping foot into my childhood home. My mom's best friend looks after it, but it's technically mine now. I will most likely sell it when I figure out my next step in life, but to do that, I'd have to pack everything up, and it just feels like too daunting of a task. So I've put it off for three years. But I'm reminded every time I go back there that I have yet to do it.

I've split the holidays between going home and spending it with Bree's family in the suburbs of Chicago, but Hannah has a point. I don't know where I'll be this time next year, but there's a chance I won't be able to come home for the holidays. I'd be silly not to spend as much time with my second family as I can before that happens.

One Monday morning in the middle of October, I get to class extra early, scared to admit to myself how excited I am to see Brody. Since I'm still on strict orders from myself not to initiate our text conversations, we barely talked over the weekend. I had typed out a message or two, but they remained unsent.

I even went as far as running to buy us both a coffee this morning, since he's done the same for me so many times this semester. But the time he usually arrives in the classroom comes and goes. As the auditorium fills, I send him a text.

Val: I hope you're on your way to class! Wouldn't want Mr. Roadie to make you his next victim!

But class starts without him or even a text back, and I start to sweat as our professor assigns the next chunk of our project. In fact, I barely hear his list of expectations over the ringing in my ears as I try to tell myself it's not a big deal that Brody didn't show.

But when the professor finishes the lecture segment of class and lets us get to work on our projects, I stare at the blank page of my notebook I flipped to at the beginning of class. No little scribbles Brody adds in the margins every class just to piss me off. No dribbles of coffee from him making me laugh as I try to keep quiet during lecture—no Brody sitting next to me even though he promised to show up for himself, for me, all semester long.

"Ms. Boyd," I hear off to the side of my table and turn toward the sound. "I assume he's already filled you in, but regardless, I received an email from your partner in the middle of the night last night that he was sick and wouldn't be here today. His inability to show will only count against him, not you."

"Oh," I say, my heart sinking with his explanation. "I didn't know that. Thanks for filling me in."

Roadie nods. "Work on what you can today, but I don't blame you if you'd rather wait until he returns."

"Will do, thanks," I lie.

Screw that. I'm moving forward without him.

He emailed in the middle of the night to say he was sick? That's got Sunday Fun Day written all over it. And he knew I'd get mad, so he didn't bother to let me know.

I rage-write in my spiral notebook for the rest of class, taking liberty to choose where our project will go from here and feeling just petty enough to hope he won't be happy with my decisions.

As soon as I'm on the sidewalk after class, I call Brody, catching his voicemail because he's too much of a coward to answer.

This.

This was exactly what I was waiting for. I knew his behavior lately was too good to be true. He practically told me his shortcomings, and I actually believed him when he said he wanted to change.

"Hey, it's Brody Ryan. Leave me a message," his voicemail says, and when the beep goes off, I let him have it.

"Yeah, hi, Brody. The only thing worse than not being worth a quick text message to let me know you wouldn't be in class this morning was knowing you let our professor know in the middle of the night last night. What, are you hungover? I'm so disappointed.

"Oh, and he assigned another part of our project today, but don't worry. I worked on it on my own, and for that reason, I made a few decisions you may not be happy with. But I'm not happy with you either, so I guess we'll be even. I thought we'd finally made it past the irresponsible choices, like letting Sunday Fun Day get so out of hand, you can't make it to class the next day?" I pause for a breath, then add. "Call

85

me back before this afternoon if you feel so inclined. I'll try to go over everything with you in the library."

I stare at my phone for a long moment after I hang up, heart beating out of my chest, wondering why I don't feel better after telling him off.

At four-thirty, my phone finally rings. I should already be at the library, but I decided not to show since I didn't hear from him all day. It would serve him right to show up and not find me there at this point. So when I answer, it's exactly what I'm expecting. What I find, though, is not even close.

"Hello?" I answer in a clipped tone.

"Val," Brody's voice comes over the line…but it's off somehow. The gravel-like quality it usually possesses has been replaced with a dry, scratchiness.

"Brody?"

"Yeah, shit, Val. I'm so sorry. I can't believe I didn't send it. I woke up and realized the text I typed out last night never sent. I'm sick—have been all weekend. My sleep schedule's all out of whack, and I think I passed out before I pressed send. I'm so sorry."

Oh fuck.

"And I listened to your voicemail. I hate knowing that was the first conclusion you jumped to, although I can't blame you."

"Brody, stop. God, I said some nasty things. I'm so sorry. Can I get you anything?" My heart is pounding overtime in my chest, my face heated with embarrassment after realizing the conclusions I jumped to this morning were completely out of line. "What's wrong? Do you have a cough?"

"Yeah, I think my roommate Isaiah passed it to me. He was suffering last week and we share a bathroom."

"Shit, Brody. I feel like an asshole. I'm so sorry I jumped to conclusions."

His voice is quiet when he answers, "It's okay."

"No, it's not. Will soup help? I can be over in half an hour."

"Soup sounds great, but I don't want to get you sick."

"Nonsense. I'll take extra vitamins. See you soon."

Chapter Twelve

Val

It's early evening, and I can hear noises coming from inside the house when I step up to the front door and knock.

Wes opens the door. "Valerie, what's up? Brody's a little under the weather. I'm not sure he's up for vis—"

I hold up my bags before he can finish his sentence. "I told him I was coming." He takes in the logo from a deli down the street, putting two and two together as he steps away from the door to let me in.

Inside the foyer, the house looks clean for a place three guys live. Aside from a few beer cans on random surfaces, and some shoes strewn about the entryway, it's fairly clean. A television is blaring somewhere in the back of the house—sports, by the sound of it.

"I didn't know semester projects consisted of nursing each other back to health," Wes says, leading me through the house. A teasing dimple pops in his cheek, and I can see why Bree fixated on him on her birthday. She still hasn't stopped asking me to get his number, but now's not the time. Either way, I'm not too blind to see he's the epitome of tall, dark, and handsome with his tall, broad build, his tan from a summer spent with his family in Florida, and full head of jet black hair complimented by a thick beard. He's his own kind of handsome.

"Yeah, well, I left him a shitty voicemail this morning on the assumption he didn't show up to class because he was hungover. Does this say *sorry I'm an asshole?*" I ask, holding up the bags with a forced smile.

He grimaces. "You know, as his best friend, that kind of behavior wouldn't have surprised me a year ago. But something's changed in him, and I think it might have something to do with you." I look up, surprised, but he just smiles and nods. He adds in a whisper, "Don't tell him I told you that, though. Use it to your advantage." He walks me to the stairs and points, "His room is the first door on the right. He's been dead to the world since Saturday, so go on in if he doesn't answer. And for the record, I think you've more than made up for the error you made this morning, so don't worry. I know he'll be happy to see you."

I try not to think about how suggestive Wes' words have been since I walked in the door as the old steps creak on my way up to Brody's room.

The hallway lights are on, and a door hangs open at the end of the hallway—someone's bedroom. But the first door on the right has no light coming from under it as I approach with caution.

Maybe I should have stayed home to let him sleep, but before I can talk myself out of staying, I tap on the door with the only free knuckle I have, thanks to these bags weighing me down.

I hear a deep breath on the other side of the door, one you make waking from a deep slumber.

"Brody," I whisper-yell, "It's Val. Can I come in?"

"Yeah," I hear him say, his voice all breathy.

As the door opens, I hear a click as a bedside lamp illuminates the space.

I follow the bare arm to a squinting, sleepy, and adorable Brody, who's propped up on an elbow in his bed—shirtless.

Shit.

"Hey," I say, sheepishly. "I come bearing…" I look down at the bags, "*Sorry-for-being-a-dick-gifts* that I hope will make you feel better—not just about what an ass I was on the phone earlier, but also physically—" I cut myself off when I realize I'm babbling like a madwoman. I take in his appearance, "You look like shit." Truthfully, he doesn't, but if I don't make a joke, I know I'll stand in the doorway ogling him long enough to embarrass myself.

He laughs, and it's husky. Like a raspy morning voice on steroids. "Thanks. You know you didn't have to do this, right?" He asks, sitting up, propping his pillow behind his back as his comforter falls, revealing his naked chest and torso.

Shit, I did not think this through.

"I know I didn't, but I wanted to," I say as my mouth dries.

He shrugs, his swollen eyes showing how exhausted he must feel. "Well, enter at your own risk. I don't want to make you sick."

"I take my vitamins like clockwork, and took an immune booster before coming over. It's not like I didn't know what I was walking into."

"In that case," he pats his bed with his hand—on a spot right next to him. A spot so close, it makes me want to abort mission.

I set the bags at the foot of his bed, rifling through them to show him what I brought. I leave the sandwich I bought myself off to the side, but hand him a large cup of chicken noodle soup, along with the deli's signature turkey sandwich.

I pull a large bottle of water from the second bag and hand that to him, too.

"I got you a whole assortment of medicine, since I wasn't sure what you had," I say, pulling vitamin-C, cough drops, Advil, and some day and night cold medicine from the bag.

"Val, you didn't have to do all this, but I'm grateful for you," he says after I've crawled into his bed to sit next to him. He leans his head back against the headboard to look at me as he chews a bite of his sandwich.

I pat his leg, then quickly remove my hand like the contact burned me. "I feel horrible about what I said today. You didn't deserve my wrath and I know you're not the guy I described in the voicemail and I felt like an explanation was necessary. I'm sorry, again. This was the least I could do."

He shakes his head, his eyes roaming every inch of my face. "No, it's not. The least you could have done was let my call earlier go to voicemail, then reply with a one-word text message. But you didn't do that. Dare I say, this is the *most* you could do—in natural, over-achiever fashion."

I smile, a little of my remorse dissipating.

We sit in a comfortable silence as we eat until Brody turns to say, "For what it's worth, I'm sorry I missed class, and that I was so out of it, I forgot to send you a message to warn you. I want you to know I'd never do it on purpose."

I finish what I'd been chewing and turn my body more toward him. "You know, I think that's why I was so mad. I jumped to conclusions, but what hurt was that I thought we'd gotten closer lately. I thought you purposely kept it from me. Looking back, I shouldn't have believed it. I'm sorry I did."

He nods, looking into his soup as he grabs another bite. "I gave you my word that I'd show up for both of us this semester, and I thought I'd done a pretty good job of building your trust so far."

"You did," I admit, only realizing how true it is after the words are out of my mouth. "You've done nothing but prove yourself to me, and the first time that trust was tested, I forgot every good thing you've done. Shit, I feel like such an asshole."

He bumps me with his elbow, a sleepy, but sweet smirk on his lips. "You're not an asshole, Val. I just want you to trust me, okay?"

"I do," I admit. "Or at least, I do now."

He smiles, moving the remnants of his meal off to the nightstand and breaking into the medicine cabinet I brought with me. "Good, because what we've got between us," he wags a finger from his chest to mine and back again, "Is important to me, and I don't want it to end on a technicality."

I finish my sandwich, trying not to read too much into the way he describes our relationship.

"Would you stick around if I went to take a shower quick?"

I gulp loudly, instantly thinking about him naked.

Shit, I should leave.

"Yeah, of course," my traitorous mouth forms the words before I even know what's happening.

He smiles, jumping out of bed and crossing the room to a sleek black dresser to pull a pair of black athletic shorts and dark blue boxer briefs from the drawers. "I promise I'll be quick, but make yourself at home," he says, handing me the TV remote.

"Actually, do you have a new set of sheets?"

His smile is sheepish, "Why, do they smell bad?" He scratches the back of his neck, "I have been laying there for a few days now."

"No, it's—" I halt. We're back into uneasy territory for me. "My mom always used to say the best thing to do when you've been lying in bed, feeling under the weather all day is a nice change of sheets."

He smiles, but shakes his head. "I'm not letting you change my sheets, Val."

"I think we're both well aware that my being here is

unnecessary. But I'm here, and I want my partner back in class as soon as possible. So where are the sheets?"

A stare down ensues, his eyes sparkling with amusement, as I try for my best death glare.

Finally, he points to his closet. "They're on the top shelf. Honestly, they might fall on you when you open the door. Good luck."

Before I can thank him, he's out the door, walking slower than usual toward the bathroom.

I toss our trash, then grab his sheets and make quick work of getting them changed.

Once finished, I flop back onto the bed with my phone in my hand.

Val: I'm in Brody's bedroom! I repeat: I am in Brody Ryan's bedroom!

Hannah: What are you texting me for then? Go get some girl!

I've tried my best to keep her informed of every new development between Brody and I, and she continually tells me to go for it, which hasn't been helpful for the part of me I'm still attempting to hold back with him.

Val: Not why I'm here, but thanks for the pep talk.

Hannah: What are you there for then?

Val: He's sick. I brought him a care package.

· · ·

Hannah: OHMIGOSH

Hannah: THAT. IS. SO. CUTE.

Val: Shut up. Don't get any ideas.

Hannah: You two are gonna bone.

Val: Nobody even says that anymore.

Hannah: Don't change the subject.

Val: Whatever. He's in the shower right now. FML.

Hannah: OMG.

Val: Stop making it a thing.

Hannah: Can I be the maid of honor at your wedding??

Val: Only if I can be yours when you and Miles get married.

I hope the message will annoy her, since she's been half in love with her brother's best friend her entire life. She insists nothing will ever happen between them, but she doesn't see the way he looks at her when she isn't paying attention.

Hannah: Who else would it be?

The water cuts off across the hall and I'm mad at myself for wasting my chance to snoop around his room. His space is tidy for how unorganized he is in every other aspect of his life. There are small piles of clothes here and there. There's a framed photo of Wrigley Field in Chicago, the only other picture is of him holding a cute little dark-haired, gap-toothed girl with bright blue eyes in a handmade, glittery foam frame on his dresser, which I assume is the niece he told me about.

Before I can peek around more, the door is tossed open and Brody steps inside shirtless, making the space immediately shrink with his presence. The sandalwood scent that wafts from him is intoxicating as I try to make eye contact instead of counting how many abs pop in his torso as he crosses the room.

"Feel better?"

"So much better," he says, flinging his body onto the mattress, bouncing me in place.

"I'm glad. I should go soon." I play with the strings around the edge of a blanket on his bed for something to focus on. "You need to get another good night's rest so you can be back in class on Wednesday."

He turns to his side, propping his head on a fist as he looks up at me. "Will you stay and tuck me in?"

I laugh, lying on the pillow next to his, half-sure he's kidding.

But then he bites his bottom lip, smiling at me as his eyes roam my face.

"Are you serious?"

He chuckles, "Yeah."

"I'm not tucking you in, you're a big boy. I think you can handle it," I tell him, making to leave the bed, but he catches my hand. I look down at him again.

"How about a cuddle, then?"

Everything in me is itching to scream *yes*, so instead, I ask, "Did you take your night time medicine yet?"

He shakes his head and I get up to grab it, along with his water. "Here," I say, holding the pills out to him after popping them out of the blister packet.

He sits up again, tossing them in his mouth and giving me a closed-mouth smile as he unscrews the cap on his water.

He throws the corner of the covers back in invitation before turning to me with a dubious expression. "Well?"

"Well, what?"

He lets out a faux-frustrated breath. "You staying or going?"

I have every intention of turning him down and walking out the door, but like they have a mind of their own, my limbs betray me. Step by step, I approach his side of the bed and pull back the corner of the comforter as Brody scoots backward with a smile on his face. Then, like we've done this a million times before, I rest my head on his chest, wrapping my arm around him as his rests on my waist. My entire body buzzes as we situate ourselves. And when he says, "Night, Val," I release a long breath, relaxing even more into his embrace.

"Night, Brody."

Chapter Thirteen

BRODY

It's been a week since Val showed up at my house to nurse me back to health. Seven days since I fell asleep with her in my arms. In the days since, I've been trying to figure out exactly what that night meant.

Unfortunately, Val hasn't been helpful in figuring it out. All I know is I woke up alone the next morning, which means she left in the middle of the night. I only know this because I always wake up randomly in the night when I take sleeping pills, and when I did, she was still lying there in my arms, her breaths coming out in little puffs against my neck, making me smile.

Ever since, she's been evading any conversation that doesn't have to do with class, like she's pulling away from the rapport we'd built leading up to that night.

Like when I messaged her the next day.

. . .

Brody: Thanks again for the care package last night—and for helping me fall asleep. I must've been out because I didn't even notice you leave.

Val: It was no problem. I hope it helps you get back on your feet.

She'd completely ignored half of my message.

Then that Wednesday, I showed up to class feeling fully recovered, thanks to rest and the meds she'd brought me. I stopped at Beans for a latte for both of us. After thanking me, she was all business, getting right to what I'd missed in class on Monday. It was as if it'd never happened. In class on Friday, I didn't even bother bringing it up.

My messages over the weekend went unanswered. When I asked what she did all weekend, she waved it off and changed the subject—then flirted with me toward the end of class.

Mixed signals much?

But it's Monday afternoon, which means we have a study date in the library. Like always, I show up a little early and I can't help but laugh when I realize that's Val's doing. It's nice, knowing I've changed for the better because she expects better from me.

This time I'm a little earlier than usual, so I take it upon myself to pick up the key for our study room at the front desk. Except when I do, the girl at the desk informs me we're not on the schedule today.

"Okay," I say, taking the news in stride. "Can I just sign up for one now, then?"

She gives me a blank look, like I requested the moon. "It's Midterms," she says nice and slow. "We're booked the rest of the week."

"Shit," I mutter under my breath. I don't want to add any extra stress to Val's plate, but it looks like we're going to have to do something different today.

I look around the lobby, and by the amount of foot traffic, I know there will be slim pickings for empty tables. Flustered, I pull out my phone to send Val an SOS.

She doesn't answer, but bursts through the front door a few minutes later. She spots me immediately, searching my hands for the key.

"Hey, did you happen to get my message?"

She looks up at me, brow adorably lifted, "No, I haven't checked my phone. Why?"

I let out a breath and tell her the news.

She palms her forehead. "This day just keeps getting better!" The words drip with sarcasm. She checks her watch and turns more fully toward me. "Sorry, that's my bad," she rubs at her forehead. "Let's head home then. We can work around my schedule tomorrow."

"Don't apologize. And I shouldn't have let you be the only one making study plans. We're partners, so it's on me as much as it's on you."

She looks at me like she's seeing me for the first time.

I look away under the weight of her searching gaze, trying to find a way out of our predicament. "Let's head to the coffee shop."

She shakes her head. "Too noisy."

"I'd say let's go to my house, but we'd have the same issue."

She eyes me, then looks at the ground as we continue to walk. "Yeah, same thing with the commons." She takes a deep breath, then says, "I guess we could go to my house. Bree has plans tonight anyway, so it will be quiet."

"You don't sound happy with that option," I point out, and she avoids my gaze. "Are you sure?"

She finally looks up at me, squinting at the afternoon sun as we reach the sidewalk. "Yep, it's all good. Come on, I'll lead the way."

"My car's on campus. I'll drive us."

I've been to this house twice, but I still haven't seen the whole thing and with the way she's been holding me at arm's length the past week, I don't see it happening tonight either.

I hold the screen door as she unlocks the house. It's clear she's more uncomfortable than she let on. She's hardly made a peep since we left campus. Or maybe she's nervous. I won't lie, I'm feeling the pressure about being alone with her again like this too. I hope the awkwardness dissipates before the night is through.

She kicks off her shoes immediately inside the door, and I follow her lead. Val sets her keys in a little dish on the entry table to the left of the door and I remove my backpack from my shoulders, letting it dangle in my hands until she gives me direction.

"Do you want anything to drink?" She asks, breaking the awkward silence. "I'll grab us a few things and you can get settled in." She answers herself before I have a chance, looks around, then turns back to me. "The couch or the island?"

She asks, but I'm already headed to make myself comfortable on the sofa.

We've just finished divvying up the roles for our homework when we hear a car pull up to the curb outside, followed by another in the driveway.

"What the—" Val starts, lifting a curtain to investigate.

We're greeted by the sound of a group of girls cackling like hens on their way to the door. Val looks at me and our expressions say the same thing: *So much for a quiet night of studying.*

Two seconds later, the front door is thrown open as Bree and four other girls topple into the entryway.

"Heeeyy!" they all call out as they turn and find Val and I on the couch together as if nothing is amiss.

Bree stops on a dime when she realizes we're here, but it isn't long before a slow smirk splits her face.

"Uh oh, it looks like we double-booked the living room," says one of the girls. She's carrying two pizza boxes and a bottle of wine, and walks it over to the kitchen island like she owns the place.

I look at Val, whose face is drained of color. Her four-leaf clover pendant at her throat is clutched in her grasp—something I've noticed she does when she's nervous or uncomfortable.

"I thought you guys were somewhere for your wine night already," she says, her eyes having an entirely different conversation with the person who knows her best in the room.

"Yeah, we're having it here because everyone else's place was occupied. I sent you a message earlier. I thought you were studying at the library."

She nods her head, and the motion comes out all twitchy. "Yeah, our study room fell through, so this was the next best place since I thought you were out for the night. I haven't even looked at my phone," she says before taking a deep breath.

"We can call it a night," I whisper to Val, attempting to break the tension-filled silence in the room.

I'm already on my feet, clearing the coffee table of my mess, shoving it in my backpack.

The ladies in the kitchen take my sudden movement as permission to fill plates with pizza and pouring wine.

"But we haven't even figured out all the details yet. We've got at least another hour of work." Her eyes ping-pong between my own and she surprises me by saying, "Let's just go to my bedroom. It'll be quiet enough in there."

At her invitation, a prickly awareness dances through my body, settling deep in my belly at the thought of being locked in her bedroom together. "You sure? I don't want to put you out."

She plasters on a smile I know is fake, then throws her hands up at her sides in a *why not* gesture. "Yeah, of course. Let's go."

Val opens her bedroom door and flips on the light, ushering me in. I waste no time making a beeline for her bed, dropping my bag off to the side and flopping on top of her queen sized mattress.

"Ahh, I could get used to this, Cupcake." I snuggle into her pillow, a puff of her signature scent billowing out all around me.

She stands near the bed, looking down her nose at me, arms crossed. "Yep, exactly what I wanted," she says, eyes reduced to slits of amber, "For my bed to reek of stinky male."

"No worries, I stink real nice. You even told me so."

Her eyebrows scrunch. "When did I say that?"

I smirk, "When you were tipsy at The Saloon on Bree's birthday."

Her cheeks immediately turn pink, but she rolls her eyes as if she's not embarrassed. "What I say when I'm drunk can't be used against me." She picks up her bag, making her way to her desk instead of sitting next to me like I'd hoped she would.

"Can I order some Chinese takeout?" I ask after a few minutes of trying to get into my work, but my hunger pangs are relentless.

"Yes, please. I'm starving," Val says without turning to look at me.

"What would you like? I'll buy."

"Sweet and sour chicken, fried rice, and at least three crab rangoons."

I type away on my phone, adding more to our order than necessary.

"It'll be here in fifteen minutes."

"Thanks," Val says, finally swiveling in her chair. "I didn't realize how hungry I was until you started talking about food."

When the food arrives, I walk out to grab it. Bree is out in the kitchen topping off her wine when she I'm retreating toward the back of the house.

"Having a good evening?" She asks, smirking from behind her glass of wine.

"Yes. And if I didn't know that tonight's study fiasco was a total fluke, I'd say you had a hand in the chaos, simply from the look on your face."

She bites her lip, failing to hide her smile. "Val doesn't bring guys back to our house, so the fact that you were here before I arrived was a miracle in itself. Her taking you back to her room surprised even me. I could say I feel bad, but the way you two were blushing as you left the living room was all I needed to see to feel better about it."

I shake my head. "I don't know what you're talking about."

She sips from her glass. "Yes you do." And just like that, she leaves the room, smiling back at me over her shoulder.

Before I can recover, Val appears in the hallway, looking between her roommate and I.

"Want to drink some wine?" she asks after Bree disappears into the living room. When I don't answer, she adds, "Or there's water and—"

"Wine's great."

She smiles, "Okay. I set up my desk as a makeshift table for us to eat at. You can take the food in there."

"Okay."

I'm surprised she didn't opt for eating in the kitchen, putting space between us like she has the rest of the week, but I'll take my wins where I can get them, even if she's still acting a little off. When I get back to her room, she's moved another chair in front of her desk, and it's clear of all homework. I pull our takeout boxes from the sack, separating our orders, taking the wooden chair so Val can have her comfy computer chair.

Val walks in a moment later, carrying two stemless wine glasses full of an orange-yellow liquid, the wine bottle tucked under her arm.

"I didn't want the girls to drink it," she says, setting one of the glasses in front of me, then the bottle between us.

"That's understandable," I say, watching her settle into her chair.

Each of us digs into our respective cartons of food without a word, proof of how hungry we are.

"This is delicious," Val says, her mouth full of fried rice. "Whatever you have over there smells good. What is it?"

"I ordered the same as you, just added egg drop soup, pot stickers, and egg rolls."

Her jaw drops, her cheeks stuffed full like a chipmunk. She has no business being so adorable.

"How will you eat it all?"

"I won't. I was planning to make you help."

With that invitation, she leans over me, snagging a pot sticker with her chopsticks, dips it, then stuffs it in her mouth.

"How is it?" I ask, watching her chew.

She washes it down with a sip of wine. "Delicious," then she leans over me again, the side of her head leaning on my shoulder. "What else you got over there?"

When we finally get back to work, Val and I sit sideways on her bed, backs leaning against the wall. I've been trying to concentrate on the work we need to finish by Wednesday, but Val's knee keeps pressing into my thigh, taking every ounce of my concentration.

An outburst of laughs comes from the living room, and Val and I both stop what we're doing to look at each other.

"Do you wish you were out there with the girls watching the Bachelor?"

She screws up her face. "I go out of my way *not* to watch that show. No thanks."

"And she chooses Brody over reality TV and wine. Noted."

She rolls her eyes. "We have our own wine," she says, holding up her glass. "And I chose school, technically."

"Ah, right."

She pushes her shoulder into mine. "What, I did!"

"Keep telling yourself that."

She removes her books from her lap, tossing them onto the mattress. "I'm gonna use the bathroom. Can I trust you in here by yourself?"

"Of course."

"Good boy," she says, patting my head, and like an abandoned puppy, I lean into her attention.

I stand as soon as I hear the bathroom door down the hall click shut. It's easier to look around her space when she's not watching my every move. I walk around, taking in all her little knickknacks.

She has a framed photo of her as a kid, sandwiched between two people who could only be her parents on her nightstand. She has her mom's amber eyes and perfectly straight-toothed smile and her dad's unruly blonde curls.

My chest hurts, knowing she's been living the past few years without them. As much as I can't stand my dad some days, I couldn't imagine my life without my parents.

I continue to her bookshelf, which is packed full of fantasy and romance books. More framed photos. Some of her with Bree, and another of a young Val with her arms wrapped around a girl with freckles and long auburn hair.

My eyes snag on an open book turned face down, like

105

she'd been so lost in its pages, she tossed it there when she realized the time.

I pick it up, lying back on her bed and flipping back a few pages to see what had her attention.

I'm a page in when she walks back through the door. "What are you doing?"

I move the book until our gazes meet. "Just seeing what's so special about this paranormal romance you were reading."

She tries to pull it from my grasp, but I hold on tight.

"This Garrett guy sure likes to growl. Are you sure he's okay?"

She huffs out a breath, rolling her eyes at me for good measure.

"If you'd put that down, I was gonna ask if you were interested in helping me finish this," she says, swishing the half-full bottle of wine we'd started drinking early. "My concentration is gone for the night, I think."

"Oh," I say, setting the book back where I found it and stuffing my books into my backpack, tossing it to the floor. Then I'm on her bed, sitting with my back against the wall, letting my feet hang off the side. I pat the space next to me in invitation.

Her eyebrows knit. "This seems like a terrible idea."

I smile, knowing she's right.

Chapter Fourteen

VAL

I settle in next to Brody on my bed, every nerve ending in my body on high alert.

If I'm being honest with myself, my mind hasn't been focused on my work for the past several hours. It feels like an important shift has already happened between us and I'm waiting on bated breath to see his next move. Instead of shutting them down like I used to, I crave them. Even if I've been trying my hardest to put some distance between us the past week after I so stupidly fell asleep in his arms.

I usually lay in bed for several minutes before falling asleep, which was the only reason I stayed. I thought I'd wait until Brody was asleep and sneak out of his room. But I was so comfortable there in his arms; I fell asleep immediately and didn't wake until the sky outside was already taking on a steely gray glow of morning.

We're sitting together on my bed a week later—almost down to the minute. The circumstances may be different this time. The tingle of excitement under my skin buzzes just the same.

Nothing a little peach wine can't fix, right?

We pass the bottle back and forth, and there's something extremely intimate about drinking from the same bottle Brody's lips have touched. Especially when his lips have never touched my own.

"Sometimes I feel like I know you well, but at the same time, I don't know you at all," Brody says, passing me the bottle.

I take a sip, then turn toward him. "What do you mean? You really think you know me?"

He shrugs, "I think so. I know you're particular about how people see you. Your appearance and anything linked to your name. You're a leader, and have a hard time giving up control of things." he gives me a knowing look, and I roll my eyes before he continues. "You're loyal to those you care about, and I have a feeling you stand up for them, too. You're like a treasure trove of feelings, but it takes a while for you to open up to new people."

His words make me feel like a butterfly pinned to a board for him to examine. We've only known each other for a short time, but he sees right through the walls I've built to keep people out.

"Was I close?"

Instead of answering, I steal the bottle from him and take another long pull, wincing at the taste.

"Sometimes you stop what you're doing, like staring at your notebook you'd been writing in, or halt in bringing your coffee to your mouth." He continues, "Like your body is saying, *oh, the audacity of this man,* but you're eerily calm. Unless I push your buttons a little longer, then you let me have it. It's pretty damn cute, cupcake."

"Why do you call me that?"

He pulls a strand of my hair taut before letting it bounce back to life. "Your hair smells like a vanilla cupcake."

I laugh, covering my face with my hands. "Oh, thank goodness."

"Why? What did you think it meant?"

I shake my head. "I don't know, but was expecting some sort of sexual innuendo."

When I sneak a peek at him, we both start laughing uncontrollably.

When I regain my composure, I say, "And for the record, you're hellbent on driving me crazy, so my reactions shouldn't be that much of a surprise to you." I turn fully toward him. "You might think you've got me all figured out, but you aren't the only one. I know you're the fun party boy of your friend group, but there are only a handful of people who truly know the guy hidden under the facade. You'd rather spend your time doing shallow things and being the life of the party so you don't have to think about the stuff that keeps you up at night. You're overly positive so no one sees you're actually freaking out on the inside."

It's his turn to steal the bottle from my hands.

"Was I close?" I ask, mimicking his earlier words.

After he takes a chug, he turns to me. "Remember that time in class I told you you sounded like my dad?"

I nod, an invisible fist twisting my gut.

Brody laughs without humor, shaking his head. "His favorite pastime is to point out every way I won't live up to his expectations. My brother's six years older than me, and he's always been studious, a real straight shooter. He's a lot like you, in the way he knows exactly what he wants out of life— had it all figured out his freshman year of high school. But I was never like that. I lost myself in sports and video games with my best friend. I rode off on my bike daily in the summer and only returned when the streetlights flickered to life. Luke spent his summers making money with the lawn service he started in middle school. He was always someone I looked up to, but we're nothing alike, you know?"

I hum in agreement, watching his Adam's apple bob as he takes another sip. My gaze trails up his neck to the stubble on his jaw before he speaks again. "My dad's trying to force me into more years of school so I can—and I quote—'make something of myself.' Says he'd be proud to have a physical therapist or occupational therapist in the family than the one thing I've ever seen myself doing with my life. I mean, it's something I'm actually passionate about." His gaze turns to mine, and I watch as he tries to school his expression. "But it'll never be enough for him."

I set my hand on his. "I was defensive there. I'm sorry for rubbing a sore spot."

He tangles our fingers, my nerves firing at his intentional touch. "You don't say." He smiles, leaning his head back against the wall.

We're sitting closer than I realized, and when his gaze flicks to my mouth, I lean closer. Our hands are so close, both settled on the blankets between us. I inch my fingers closer until I'm touching his hand. His tongue peeks out to wet his lips as he threads our fingers together.

His head dips, his peach wine lips meeting mine in a soul-crushing kiss. It's like he's been dying to do this forever, and his will finally failed to keep him away. His hand finds my lower back, pulling my body closer. I go willingly, moving my hand to his shoulder, letting it slide across the planes of his chest. My skin tingles as if I've finally found my superpower in touching him—electricity coursing through my veins. When I reach his abdomen, the muscles underneath ripple under my fingertips.

When he deepens the kiss, his tongue exploring as it slips across my top lip, my brain is practically mush—my body like putty in his skilled hands.

Then I'm falling forward as his back slides down the wall,

finding my mattress until I'm half lying on his body. I faintly hear the sound of glass sliding on wood as he sets the wine bottle on the ledge of my headboard, his free hand pulling my leg over his hip until I'm straddling him, then landing on my lower back and pulling me into him.

His hands move to the sides of my face, and he's holding up my weight as he gently pulls my face from his. My eyes open slowly, surroundings swimming in my vision as if I've been drugged, then coming back all at once.

"Even better than I imagined it," his gaze bouncing back and forth between my own. Usually hazel, his eyes are bright green leaves in a rainforest newly quenched of their thirst.

"Yeah, me too."

"You've thought about this?"

I look down at his lips, the lower one more plump than the top—perfectly kissable. "Like that's even a question."

He grins, a flash of white teeth and dimples, then his lips rise to meet my own again. We both inhale at the contact. One hand finds my ass, sliding down my curves until my thigh is tight in his grip. Desire trickles through every inch of my body, pooling low in my belly. I regret wearing my thinnest pair of black leggings today. Every movement, every touch might as well be on bare skin by the way it feels. His tongue dances with my own as his hand snakes back up my body until it's underneath my shirt, his hot fingertips pressing against my lower back and leaving me breathless.

One finger dips below the clasp of my bra, the simple touch suddenly switching my brain back on. Our lips disconnect with a pop as I sit up, putting distance between his dangerous mouth and my own.

He's half pride, half worry, like he's afraid I'll spook if he makes a sudden movement, proof that he knows me too well. It's taking everything in me not to kick him out of my house. I lift to my knees, preparing to remove myself from his lap, but his hands clamp down on my thighs, holding me in place.

"Don't go yet," he says, the smile dropping off his face as those eyes rove every visible inch of my body, making me feel self-conscious.

I settle back over his hips, his hand only moving when he's sure I won't leave. His thumb brushes my cheek. "You're beautiful, you know that? I've thought so since the moment we met."

"You mean your first impression of me wasn't that I was extremely clumsy?" I ask, watching his mouth spread into a grin.

"Not even close."

Chapter Fifteen

BRODY

"You're smiling again," Wes says, making me lose count of my arm curl reps.

The last time he mentioned it, I evaded his questions because I wanted to keep the new developments between Val and I to myself a little longer, but Wes has a way of extracting the thoughts straight from my head, so I know it can't last much longer.

"I noticed you were out pretty late last night. Unless you forgot, I had the night off and was still awake when you tip-toed into your room. Where were you all night? I thought you were studying?"

"I was."

"You studied until midnight?"

I roll my head on my shoulders, stress pulling the muscles there taut, and set down my dumbbells. I turn my body to face Wes head-on. "I studied for most of that time, yes."

"So you were with Val?"

I release a heavy breath. "Yes, Wes. Okay? Is that what you wanted to hear?"

His nagging curiosity morphs into innocence. "You act like I wasn't trying to get an answer out of you since we woke up this morning."

"Maybe I want some things to be mine and mine only, you know?"

"Something happened, didn't it?"

With a simple question, I'm transported back to last night, sprawled on Val's bed with her thighs straddling my hips.

"Dude. I swear, if you get a boner right now, I'll smack you right across the face."

Wes' words hit me like a splash of cold water. "We kissed, okay? End of story. Stop fishing for details. I respect Val too much for that."

He moves to grab his next set of weights with a smirk. "I knew something happened, just wanted to hear you admit it."

"Jackass."

I think about Val throughout the rest of my workout. Tuesdays and Thursdays are the days of the week we've found it's impossible to see each other, because of Val's early classes ending right before mine start, and my lab that runs well into the evening. So as much as I long to see her after everything transpired last night, I know it won't happen.

I sent her a text as Wes drove us across town to the gym. I've been trying not to look at my phone every five seconds since we got here, but I know she usually wakes up right around this time every morning. I don't want to come on too strong and scare her away, but I'm dying to know what she's thinking.

I somehow manage to keep my phone pocketed for the rest of our workout, but it doesn't stop a smile from spreading across my face when I finally open it to see her name on the screen.

Who knew a simple good morning text could make you feel so damn good?

But I should have known the feeling wouldn't last long, because when I'm back at the house, returning to my room straight from the shower, I hear my phone go off.

I practically jump at the sound of it, excited Val is keeping our conversation going during her busiest day of the week.

But when I pick it up, it's my dad's name on the screen.

Dad: *Midterms this week, it's about the time to work a little harder for your grades. If you're struggling, I think you can spare a couple afternoons with the roommates to find a tutor. You need passing grades this semester or you won't be graduating, come May.*

Yeah, dad. I'm only having the best semester I've had in college. Thanks for asking. Pretty sure I've got it handled.

I don't even bother with a reply, knowing he'll think I'm too irresponsible here at school to send him a text back, but I don't care. Let him think that. He's never bothered to know who I truly am, anyway.

Val's face floats into my mind. The words we shared last night—the most vulnerable I've felt in front of someone in a long time—float around in my head. I hate feeling that way, yet she made it easy to lay all my cards out for her to see, and it wasn't as scary as I thought it would be.

I suppose that's the reason I kissed her too—as badly as she tries to fight it, things between us just feel effortless.

The thought of her is enough to flip my mood back around. And as I walk into my evening class, I vow to talk to her tonight before my head hits the pillow.

Chapter Sixteen

VAL

"So, I'd apologize for surprising you guys last night, but it seemed like it went well, so I'll stay quiet."

I release a breath and turn to her, standing at the sink scrubbing the wine glasses. A perfectly groomed eyebrow lifted. I just returned to the house after a long afternoon of studying.

My mind has been racing with thoughts of Brody since I woke up this morning, so I might as well spill the beans to get some of this off my chest. "Nothing happened," I tell her, knowing it couldn't be further from the truth.

"Your face says otherwise."

I walk down the hallway to throw my bag in my room, freezing at the sight of the bed, and the empty bottle of wine still sitting on the back of the headboard where he placed it. As if Brody hasn't already infiltrated every part of my life, my room is no longer safe, either.

I've done a great job keeping people out of my heart this

far into my college experience, but somehow Brody snuck past my defenses.

Instinct is screaming for me to run away, but there's a slow ember lit in my chest, faintly crying for me to *try* for once. The way he looked at me after we kissed last night—the way he's looked at me since the day we met—is all I could think about today.

Could this be real? Whatever this is between us?

I resist the urge to jump back under the covers in the hopes that his scent is still lingering in the sheets, walking back to the kitchen for a conversation I'm not ready to have.

Bree is drying a glass when I sit down at the island. "Things happened, but not where I know your dirty mind went to."

She giggles, proof that I know her well. "Excuse me for hoping you finally hooked up with someone, okay? It's been a long time."

"So I've had a bit of a dry spell the past few years. Thanks for reminding me."

She shrugs, stretching to put the wineglasses away. "If I didn't, I swear you'd stay complacent forever. I don't want that boring of a life for you. Quit stalling and tell me what happened."

I drop my head into my hands, then meet her eyes. "He kissed me," I stare off into space, recalling his lips on mine. "Like really kissed me, and I didn't want him to stop."

"So, why did you make him stop?"

My brows jump as I look at her. "What makes you think I was the one to slow things down?"

She smiles. "You mean Miss Control Freak loosened the reins and let Brody take the lead?" she rolls her eyes and continues, "You forget I know you. Besides, I've seen the way he looks at you. He's got it bad."

"You've met him twice. There's no way you'd know that."

There's a smug look on her face when she shrugs. "Only

two times, and if he's looking at you like that when I'm around, I can only imagine how he does when I'm not."

I drop my head to my hands and groan. "Yeah, it was me who slowed things down."

"So, what's your next move?"

I wipe my hands down my face. "I've been trying to figure that out all day."

She gives me a look. "Let me help you, then. He *likes* you." She lets that information marinate before adding, "There's nothing wrong with thinking through life-altering decisions, but make sure you don't get stuck there inside your pretty little head and forget to live."

"Yeah, but—" I start to defend the warring feelings in my head, but she interrupts me.

"Tell me something. How'd it feel?" She rubs the spot above her heart with a fist. "Did it stir something inside you?"

We look at each other for a long time as I try to ignore the affirmative answer already bursting from my chest.

"Because that feeling doesn't come around often. It would be smart to jump on that feeling instead of holding him at arm's length until he decides it's not worth his time."

"It's not that easy, Bree. I've got my entire future to find someone. I'm here to figure out my next step in life, to find a career, not to find a boyfriend."

She rounds the counter, sitting down in the stool next to mine. Her hand covers my own. "And that's a brilliant point, Val. But what if on your way to one dream, fate brought you another? You've always been a planner. Hell, it's going to be your future career. And you've always had these contingency plans in place just in case disaster strikes, and I get it. Expecting the worst possible outcome in every situation is a trauma response. Given your past, I can't blame you. All I'm saying is, maybe you should make a plan for what to do when things go right. It can't hurt to keep an open mind about it, because I've known you since the moment we stepped foot on this campus together, and not once have I seen you consider a man the way you are right now. This guy has brought you to your knees, and I'm pretty sure there's a good reason for that."

I sit there speechless, because I know there's nothing I could say.

"My advice?" she continues, "Talk to him. Even if it's only to say exactly what you just told me. Be scared, be worried, be excited, but do it *with* him. Don't shut him out. You owe that to both of you."

I nod, even though what she's just suggested is easier said than done.

———

Later that evening, I'm lying in bed reading a book since it's one of those rare nights I don't have homework to do, but I'm finding it impossible to concentrate when the smell of his cologne wafts from my sheets each time I flip the page.

After rereading the same paragraph for the third time, my phone rings.

Fully expecting it to be Hannah, I answer without looking at the caller ID.

"Hey, what's up?"

"Val, hey." The voice on the line is deep and husky, rather than the soft, familiar one that was the soundtrack to my childhood, my heart stalling when I realize who it is. "How was your day?" Brody asks.

"Oh," I say, my brain trying and failing to comprehend the fact that Brody just called me. "Hey, Brody. It was good. How was yours?"

"You sound like you were expecting someone else," he says, laughing to try to play it off.

"Oh, no, I just assumed it was my friend, Hannah, because she's the only one who usually calls me."

His deep breath blows into the microphone and into my

119

ear. "Yeah, sorry. Is this weird? I've just been thinking about you all day, so I thought I'd call you to see how you're feeling about, uh," He pauses, like he's afraid to bring up the elephant in the room, "last night. Before we see each other in class tomorrow, I wanted to talk about it. I've been lying in bed trying to get into an episode of Seinfeld, but I can't concentrate."

"Oh," I say yet again because it's apparently the only word I know how to say anymore. "I'm having the same problem trying to get into the book I'm reading."

"Really?" He asks as if it surprises him.

"Yeah."

"Huh. Well, let me start by saying I enjoyed last night. I'd definitely do it again."

"You would?" I ask, sounding far more excited by the prospect than I meant to. Because I am. This guy who I've been infatuated with for years is attracted to me? *Don't forget you're leaving,* my conscience chimes in, keeping me grounded, as always.

"Yeah, would you?" The vulnerability in his voice makes me dread what I know I need to say.

"Yeah," I say before my mind catches up with my mouth.

"Why does that sound like it comes with a but?"

I take a deep breath. "But there are so many reasons this can't happen between us."

"Like what?"

"Like the fact that we're partners in class. If things go wrong, the rest of the semester will be a disaster."

"I'm willing to take that chance. Next."

"Okay, how about the fact that I'm leaving as soon as I graduate? What then?"

"We cross that bridge when we come to it."

I drop my head into my hands in frustration, even though he can't see me. "Brody, that kind of thing might work for you, but in case you haven't noticed, I'm a planner. I think things through before I jump. I plan out my life, and things that don't match up usually get thrown to the wayside."

"When do you shut off the planning side of your brain and just let yourself live?" He asks, frustration sneaking into his tone.

Never. "Sometimes, but I haven't had a relationship in years, and I'm not looking to start now."

Surprising me, he says, "I admire you for trying to plan out your life to the minute, but why do you let those plans keep you from pursuing something standing right in front of you?"

"Brody," I say with a sigh.

"Val," he mocks, his playful teasing breaking through the tension building. I can hardly believe it's helping, rather than hindering me at this moment.

I'm still combing over that thought when I hear him say. "Val, you still there?"

"Yeah, sorry. What were you saying?"

"What do you say we explore what's happening here? Will you go on a date with me?"

Champagne bubbles dance in my belly as I tear my phone from my ear, kicking my legs in the air, my cheeks sore from my smile.

Before placing my phone back at my ear, I take a deep breath to collect myself.

"Okay, yes. Let's do it."

Chapter Seventeen

BRODY

I've been looking forward to this day since Val agreed to our date.

It's Saturday night. We reached a checkpoint in our project yesterday, and Val seemed just as excited about tonight as I am when we went our separate ways after class.

I dab some cologne in all the right places and send her a quick text to let her know I'm leaving soon.

The text has barely gone through before my phone is ringing. I smile when I see her name on the screen and answer.

"Hey, you ready?" I answer.

She lets out a deep breath on the other line. "Brody, I'm having a bit of a crisis here. I don't think tonight's gonna work."

My shoulders immediately slump, but instead of letting disappointment leak into my voice, I collect myself and ask, "Okay, what happened? Is it anything I can help with?"

She laughs, but I detect no humor in her tone when she

says, "Not unless you want to drive with me for two hours to pick up my best friend."

Two hours of uninterrupted time with Val? Count me in. "Of course I want to. I was already planning on hanging out with you. So our plan changed, big deal. I just gassed up my vehicle, so I'll drive. You figure out the details. I'll grab us some food for the way. See you in fifteen minutes."

"Are you serious? You don't have to—"

"Val," I say, speaking over her, because I can tell she's veering into panic mode. "I know I don't have to, but I want to. Like that time you nursed me back to health, remember?"

She releases a long breath. "Brody, thank you. You're the best."

Thirty minutes later, we're on the road, headed to a tiny town in the middle of nowhere, about thirty minutes from our hometowns. I still can't believe the chances that this girl I've spent my every waking hour thinking about lately grew up down the road from me.

Val breaks into my reverie, unwrapping our tacos and filling me in on the current predicament.

"Hannah hasn't had the best of luck when it comes to love. She desperately wants to find someone, but as I've tried to tell her, she finds all these guys in the wrong places. Tonight's guy slipped her his number while she was at work. He picked her up while she was ringing him out at the cash register. No wonder she quit. Who does that?"

I laugh, trying to imagine it. "Creeps, that's who."

"Exactly!" She yells, throwing her hands up in the air. "No one wants to be hit on at their job by a random stranger. One, you're there to get a job done, and two, we're taught to be professional in the workplace, which means we have to be nice to this customer even when all we want to do is tell them to screw off already."

I laugh at her rant. "It seems like you're speaking from experience."

I see her shake her head aggressively as she chews a bite of her taco. "Yeah, it happened to me twice at my internship over the summer. One guy was even there with another woman. It makes me sick. Knowing Hannah, she agreed to a date just to avoid the awkwardness of having to tell him no."

I chew on a bite of my taco, but my stomach turns sour at the thought of Val getting unwanted attention at work.

"Speaking of dates, thanks to me, tonight's not much of one anymore, so no pressure, right?"

"Are you kidding me? I love road trips." I admit.

She laughs, "Oh yeah, that's right. What's your favorite part?"

"Good company," I say, looking at her pointedly, then I hold up my taco, "good food, and good music. The three staples to a quality road trip."

"Well, in that case," she says, grabbing my phone, playing chill music quietly through the speakers. "May I?"

I unlock it with Face ID, then give it back to her.

She gets into my music app, my alternative rock playlist rumbling through the speakers a moment later.

My thumb taps against the steering wheel along with the intro to one of my favorite songs. "I didn't know this was your genre," I say, turning away from the road long enough to see her wiggling in her seat to the beat.

She laughs. "Yeah, you can blame Hannah for that. We listened to it all the time when we were in high school because her older brother and his best friend got her into it. They even took us to a concert for her eighteenth birthday."

"Which band?"

"Breaking Benjamin. We were obsessed. Knew every single word to their album that came out back in high school."

"A rocker chick, never woulda guessed it."

"Believe it. And it wasn't my first rock concert, either." She looks out the windshield with a wistful smile. "My parents took me to a Red Hot Chili Peppers concert when I was a freshman in high school."

"Was it amazing?"

"Best concert I'll ever go to. And I'm glad I have that memory with them now." She shakes her head and laughs. "I rolled my eyes the entire way to Minneapolis as my dad blared all their albums in the car, playing the drums on the steering wheel. But I love remembering that moment. It was him in a nutshell. They were so in love with each other, too. I sometimes forget that I'd always wanted something like what they had."

"It's not too late to find it, you know," I say, hoping it's clear I'd be first in line if she's taking applications.

She swivels her gaze toward me. "Sorry. This conversation really isn't first date material, is it?"

"We're friends too. Talking to your friends about your dreams isn't a crime."

"You know, now that I think of it," Val sips her drink to wash down the bite she'd been chewing. "They were friends first, too. My mom always said it was the best way to fall in love."

Then, as if she realizes what she just insinuated, she covers her mouth, big eyes meeting mine. "Okay, I'm just going to stop talking now. I'm sorry. I wasn't trying to say—"

I grab her hand that's resting on my center console, squeezing it as I say, "Val, it's okay. Please stop apologizing. I'll try not to read too much into it."

———

When the heavy steel door at the entrance of the bar Hannah's hiding out in slams shut behind us, I spot a girl with long auburn hair sitting at the bar talking animatedly with a bartender with salt-and-pepper hair.

She screams when she spots Val, throwing herself at her

best friend. "You came! Ugh, you're the best!" From her elongated syllables and high voice, it's obvious Hannah's tipsy.

"Of course I'm here. You ready to go?"

"Yes, I just need to say goodbye to my new friend, Jimmy, here. Bye, Jimmy!"

Val turns to him, "Jimmy, thank you for taking care of my best friend until we arrived."

He waves off the praise, saying, "No worries. I've got a daughter your age, and I'd hope some fella would do the same for her at a time like this. You kids have a nice night."

When we're almost to the door that Hannah finally realizes I'm here.

She sucks in a loud gasp, "Brody? I didn't know you were coming! Wait," she looks over at Val.

"Tonight was date night, but he decided to help me when I told him what happened."

She gasps even louder at that as we step out onto the sidewalk. "Shit, I completely forgot you told me." She says, pulling Val by the arm.

Val wraps an arm around her, pulling her into her side. "Hannah, he knew how important it was for me to come and get you. He wanted to help. It's okay."

Hannah turns to me, "I'm sorry for ruining date night, Brody. If it's any consolation, she's been wanting to go out with you forever."

I turn to Val, who looks like a deer in the headlights at her best friend's drunken slip.

I smile, "Forever, huh?"

The closer we get to Val's hometown, the quieter she gets. She'd been singing along with the music and chatting with Hannah for most of the ride, but she's noticeably tense as I pull into town.

"Just let me know where to turn," I say.

Val nods, but doesn't look at me. "Keep going straight."

"Wait!" Hannah yells from the back seat, her head suddenly appearing between us. "Turn here so we don't go by—"

I slam on the breaks at her chaotic directions. By the time we're stopped, I'm already past the intersection.

"Hannah, it's fine. Brody, keep driving," she says, but her body language says differently.

She's picking at a loose thread on the thigh of her jeans as if she can't bear to look out the window.

We slowly start rolling down the street again, but I still ask, "Are you sure?"

Before Val can answer, Hannah chimes in from the backseat. "I'm so sorry. I didn't think this through. I didn't know who else to call." She's in hysterics. "Well, I did, but the last time Miles picked me up in an emergency, things got weird between us. I should have dealt with the weird instead of making you come all this way. I'm sorry."

"I'm okay, Hannah. I promise."

They're having a conversation right in front of me, but I'm still not following.

But when Hannah's hand lands on Val's shoulder as she looks out the window with tears in her eyes at a small white house with black shutters, I think I've figured it out.

Not knowing what else to do, I reach for her hand. She surprises me by lacing her fingers through mine and squeezing tight for the rest of the drive.

"You guys are more than welcome to stay," Hannah says when we're in her parents' driveway. "I'm sorry again for ruining your date night."

It's late enough that if we left now, we'd get home after midnight.

Val turns to me, eyes still a little puffy. "Would you be okay if I went to say hi quick? I haven't seen Hannah's parents in a while."

"Yeah, go ahead. If you want to stay, I could always stay at my parents' for the night." Even as I say it, I dread following through with it. I don't do well with having my dad sprung on me like this, and he'd be the same way if I showed up at his house unannounced.

"Let's go say hi quick and see what happens, okay?"

I follow Hannah and Val into the house, which has a wide open floor plan with a mud room that opens into the living room. Who I assume are Hannah's parents and two guys who look a couple years older than me are all sitting at the large island in the middle of the kitchen with drinks in front of them.

"Valerie, is that you?" Hannah's mom asks, the words coming out in a gasp.

"Yep, it's me," she says as she gets closer to the kitchen. "Get over here and give me a hug."

The rest of the guys in the room pipe up with varying degrees of, "Hey, Val!" And she hands out smiles and waves over Hannah's mom's shoulder.

I try not to shrink under the stares coming from the guys across the room and focus on the emotion in Hannah's mom's voice as she talks in hushed whispers. Val clearly means a lot to this family, which begs the question, why is she in such a rush to leave them behind?

Hannah's dad walks around the island to kiss Val on the top of her head and squeeze her while she's still in his wife's arms. Then he's on his way to me, hand outstretched. "Hello, there. I'm Hannah's dad, Bobby, and that's my wife, Jenn. You must be a friend of Val's?"

I shake his hand, nodding as Val looks over her shoulder at me. "Yes, sir. I'm Brody Ryan. I grew up in Freeport, actually. You have a beautiful home."

"Thank you, Brody. Tell me why your name sounds familiar."

I make a face, unsure. "I played sports in high school. My dad is an investment banker in the next town over."

"Did you play baseball?" The lanky guy sitting at the table asks. "You do look pretty familiar."

"Yes, I did. Malakai Moore was in my class," I mention because he's somewhat of a local legend, having made it past baseball at the college level and into AAA. "He's my best friend."

Bobby snaps his fingers. "That's right. He still playing in the minors?"

"He is. He just finished up a great season. I have a feeling he'll be in the majors in no time."

"Oh, wouldn't that be something?"

"You were one of those little freshmen that kicked our asses our senior year," the lanky guy says.

I grimace. "Yeah, we were pretty good at baseball. Sorry about that," I say, and the rest of the room laughs.

He reaches out his hand and I take it. "It's nice to meet you, Brody. I'm Holt Hawkins, Hannah's brother. And this is my friend Miles O'Harrow."

Miles doesn't say a word, just shakes my hand. I'm not sure if he's just quiet around new people, or if it's the norm for him. But Holt doesn't seem to have any trouble filling the silence.

"Nice to meet you both."

We're all seated around the roomy kitchen island when Holt asks Hannah, "So I take it your date didn't go so well if you needed rescued?"

Judging by the look Hannah gives him, she didn't want this to be public knowledge. Unfortunately, that doesn't stop him from continuing. "Was this guy worse or better than that guy who took you to the place his ex was a server to make her jealous?"

"Wait," Jenn says, looking between her children. "You went on a date tonight? Where—with who?" With each word, her voice gets more and more frantic.

"Mom, don't worry about it. I escaped to a bar where the bartender was close to your age and treated me like his own daughter until these two showed up."

"The real question is, what the hell are you doing, going on a date with someone you need to escape from?" Miles asks, joining the conversation for the first time since we walked in the house.

"I know," Hannah says, looking down at her entwined fingers. "I learned my lesson, so can we drop this, please?" Hannah asks, looking around the table at her family. "I just want to forget it ever happened. Val and Brody were kind enough to cancel their date night and pick me up. I'm here, safe, and I brought Val home with me. That counts for something, right?"

"Of course we're glad to see Val, honey," Bobby says. "We just want to know you're okay."

"Exactly," Miles agrees.

"I am," she rushes to say, looking anything but as she pushes back her chair and stands. "I'm gonna go change."

The room quiets at her departure.

As everyone swirls their drinks around awkwardly, I watch Miles, who looks about ready to jump to his feet and follow Hannah into the back of the house.

"Do you want to stay the night, or do you feel comfortable driving all the way back home right now?" Val whispers, but with the room as quiet as it is, everyone hears.

"Oh, you guys are more than welcome to stay. Val can sleep in Hannah's room, and we've got an extra bed for you, too." Bobby says.

Val and I look at each other for a moment, trying our hand at telepathy and failing.

"That's it. I'm making you both a drink so you don't have a choice."

When he leaves his chair for the counter where he's got all the makings for margaritas, Miles excuses himself to go to the bathroom, although I have a feeling he's going to find Hannah.

Chapter Eighteen

VAL

Sitting in the middle of a group of people I've always considered family is not how I expected to spend my night, but I can't say I'm mad about it.

It was touch and go there for a second when we were rolling into town, but now that I'm here—with Brody, no less—I curse myself for not coming back more often in the past few years. I know my reasons for staying away, but these people I'm surrounded by are plenty of a reason to visit. And there's a part of me who mourns for all the time I wasted being too scared to face the things I left behind to enjoy the good parts I'd let myself forget.

When Hannah returns to the table with red-rimmed eyes, closely followed by Miles, who I hadn't seen leave the room, I scrunch my eyebrows at Hannah, trying to have a conversation without words. She gives me a quick shake of the head, which means I'll be waiting until later to hear what this is about.

Bobby Hawkins' drinks are nice and strong, as per usual,

so Brody and I are stuck here. I feel kind of bad that he drove me all over the countryside tonight, but oddly enough, he seemed to enjoy himself. Even now, he's smiling, talking to Holt and Bobby.

Having him along tonight meant more to me than I think he realizes. It wasn't the first time that his easy-going spirit helped put me at ease in a time I'd otherwise label as a crisis. If I'd come alone, I would have driven myself into a frenzy, worrying about Hannah's safety, even though she was perfectly safe.

As soon as she called, I knew I was going to have to call Brody and cancel. It didn't cross my mind that he'd be game to come with me to help someone he didn't even know. I shouldn't have been surprised.

"You look comfier," I say to Hannah when she sits next to me in sweats.

"I am." she looks across the table and I follow her gaze to see everyone but Miles is in a conversation. "I'm so pissed Holt had to say something," she whispers. "He has no filter sometimes."

"You don't say." I slide my margarita in front of her and she sucks down a large gulp.

"Thanks."

When Hannah's parents go to bed, the five of us still remain. It becomes clear quite quickly that Holt is the most tipsy of all of us because he hasn't noticed the tension surrounding Hannah's date.

"So who was this guy you went out with tonight, Hannah?"

She'd just finally started loosening up again, but her shoulders practically hit her ears at Holt's question.

"Can we just let this go, please?"

133

"No," Holt says, elbowing Miles with a smirk. "Right? We need to know whose ass Miles will be kicking tomorrow."

Hannah and Miles share a look I can't quite interpret before Miles says, "No, man, I think we should just drop it."

This has always been the dynamic between these two. They're super-protective of Hannah—and me, when I'm around. I've tried to tell her it's why she can't get a good date around here.

Miles is the strong and silent one, Holt is the little ankle-biter dog that instigates everything. They even each other out.

"Oh come on," Holt says. "At least tell us what you two were going to do."

Hannah squares her shoulders and faces her brother. "We were supposed to go to a concert, but he said he needed to make a quick stop first. I didn't think much of it until we stopped on the side of the road and he asked me if I wanted to go halfsies, or if I was a cheap date. My first thought was that he was talking about alcohol, but then he tapped his nose and I realized what he was really asking. He was at his dealer's house picking up his shit for the night. I just told him I was good, then got out of the car and ran to the nearest public place, which happened to be a bar and called Val. Is that explanation enough for you?"

Holt's speechless, his mouth hanging wide open, his brotherly brain short-circuiting.

"I'm just glad you were smart enough to get out of there and call someone," Miles says, looking at Hannah like there's no one else in the room. "I'm glad Val answered and came to help, but I hope you know you can call me if, God forbid, something like that happens again. Besides, if Val still plans on moving away after college, you'll need someone new to rely on for stuff like this."

I've been saying it for years, but hearing that out of someone else's mouth sends a hole right through my chest.

Brody must've noticed, because his hand is in mine under the table before I can recover.

"That is still your plan, right?" Miles asks, apparently seeing my reaction as well.

I feel like a deer in the headlights as all eyes at the table turn to me, waiting on an answer I've been second-guessing lately.

I stare at Miles long enough for Brody to squeeze my hand, reminding me I need to answer.

"Um, yeah, I think so."

"You think so?" Hannah asks, confused because the answer has always been a resounding yes in the past. "What changed?" But before I can fabricate an answer, she finds Brody's hand intertwined with my own in my lap, and smiles as if she's found it.

"Alright, Holt, I think it's time we head out for the night. Val, it was good to see you. Don't be a stranger. And Brody, nice to meet you."

I nod, trying to process how many words in a row he just said. "Yeah, it was great to see you," I say as Hannah and Brody murmur their goodbyes.

"Let's go," Miles says, smacking Holt on the back.

He tips his glass, finishing his margarita, then stands. Saying his goodbyes on the way to the door.

"Go show Brody the guest bedroom. I'll lock up after these two."

After she follows Miles and Holt, I turn to Brody, butterflies flapping their wings in my belly at the thought of getting a moment alone.

I take his hand and lead him down the hallway I've walked down a million times in my life.

"Your humble abode for the night," I say with my arms spread wide when we walk through the guest bedroom door.

"Looks perfect," Brody says with that smirk I can't get enough of lighting up his face as he closes the door. "And since I was robbed of the chance to take you out tonight," he says, his finger leaving a trail of electricity in its wake as he pushes a curl behind my ear. "I was wondering if I'd get a moment with you to do this..." he whispers as his nose inches toward my own until we're touching. Then his forehead follows suit, his hands landing on either side of my face.

His small touches have me panting in anticipation by the time our lips finally brush.

The scent of his cologne tickles my nose with him this close. My hands have a mind of their own as they move from the short, soft hairs of the back of his head, down his back, to wrap around his waist. His get tangled in my hair, and my stomach dips as he deepens the kiss.

When we pull away breathlessly, he leans his forehead on mine and says, "I've been wanting to do that all day."

I chuckle, "So have I. I'm sorry our day didn't go as planned."

"Don't be. I still had a great time. It was fun to see you with Hannah and her family. Everyone's great, and you know what?"

"What?"

"I could tell everyone missed you."

Chapter Nineteen

BRODY

The week following our impromptu visit with the Hawkins family turned out to be the week from hell. Two exams, and a ten-page paper are finally in my rearview. It's Saturday morning, and Val and I have another checkpoint due by midnight tonight for our class project. My head's been buried so deep in my books, I've barely had time to talk to her, even though she's been sitting across the table from me most of the week. She's been itching to get this done since it was assigned, but I had no wiggle room in my schedule unless I wanted to fail an exam.

So against my personal code of ethics, Val managed to get me into the library on a Saturday after all. And early at that. She also promised that if we get our work in on time, we can celebrate by going out. A bit of a first date redo, if you will.

She insisted on having coffee duty this morning, but I didn't come empty-handed either. I take her hand after she passes me my coffee, dropping my lips to hers with a quick kiss. "Good morning."

Her smile is infectious. "Good morning to you too."

I'm still not over the fact that I get to kiss her when I want to. I pull on her hand, leading us to our destination.

"Wait, our tables are back that way," Val says, catching on.

"I know, but I want to show you something."

Her brows pinch, uneasy with me switching the plans on her, but I think she'll enjoy the outcome. I was walking around the library the other day between classes—because that's who I am now, apparently—when I stumbled upon a hidden gem.

"Not much further," I say, leading her through the stacks.

"Is this where you kill me?" She whispers, wrapping her free hand around my biceps. I can't even put into words how good it feels to have her hands on me.

"Why would I kill you, Val? I like you too much."

I turn back with a smirk to find her smiling at me, but her attention is stolen quickly when our destination comes into view.

"Brody," she smacks my arm in excitement. "How on earth did you find this?"

I turn to assess the space, glad to find it free of people this early in the morning. There's a huge window with a couch in front of it, side tables on either end. The room itself is small and cozy. Green plants litter the walls along with literary posters in extravagant gold frames. The walls are dark, but the room is still well lit.

I lead her in, setting my bag down on the floor at one end of the couch. "I had some time to kill the other day between classes."

"So you came to the *library*? Who are you, and what did you do with the guy I met at the beginning of the semester?"

I shrug. "He met a cute girl who changed him for the better."

Her eyes are sparkling when she smiles up at me. "Yeah, well, the girl changed too."

"Oh yeah? How so?"

"The cute boy helped her step out of her comfort zone," she leans into me, her hand on my chest. "And despite her aversion to change, she's finding that she quite likes it."

She lifts onto her toes as our lips come together. I lose myself a little more in that kiss, something I've found happening a lot lately. In bits and pieces, this girl has stolen my heart.

―――――

With Thanksgiving break next week, it's getting down to the wire as far as grades go. This is the point in the semester I usually wake up to my responsibilities and realize how terribly I'm doing in my classes, then fret about it for the rest of the semester, but it's like a weight lifted off my shoulders as I check over my classes online while waiting for Val to return after a bathroom break.

Going through all four classes I'm enrolled in, I find that my lowest grade of the four is a C-plus that is teetering on a B-minus. A far cry from the lead ball plummeting when I'd check my grades in the years leading up to now. My hands do an excited drumroll on the table and I turn at the sound of footsteps.

Val smiles, an eyebrow lifted. "What are you so excited about?"

I wave her over. "Come look."

She cuddles into my side to look at my screen. "Holy shit, Brody! An A, two B's and a C-plus? Who knew you had it in ya, huh?" She plants a quick kiss on my cheek.

I've told her about my past struggles when it came to my classes, so she knows I'm used to C's at best. "I owe it all to you for kicking my ass into gear, Val. Seriously."

She squeezes an arm around my waist and I hug her back, leaning my cheek against the top of her head.

Later, I finish my half of our work, slapping my laptop shut, earning myself a glare from a startled Val.

"I'm finished, need help?"

"I'm good," she mutters, already typing again.

"What should I do then?" I ask, uneasy with nothing to keep me busy for the moment.

"You can just go, if you want."

That suggestion makes my brow lift. A few months ago, I would have jumped at the opportunity. Now, though? Not so much. "I don't want to leave you here. I can wait."

Her head pops up quickly, as if she hadn't expected to hear me say that. *That makes two of us.*

She recovers quickly. "Okay, so grab a book and read while you wait for me to finish."

I peek around her, snagging the book she set next to her when we sat down, but I don't get far before she rips it out of my hand. "Not that one!"

I drop a hand to my chest, as surprised as I am appalled by her behavior. "Okay, then, which one?"

She tosses her hands up at her sides. "I don't know, pick one. We're in a building full of them."

I snap my fingers, pointing at her. What a genius. "Of course. I'll be right back," I say, lifting to my feet and making my way to the stacks I always find Val meandering around when I show up late for our study dates.

I find a cover that looks familiar, something she's read before. By scanning the back cover, it sounds like a YA love story. Not sure that's my cup of tea, but I'll try it.

I check it out at the desk and walk through the stacks back to Val.

She smiles from behind her computer as I approach. And I lean in for a kiss before I sit down, surprised when she lets go of her laptop, moving her hands to the sides of my face to deepen the kiss.

My eyelids droop when I pull away. "Damn, what was that for?"

Her shoulders jump as her attention lands back on her laptop, as if the moment never happened. "You look hot with one of my favorite books in your hands. Book nerds are sexy. Your glasses, the book—it all just works."

I plop back down in my spot, "Well, consider me a book nerd, then."

Chapter Twenty

BRODY

We finish our work in plenty of time, so date night is a go.

Two hours later, I'm in an Uber pulling up outside her place, and I see her walking through her house toward the door before I can even meet her there. I get out and open the car door for her, anyway.

"You look great," I say, taking in her jeans and wedge boots. Her wayward curls are more uniform than usual.

She smiles, resting a hand on my chest when she's right in front of me. "Thanks, you aren't so bad yourself." She rises to her tiptoes and kisses my cheek, then she buries her nose in my neck and says, "And you smell good."

I smile and pull her back into me when she tries to get in the car. "Thanks, but you didn't seriously think you were getting away that easily, did you?"

She smirks, knowing exactly what she's doing to me. Before she can protest, I lean in and kiss her for real. When her tongue finds mine, I feel a twinge low in my belly that makes it hard not to turn around, take her inside and explore that a little further.

As if she can read my thoughts, she pulls on my hand and we both fall into the Uber.

In true Val fashion, she starts making small talk with the driver. I've never wished to be alone in a vehicle with someone more than I do now. But I chose an Uber in case we drink too much tonight.

The pizzeria is loud when we walk in. The usual Saturday night clientele, rowdy on beer and pizza. Maybe not the best spot for a first date, but it was the best option with such late notice.

"What's your favorite kind of pizza here?" She asks, when we're seated, flipping open her menu.

"I usually get the chicken Alfredo, it's hard to beat. Have you ever had it?"

She laughs and shakes her head in disbelief. "Brody, did we just find something we agree on?"

I smile, "Your favorite too?"

"I would have judged you for wanting anything else. I hope you're also cool with cheesy breadsticks."

"Double the cheese, double the fun," I say, glad she's not suddenly putting on that annoying 'I barely eat' persona since we're on a date. I've seen her throw down some food, and it's impressive. I don't know where she holds it all.

"After all that work we got done today, I swear I could eat one of everything."

We're not even halfway into our beers by the time dinner arrives at our table. With the way Val is practically salivating at the sight of it, I'm no longer feeling insecure about pizza and beer for date night. I should have known better.

"Which one do you want?" I ask, picking up the spatula that came with the pizza and Val's plate.

She smiles sweetly, then points out the biggest piece. I

laugh as I plate it for her and throw the next biggest piece on my plate.

"Ermagherr," Val says with a full mouth of cheese, her eyes rolling back into her head. "This is delicious. Best. Date. Ever."

That has me smiling. "Yeah?"

"Yes. Keep feeding me and I'll give you a pizza my heart."

I halt my fork halfway to my mouth. "Oh, she's got jokes."

"Dad jokes are the best jokes, or at least that's what Evan Boyd always used to say. I learned from the best."

I laugh, "Well, he was right, they're pretty great."

She takes another bite, smiling. "I know."

Once we've both downed our fair share of carbs, we're mirroring each other's posture as we each lean back in our chairs, unable to eat even one more bite.

Val takes a deep breath. "You might have to roll me out of here."

I lift a brow. "Well, I guess we'll be here a while then, because I don't think I can move either."

She smiles and we both sit there in a food coma until our waitress returns to the table.

"How are you two doing over here?"

"Can I get another beer?" Val asks, sliding her mason jar across the table in her direction, going after what she wants, as usual. It's a major turn on for me. She's so damn sure of herself, and part of me kind of envies that side of her.

"Of course," the waitress says, turning to me to add, "How about you?"

I figure we'll be here for a while, so I sit up a little straighter in my chair and place my glass in front of her too. "Yes, please."

We sit there for a while, nursing our beers and talking

about some of the most random topics. Soon enough, our beers have been drained, the bill has been paid by me, and I look expectantly across the table.

"Where do you want to go tonight?"

"Why don't we just start walking and see where the night takes us?"

Um, Miss Plan Everything wants to be spontaneous? Count me in.

I reach out my hand and she takes it, a smile lighting up the beautiful features of her face. "You lead the way."

Val shivers as soon as we walk out onto the sidewalk, the wet, cold, winter night holding the promise of eventual precipitation. I drop her hand, wrapping my arm around her for warmth instead. She wastes no time leaning into my touch.

"Thanks," she says, teeth chattering as she wraps her arm around my waist. I wish I'd brought a coat for myself now, just so I could share it with her.

"I should have covered up more, given tonight's forecast."

The deep-V of her sweater may not be keeping her warm, but it looks amazing on her. Besides, I have no complaints, having to hold her close. "No worries, I've got you."

She smiles up at me, her amber eyes sparkling in the streetlight. I can tell she's about to speak, but the thump of the bass in the building we're passing steals her attention.

"Do you hear that?"

"Do I hear what?"

Her eyes are wide with wonder as her jaw unhinges, pointing to a sign on the door of a dance club I've never been to, its walls practically vibrating with the effort to contain the music thumping inside.

"I think I found our plans for the night."

All Out 80s, the sign boasts. I use the arm slung over her shoulder to turn her toward the door, holding it open to let her through first. "Dancing it is, then."

I pay our cover after the bouncer checks our IDs and

stamps the backs of our hands with a smiley face that'll be there next week. The music magically turned three times louder as we entered the space. I follow Val, who's shimmying her hips on her way up to the crowded bar.

The lights are going a hundred miles a minute to keep up with the song playing. The song itself sounds familiar, even though I can't quite place the name or band.

"This is so magical," Val's awestruck whisper is barely audible over the music.

The place is bustling with people, the perfect excuse to take her hand. And I do exactly that on our way up to the bar. I watch as she looks down at the connection, then back to me with a smile.

I get immense joy out of the way she bounces with each step in time with the music. It's clear she has rhythm, but only busts out the moves on rare occasions. The only other time I've seen her even close to this free was the night of Bree's birthday.

The song changes, and she belts out the lyrics to a song by A-Ha that I haven't heard in a while.

I love seeing her this way. Especially after seeing her quiet and reserved all week at school.

Once we find a table, she does plenty of shoulder shimmying as she nurses her beer, watching the patrons out on the dance floor.

"Do you want to go out there?" I ask, after watching her for a while.

She gives me a shy smile, holding her beer up to me and says, "Not yet. I need more liquid courage."

I hold out my drink to her, "To a night of letting loose after a week of hard work."

She clinks her bottle with mine and we both take a quick chug.

A few minutes later, she's in the middle of telling me a

story about Bree when "I Wanna Dance With Somebody" by Whitney Houston starts blasting through the speakers.

She stops mid-sentence with a loud gasp. "Oh my god. It's time to dance!"

She's up and out of our booth before my brain recovered from the mental whiplash, pulling me in the direction of the dance floor as Whitney belts out her first, "Woo!"

I follow her into our own spot out on the dance floor and it's like the rest of the world around us blurs to a dull roar as she pulls me in close and starts to croon the lyrics, wrapping her arms around me. Mine follow, settling around her waist as we find a rhythm together. Her hips shake with the beat and I follow her lead, smiling ear to ear at the pure ecstasy I find in her expression.

I want to bottle up this moment only to uncap it down the road after she's discarded me. Because there's no way I'll be able to keep someone like her for long. She's got her plans after college, and no matter where this goes in the near future, I'm afraid our relationship is like a ticking time bomb. Every time I ask myself if I'd be willing to follow her anywhere, the answer deep in my chest is a resounding *yes*. But I know it's too early for rash decisions like that, because although I've got her in my arms, she could slip through my grasp just as easily.

Her hand lands on my face, breaking through my thoughts. Her hand rakes through the hair at the back of my neck as she pulls me in for a quick kiss, right there in the middle of the dance floor. I hold her tighter to me, sending a wish into the universe that I can actually keep her.

She smiles up at me as she pulls away, and before long she's singing with such abandon, she doesn't notice that my hands are the only thing keeping her upright. When the song ends, her eyes pop open, and she looks up at me like she's coming off a high. Her smile takes up her whole face before she hugs me, and for a moment, it feels like it's just the two of us out here on the dance floor.

While we'd been inside, the snow that had been predicted for the day finally fell. It's not unusual for the end of November in the Midwest, but it still feels premature, covering the ground in a glistening layer of white. There's something about freshly fallen snow that makes the world seem so silent, making the walk to the corner to meet our Uber feel surreal, the only sound the crunch of snow beneath our feet.

"It's gorgeous out here," Val says, looking around.

Her usually buttoned-up appearance is nowhere in sight, although we're both practically sober. Sneaking a look in her direction with her hand in mine, I wonder if maybe she needed a night like this as badly as I did. Tonight I got to see her let logic fall to the wayside and do what she wants without second-guessing everything. Day to day, it's like she calculates every little moment of her life to make sure it all adds up to help her future self. But I watched her become boneless out on the dance floor, shut her eyes to the outside world, and lose herself in the music. I just wish she'd silence those inner voices and do the same with me.

We find the car waiting and shuffle into the backseat, our thighs touching as we settle into place. I don't move to put space between us, and neither does she, instead leaning on me with a hand on my knee as I put my arm around her shoulders.

"You wanna come to my house for a bit?" She whispers as the car begins to move in the direction of her place.

I look at her for a long moment, trying to decipher her expression from the beams of light that pass across her face as we make our way down the road.

Before I can answer, she adds, "Bree went home for Thanksgiving this morning, so it would only be the two of us."

My eyes roam her face, detecting nothing out of the ordinary as far as nerves. My insides are bubbling under the surface like a fifth-grade volcano project about to erupt. "Yeah, I'll stick around for a bit," I say, trying to hide that fact.

Chapter Twenty-One

VAL

Now that Brody's kicked his shoes off and is following me into the kitchen, my nerves are at an all-time high. We've essentially spent the entire day together between the library, the pizza place, and the dance floor. I was hesitant to let the night end, especially when I knew I'd be coming home to an empty house. But standing toe to toe, sipping water in front of my sink, the atmosphere is charged and crackling with possibility.

To make matters worse, he chugs his in seconds and sets his glass in the sink. Then he leans against the counter, staring at me. I avoid his gaze, forcing myself to go slow with the rest of the water in my glass, prolonging the silence. When the last drop falls on my tongue and I take my time retrieving his glass and setting them both in the dishwasher to the left of the sink.

The door clicks shut and I turn slowly, feeling his attention on my every move. When I finally meet his gaze, it's dark and probing. Exactly what I'd been afraid of. He reaches across the space between us and takes my hand, tugging until I finally fall into his chest. He kisses my forehead. "Whatever you're over-thinking about up there," he taps the crown of my head. "Stop. I know something inside you flips into high alert every time I'm in your personal space, but you're in charge here. Hell, I've had an amazing day with you, and will leave right now if you tell me to."

My hands link behind his back as I lean heavier into his embrace. "I don't want you to go yet." I don't realize how much I mean the words until they're out of my mouth.

I'm just so afraid to lose myself in this relationship. Everyone I love leaves, and I don't want him to turn out to be another heartbreak. Because what happens when he finally succeeds in breaking down my walls to find all the parts of me I've been trying to hide away from the world? Will he leave too?

Don't put this on him. If anyone's leaving, it's you.

My conscience has been a loud voice in the back of my head these past few weeks, reminding me of my post-graduation plans. Is it even worth trying to start something with Brody if I don't plan to stick around?

"You're doing it again," Brody says, his fingers combing through my hair in the most comforting way as he leans his head on top of mine.

"I know, I'm sorry. I can't help it."

"No need to apologize. But instead of keeping it all internalized, why don't you try talking to me about it? Maybe we can figure out whatever's bothering you together."

I snuggle further into his chest. "I don't know if that's possible."

"Try me."

I lean back, looking up at him, surprised by the sincerity I find in his expression. I take his hand, leading him to my bedroom, my heart beating harder with each step I take.

I settle onto my bed, leaning against the headboard as Brody hovers above me with a million questions in his eyes.

"I thought this would be comfier than the kitchen

counter," I say by way of explanation. For myself as much as for him, pulling him down next to me.

We situate, both lying on our sides, face-to-face. My head is propped on my pillow as Brody holds his head up on his hand. "So, what's up?"

I take a deep breath, focusing on a point on his chest. "I guess, I'm just wondering where, exactly, we go from here."

His fingers comb a stray curl out of my face. "Would it help you figure that out if I told you what I'm thinking?"

A jolt of electricity shoots through my nerves. Am I ready to talk about this? Two weeks ago, the answer would have been no, but something in me has changed since then.

"Yeah, I think it might, actually."

"Okay," he says, suddenly looking nervous, but his hand remains on my hip as if the connection is grounding him. I understand the feeling. "Well, these past few weeks have been great, and I'd like to see where things go between us, Val. Because I," his eyes bounce between my own. There's vulnerability in his gaze and I move closer to him without consciously deciding to. "I feel like there has to be a reason we met."

I stare at his lips, digesting his words before he quickly adds, "And I haven't forgotten what you told me months ago —your plan for after graduation. I still don't know what my next move will be, or if I'll be able to crawl out from under my father's thumb long enough to do what I want to. But I'm going into this with an open mind. And I'd love it if you could do the same."

I nod, placing my palm on his chest, right over his heart, and say, "Okay."

"Yeah?"

"Yeah. I think Bree said it best when we were talking a couple weeks ago—I haven't spent this much time thinking about a guy since I met her in the dorms freshman year. And there has to be a reason for it."

Brody smirks, his vulnerability replaced with something more familiar before he leans in, carving a line down my nose with his own before his lips land on mine. The kiss deepens quickly, like he's as desperate for a deeper connection as I am. His tongue swipes across my lip and I open for him. My hands roam the parts of his body that I don't know well enough yet—his muscular chest and shoulders, down his back.

Soon enough, I move my leg until it's hitched high on his hip and press myself into him until I can feel how badly he wants me. He groans against my mouth as his fingers find the hem of my sweater, inching their way up my bare back, and stops under the clasp of my bra as he pulls me ever closer.

After years of avoiding this type of connection, I forgot how good it feels to be wanted like this. The breathlessness that comes with these passionate kisses—the desperate feeling to be as close to him as I can get and having it actually be reciprocated.

Brody pulls away, and it's the last thing I want.

"What are you doing?" I ask as his eyes search for something in my expression.

"I didn't want to get ahead of myself," he says between breaths and slides a hand down his face.

"I don't want to stop."

His eyes bounce between mine. "Are you sure?"

I push his shoulder until he's flat against the mattress and straddle his hips. I pause right before our lips touch. "Yes, I'm sure."

My curls fall around my face as I look down at him, but he brushes them away, holding them in his fist at the side of my head. If there was any question whether his feelings matched those swirling inside my chest, that thought is put to rest by the way he's looking at me.

I'm in deep, but what I never stopped to realize is that so is he. And that only makes the decision to move our relationship forward easier. Because no matter how scared I am of the outcome, we're in it together.

"You're so beautiful," he says, one hand on my hip to hold me in place, the other trailing down my neck toward the V in my sweater. When it settles at my other hip, my patience wears thin. His hungry eyes take in my every move as I pull at the hem of my sweater, ripping it over my head to toss it carelessly behind me. I've been trying to go slow with him for so long, the steely patience he's practiced for months is even driving *me* crazy. It's a wonder he's still interested in me, but the waiting ends now.

When I finally have the courage to meet his eyes, they're blazing bright green. His fingers latch onto my hair at the back of my head as he pulls me in for a slow and sensual kiss.

I pull away, leaning back and pull him up enough to get my hands under his shirt, borrowing his playful smirk as I run my hands up every inch of his torso, the soft material bunching along my wrists as I go. His gaze is wide open as I pull his shirt over his head, letting it join mine on the floor.

He sets his glasses on my nightstand, and I realize it's the first time I've had an unobstructed view of his entire face up close. He looks different, but still so beautiful.

"Will you be okay without those?"

"I can see everything I need to," he says with a wicked smirk.

My cheeks heat.

We sit there, staring at each other for a long moment before Brody's fingers are dipping under the strap of the lacy black bra I'm glad I decided to wear tonight. His touch grazes the cup of my bra, but his eyes stay glued on my face, watching my every reaction. I gasp, unable to help myself when his thumb shifts over my nipple.

Spurred on by my reaction, his fingers find the clasp in the middle of my back, his searching gaze asking questions that don't need voiced out loud. With my subtle nod, he pops the clasp, letting the straps fall down my arms before he shoves it down the rest of the way like his will has finally broken. He pulls me in for a kiss as I hear my bra hitting the floor with a thud behind me.

Before I can blink, he's got me lying on my back and his kisses grow deeper as his hands learn every new part of me. We're both breathless when he pulls away, his gaze meeting mine quickly before he's trailing kisses down my neck all the way to my chest. A moan leaves my lips when he begins working his tongue over my sensitive nipples. It's like there's a direct connection between each open-mouthed kiss and the place where I want him the most.

"Brody," I whisper. His head lifts, and I miss his touch immediately. "Don't stop."

His eyes are half-lidded as his hands lower to the button on my jeans, yanking them down my hips. His touch soft and sensual as he explores every uncovered inch of my body. "Beautiful," he repeats, meeting my gaze as he pulls my jeans past my feet, tossing them to the floor.

Between the way he looks at me, and the comfort I feel in his presence, baring myself to Brody is easier than I ever imagined.

When his fingertips finally dip between my legs, I know there's no turning back for me. He presses my thighs apart with his own, his mouth returning to mine. I deepen the kiss, desperate for his touch, every nerve ending in my body firing at once as his fingers massage circles over my bundle of nerves.

My fingernails graze his back before my hands move to his belt buckle, undoing it with urgency. The clanking of metal on metal the only sound in the room as I shove his jeans down over his hips. He moves off the bed to let them drop to the floor.

My brain makes an appearance through the fog of lust,

finally realizing one problem—"do you have protection?" I ask, sure I'll cry if we have to stop.

He grabs his jeans, digging into his back pocket for his wallet and resurfacing with a foil square, holding it in the air like a golden ticket, making me laugh. He tosses it on the bed, his gaze caressing every inch of my body before his hands join in, starting at my neck, down my shoulder and arm until our hands are linked. He rests his forehead on mine as I wrap my arms around his back and he presses himself against me. The lack of layers between us creating a new type of friction as our hips move in unison and his lips land on mine.

It's been so long since I've let someone in like this, so it's hard to tell if my memory isn't serving me correctly, or if I could have truly forgotten what it feels like to surrender to the crackling electricity I feel when Brody touches me.

No—I'm sure I've never felt like this in my life.

"You okay?" Brody whispers against my skin, trailing kisses down the line of my neck.

"Yes. Are you?"

He smiles before flicking his tongue against my nipple. "Never better."

I watch him there for a moment before getting brave as I inch my fingers past the waistband of his boxers. His licks and kisses become little nips against my skin as I take the length of him in my hand, using the sounds he makes as direction.

"Fuck, that feels good," he says before his fingers find my slick center. My hips move against his hand, chasing that feeling that lies just barely out of reach.

His touch is suddenly gone, making me want to cry out in frustration, but in a few swift motions, the remainder of our clothes hit the floor.

Brody rolls on the condom and leans down for a kiss, pouring more passion into it than any kiss he's given me before. When a moan escapes me, he springs into action, spreading me wider. His eyes find mine as he glides against me, friction building between us.

"Please," I plead breathlessly, and he listens, lining himself up and pumping his hips until we've become one. Then our bodies take over, moving in unison as if this isn't our first time. His heavy breaths heat my neck, goosebumps prickling across my skin. Every nerve ending in my body fires off at once as he kisses me like a soldier who's leaving in the morning. The pressure builds, and suddenly there are bursts of electricity singing through every inch of my body. He pumps his hips even more wildly as his mouth crashes to mine in a hot, wet kiss, followed by his own release.

He's breathless as his body becomes a dead weight on top of me and we both wait for our heart rates to return to normal.

"Damn," he says, kissing my shoulder.

"Damn is right," I say, pushing sweaty strands of hair away from his face.

He nuzzles into my neck, "That was—" he starts, peppering little kisses against my skin, lifting on one arm and finding my gaze.

"Better than my dreams," I finish for him.

"So you're saying you'd thought about it?" He asks, mirroring his question the night he first kissed me.

I make a show of checking out every bare inch of him. "Uh, yeah."

He laughs, kissing my forehead. "Good."

Then he flashes me a sated smile before he collapses onto my chest. It's hard to say how long we lie there, tangled limbs before Brody props up on all fours, taking in the sight of my body like a starving man. His lips find mine suddenly, tongue tangling with mine before we disconnect with an audible pop.

"I'll be right back."

I watch his bare cheeks as he leaves the room, still half in shock at the events of this entire day. But when the door clicks shut, I throw the comforter over myself and smile like an idiot. Never in a million years would seventeen-year-old me believe that this could happen—that the boy who I dreamed of in baseball pants would someday notice me. Or that my feelings for him would grow to be so much more than a crush.

Chapter Twenty-Two

BRODY

The next morning, I wake up disoriented by the light shining in my eyeball. I sleep with my blackout curtains closed.

Did I pass out with the light on?

I blink my eyes open, confused by the unfamiliar ceiling fan above my head.

That's when I realize I'm sweating—and there are small puffs of air hitting my neck. I reach up to feel the weight against my chest. It's an arm, and it moves as soon as I make contact.

"Mmmm," comes a familiar voice, and I look down to find Val blinking one eye open against the morning light. "Hi," she says as I roll onto my stomach, leaning in front of the brightness to block it from her eyes.

"Morning," I say, taking in her sleepy state, as all of last night's festivities come flooding back. I place a quick kiss on her cheek.

"You stayed," she says, sounding alarmingly surprised.

"Of course I did. Why wouldn't I?"

She shrugs, recoiling into that shell she's used as a shield ever since I met her. I guess I shouldn't have expected that her giving me her body last night would automatically mean she'd trust me with her heart too, no matter how much I wish it were true.

Last night.

I expected to be here maybe a half hour, tops. She's taught me well in past months that I can only push her so far before she shuts down on me, so when she led me to her bedroom, it was the last thing I expected after spending the entire day together. I was just happy she'd agreed to let me take her out last night. The rest of it was unexpected.

Watching her come undone underneath me was unlike any experience I've had with anyone else. Probably because she's always in control, and last night, she let me have it instead. She was so responsive to every touch, showing me what she liked with the way she reacted. I'd never thought far enough into what she'd be like, laid bare in front of me, but it was so much more than I ever expected.

I kiss her bare shoulder, "Babe, wake up," I say, but her eyes are closed and I only get an unintelligible noise in response.

I plant another kiss just below her collarbone, lifting to see if she reacts. Nothing.

The next one is on her neck, and I linger there, swirling my tongue. This causes one eye to open. Her brow lifted. "Brody, let's sleep a little longer."

"Nope," I say, moving my body on top of hers and swirling my tongue on around her nipple, raised from being exposed to the cool morning air. I stay there, flicking my tongue until she squirm underneath me, eyes lifted to watch her reaction.

Her hands move to my back, kneading my shoulders and giving me all the reaction I needed to know she's enjoying this. When a moan escapes her, I switch sides, giving that peak the same attention. When she finally lifts her head to find I'm already watching her every reaction, she lets it flop back onto the pillow.

"What are you doing?" She asks breathlessly.

"I was trying to wake you up, but now that I succeeded, I'm going to make you feel good."

"What?" she asks, our bare bodies causing sweet friction as I disappear under the covers, settling between her legs, spreading them apart.

"Brody, wait——" She says just as my mouth lands between her thighs, causing her to squeak out a little, "Oh," as I move my make slow languid circles against her sensitive bundle of nerves, learning what she likes from each sound she makes, her hips bucking against me involuntarily.

"Oh my god," I hear her whisper like I wasn't meant to hear it, but it has me adding two fingers to her slick heat. She moans, and I peek up at her to find her mouth parted, eyes squeezed shut, lost in the feeling. I love getting her out of her own head, just for a moment. I've never seen a sight so beautiful as Val when she finally lets go. I hope I can be the one to help her see it's okay to put her to-do list to rest every once in a while and live the life she's put on hold for so many years.

When was the last time she came apart like this? And more importantly, *has* she?

Her fingers grip my hair as she gets more vocal, and I know she's getting close. Then suddenly, her body slumps against the sheets.

She pulls me by the shoulders and I wipe my mouth against the back of my hand and kiss every inch I climb until I reach her lips.

"You awake yet?"

She laughs breathlessly. "You could say that."

"How'd that feel?"

She covers her face with her hands, but not before I witness the blush that spreads across her face.

"Are you okay? I didn't hurt you, did I?"

"Ibneverdunthatbefore," she says from beneath her hands, but it comes out garbled.

"What?" I ask, gently prying her hands away and wait until she meets my gaze.

"I said I've never done that before."

My eyebrows jump before I can think better of it. "And did you like it?" I ask, although all signs point to the fact that she did.

"No, no. I did," she says, aggressively nodding her head. "I liked it, Brody, I did. I—" Her hands move to her face again, hiding from me.

"What is it?" I take her by each wrist, pressing them against the pillow above her head. "Don't make me tickle torture the answer out of you," I move my hands just below her ribs, punctuating the threat.

"Don't you dare," she throws her best glare my way, but it doesn't faze me. I press my fingers the tiniest bit into her flesh there. She gasps, body flailing. "Okay, okay. I was just gonna ask—did *you* like it? I've never had someone that...close before," she says, screwing up her face with the explanation.

I can't help it—I laugh. "You tell me if I liked it," I say, rubbing my hard length against her hip as proof. "I know things between us are pretty new, but trust me when I say I thoroughly enjoyed myself. But if you don't like it—"

"No!" she says, wriggling against my grip. "I never said I don't want to. It's just new for me," she shakes her head frantically, "Forget I mentioned it."

"Pretty sure I'm never going to forget you telling me that my tongue is the first one that has ever made you come. Sorry, that's engrained for life," I say, tapping my temple.

"Ugh, Brody," she says, turning her head until it's half hidden in her arm, like talking about it makes her uncomfortable.

I laugh against her lips until she wraps her legs around my

waist, her arms encircling me in a death grip after I finally let her go, deepening the kiss. She rolls us over until she's straddling *my* hips.

A sly smile curves her lips before she kisses my chest, climbing lower. "Your turn."

"I'm gonna miss seeing you every day," I admit later when we're cuddling on her couch, with a pizza box on our laps.

"It's only a week, Brody."

I take a deep breath, thinking about everything that awaits me in the week ahead. "I know."

"Are you nervous to see your dad?"

I nod. "Yeah, he's been blowing up my phone about my grades and I haven't texted him back even once. I'm sure the suspense is killing him."

"Brody," Val says, wiping her napkin across the corner of my mouth. "I know you two don't see eye to eye, but are you sure you want to make things worse with shit like that?"

I shrug. "It's my last line of defense against him. If I instigate things, at least he's got a real reason to be angry."

She snuggles further into my chest. "I'm sorry he makes you feel that way. I wish you were going to be at your parents' over the holiday so we could still see each other when we want."

My brother, Luke, and his wife, Kaitlyn always host Thanksgiving at their place in the suburbs of Des Moines. "I know. At least you'll have fun with the Hawkins family, though."

"I feel bad for saying this, given your circumstances, but I'm excited for break. But for what it's worth, I'll miss you too."

I kiss her hair, burying my nose in it for a prolonged

moment. "I know it's a little early to talk about it, but do you think you'll be going back there for Christmas?"

She sets the piece of pizza she'd been nibbling on back in the box, then turns to me. "I guess I don't see why not. Why?"

I dust my fingers off on my napkin and pull her back further into my chest, wrapping my arms around her, mostly so I don't have to be vulnerable with her eyes on me, "I thought maybe you could stay with me and my family. You'd still be able to come and go as you please, and spend time with Hannah and her family. But I'd also love if you could come to Christmas for my side of the family."

She sets the pizza box down beside us and turns around in my lap until she's straddling my waist with her arms around my neck. "That sounds like it would be fun."

"Is that a yes?"

She kisses the tip of my nose. "It's a…let me think about it?"

The fact that it's not an immediate yes is a little disappointing, but I understand why. "Of course. Take the time you need, then let me know."

She smiles. "Speaking of taking time, what time do you need to leave?"

I check the time on my phone. "I've got about thirty minutes, give or take."

"Just enough time," she says, jumping to her feet and pulling on my hand, leading us back to her room.

"You're insatiable."

She turns when we reach her bed. "Are you complaining?"

I guide her back onto the mattress, leaning over her with my hands on either side of her head. "Not one bit."

Chapter Twenty-Three

VAL

I'm still riding the high of the past several days when I'm getting settled at the Hawkins residence.

"So fill me in on the Brody situation," Hannah says when we make it into her room where we can talk without listening ears.

Although I can't see, I know my cheeks heat at the mention of him.

"That good, huh?" She asks. "Something happened. It's written all over your cherry-red face."

"Uh, yeah. He took me on a date over the weekend."

"And," she says, rolling her hand in a *keep going* gesture.

"He stayed the night...things may have happened."

She throws both hands up in the air like a fan in the stands at the World Series. "Are you saying what I think you're saying?" She asks, making a circle with one hand, her other pointer finger at the ready. I grab her wrists before she can take it any further."

"Yes, now stop it."

"Oh my gosh! You're living teenage Val's dream! I can't believe it."

"He's even more amazing than I thought he'd be, Hannah."

"In bed? You lucky bitch!"

"Well that, yes. But I actually meant in general. Back in high school, I thought he was hot. But it was a surface-level crush. I never stopped to think about the type of person he is, and now that I know, I'm in serious trouble."

"You aren't in trouble, you're in looove," she says, drawing out the word. "And if you aren't there yet, you're about to be. Mark my words."

"I don't feel platonic feelings toward him. I'm still figuring out exactly what it is. But for now, we're just having fun."

"So, are you two exclusive?"

I shrug. "We've never labeled things. Do you think this whole thing is a bad idea?"

"Enjoying someone's company—and a few orgasms along the way—is never a bad idea."

"But I'm leaving in less than six months."

"Are you?"

Am I? "Yes. Despite meeting him, I'm not putting my own life plans on hold."

"And I understand that, I do," she says, holding out her hands like she's preparing for an attack. "But is that really what this is? Your life plan—or are you just running away from the memories home holds?"

"What do you mean?"

She takes a deep breath. "Come on, Val. You've avoided this place for years. And as much as I can understand why, I think it's something you'd be better off facing head on so you can heal."

"Hannah, I'm never going to fully heal from losing my parents as a teenager. That's not how trauma works."

She covers her face with both hands, her ivory skin turning splotchy and red with the uncomfortable topic at hand. "I know, and I'm sorry. I'm not sure how to make these words come out right."

I stare at the floor, waiting for her to continue, although I'm not sure I'll ever be ready for where this conversation is leading.

"Before you leave this place behind, you should at least give it a fighting chance."

"And how do I do that, exactly?"

"You come home more often. You spend time with the people here that love you. You give that boy who makes you feel like you're on top of the world a fighting chance at a future with you. And I know you're not going to like this last one, but you need to go back to the house."

"No," I say, immediately shaking my head. "When will you let this go, Hannah?"

"When you *try*, Val. I've been supportive since it happened. I've visited you at school and kept my mouth shut when you make me feel like a burden when I ask you to visit. I understood your heartache. Hell, I watched the aftermath of it all, Val. But there's always been this nagging feeling inside of me telling me I should talk to you about it more, even if you push back. To give you some tough love before it's too late, because I don't want you to run away, if that's what you're doing."

"I'm not running away," I say with false bravado, because it's taken me this long to question if that is actually my motive.

"Are you sure about that?"

"Yes," I say, but for the entirety of the week, I keep running her words over in my head. And the crazy thing is, they start to sound more and more true.

The week off for Thanksgiving went quickly, but the quality time with Hannah was something I didn't realize how much I needed. Although her probing questions made me uncomfortable, they've also got me thinking of my future and the authenticity of the dreams I always thought were mine.

The two weeks that follow fly by in similar fashion, classes are done, and holiday break is so close, I can practically smell the turkey in the oven—at least I assume that's what I'll eat on Christmas. I guess I won't know until my plans have been finalized.

"Oh my gosh, listen to this," Brody says, walking with his hand in mine, both of us a little tipsy—although the bitterly cold air is sobering me up quickly. We've been at The Saloon celebrating the end of the semester with our friends, but left Isaiah, Wes, Bree, and a few of her friends behind since the most time we've spent together lately was while studying for finals.

Brody's been refreshing his grades all night waiting for our presentation grade to pop up, since Professor Rhode promised to have them up by the end of the day. He just informed me, rather excitedly, that we earned an A-minus. I don't know what I'm more proud of—the grade, or the studious monster I created who checks his grades at the bar. "After reprimanding one of you on the first morning of classes, I was worried you two would make for a horror story to tell my future classes—"

I pull his phone in my direction to get a look at the screen. "There is no way he said any of that," but when I get a good look, I realize he's been reading our feedback word-for-word. "Wow, okay. Continue."

"You two made a great team, surprising me with your hard work and commitment," he turns to me. "Did you hear that? Professor Roadie thinks we make a great team." He tosses his arm over my shoulders and leans his head against the top of mine. "He knew we'd end up together as well as I did, it seems. Maybe he wasn't so bad after all."

"Words I never thought we'd say."

When we're a half block from his place, Brody says, "So you still haven't given me an answer."

I know exactly what he's hinting at, but play dumb. "An answer about what?"

Brody pulls me in, chuckling because he knows exactly what I'm doing. He's already asked me three times this week, but I've found a way to change the subject each time. He presses a kiss to the crown of my head, "About Christmas! I'm starting to think you're scared to be seen with me."

"Would someone who's scared to be seen with you do this in public?" I ask, pulling at the collar of his coat until his lips land on mine, kissing him with abandon, right there in the middle of the sidewalk.

Our tongues tangle and I think I've finally shut him up until he pulls away, eyes heavy as he looks at me for a long moment before pulling on my hand and we're walking again. "You evil woman. You can't just use your kisses to disarm me. I need *answers*."

I'm not sure what's been holding me back, but it's time to put this beautiful boy out of his misery. "I'd love to go, if you'll still have me."

He stops, turning me by the shoulders to look me in the eye. "You're serious?"

My shoulder jumps in an attempt to play it cool. "Yeah, of course!"

His smile is huge as he pulls me in and swings me around the sidewalk. When he sets my feet back on the ground, his hands find my hips, pulling me against him. "I'm so excited, you have no idea."

"Yeah, well, I'd kiss you to show you how excited I am, but I think you need to get me inside before I freeze."

"Say no more, milady," he says, picking me up with an arm behind my knees and back, carrying me in his front door,

and as soon as I get you warmed up, consider yourself
ravished."

Chapter Twenty-Four

Brody

"I'm hungry," Val says as soon as we kick off our wet shoes at the door. "Do you have anything to eat?"

I squint, trying to think of the last time I actually went to the grocery store. With how busy I've been, eating out has been the most convenient. I'm sure if I went to the fridge, I'd find sour milk. "Depends what you deem edible," I say with a grimace.

"Okay," she says, sneaking her fingertips under my shirt until all ten of her icy fingers are pressed to the small of my back.

I shiver, trying to look intimidating, hoping it will persuade her to remove her frozen phalanges from my skin. Spoiler alert: it doesn't work.

"Val," I say in a warning tone.

"What did I say about using me as your warming pad?"

Her grin grows wider. "You said it makes you feel needed, and to do so anytime I please."

I press my lips together. "As much as I love catering to your needs, that is definitely *not* what I said."

She scrunches her face, thinking it over. "That's definitely how I remember it," she says, sneaking her fingers under the waistband of my jeans. That's when I tap out, pulling her hands from my back.

"Do you want to eat my food or not?"

She chuckles as I put one of her hands in both of mine, trying to warm them that way. "Yes, let's find food."

I pull open the fridge, and just as I expected, it's a barren land of forgotten food and condiments...and of course, beer. "Looks like we've got a whole lot of nothing."

She peeks over my shoulder. "Come on, Brody. Have a little imagination! There's plenty here to work with," she says, opening a drawer. Tossing a few things in the garbage, but ultimately finding some decent stuff.

She pulls a plate from their place in the cupboard because she's been over enough now that she knows everything's location. That fact makes me happier than it probably should.

I grab us water then stand back, checking out her ass every time she bends to find something in the fridge, letting her do her thing.

When she slams the fridge shut and turns around carefully with the plate in her hand, I realize she's made a charcuterie board, of sorts.

An array of meats and cheeses, because I bought the variety pack of cheese slices the last time I went to the grocery store. Grapes, blueberries, small pickles—I don't know how she came up with half of it. They weren't mine, but she even snuck green olives on the plate, a fact that makes me a little squeamish, if I'm honest. What were those even doing in the fridge?

She takes a step toward the stairs, but stops, handing me the plate. "Wait, one more thing," she goes to the snack drawer, grabbing my box of Cheez-Its, then skips back to me. "Gang's all here."

She pulls on my hand, leading us to my room.

———

"Okay, be honest," she says, popping an olive in her mouth after we've been settled on my bed for long enough to polish off half the charcuterie board. I'm trying really hard to concentrate on her words, rather than what she just put in her mouth. "When we met at Beans, did you really think we'd end up here?"

That gets my attention off the olive for the moment, and I chuckle at the memory of that day. "After I let you walk out the door, I was ninety percent sure I'd never be able to find you again."

She smiles. "Why didn't you chase me?"

"Because I thought you left because I creeped you out."

"What?" Her voice is so high-pitched, it squeaks.

I shrug. "You looked pretty content before tossing your coffee at me—"

"I did not toss my coffee. I knocked it over."

"Before you *knocked over* your coffee," I say with a wink. "Then I sat down to talk to you, and just when we were about to get to know each other, you high-tailed it out of there. I was actually a little scared when you sat down at my table on the first day of school. Thought for sure you'd find a far-fetched reason that I showed up in your lecture to creep you out."

She shakes her head like I've had it all wrong this whole time. "It wasn't that you crept me out. I was taken by you, and trying to fight those feelings. I have to say, I think you held out for a very respectable amount of time."

I nearly snap my neck to look at her. "You drove me crazy for weeks, Val."

Her hand lands on my shoulder. "I know, I'm sorry. If it helps, I was fighting with myself about it the whole time."

She moves across the comforter and into my lap, setting our plate off to the side.

"So you're saying I've still got it?"

She brushes my too-long bangs back. "Oh yeah. You've still got it."

Her forehead presses against mine and just before her lips find mine, I gently push her to arm's-length.

"Olives!" I yell, by way of explanation.

"What?" she says, offended that I pushed her away in an intimate moment.

"I'm sorry. It's just that you—" I turn to look at the offending plate on my bedside table. "You ate olives and I hate olives. I think they're disgusting, and I was gonna try, but I don't think I can kiss you when you taste like them."

Her eyebrows rise higher and higher throughout my entire monologue, but it's too late to back down now.

"So what, you want me to brush my teeth before I kiss you?"

I purse my lips, thinking that over. "That would be great, actually."

She removes herself from my lap completely, jumping off the bed and stepping back a few steps for good measure. "You're actually serious?"

I palm the back of my neck. "Why do I feel like this is a trick question?"

As if she wasn't already surprised, her face drops further. "Wow!" She turns on her heel, heading straight for my bathroom across the hall.

"Wait," I say, popping out of bed to follow, but before I can open the door, there's an audible click of the lock. "Val, I'm sorry. It's like you, with letting me borrow your favorite writing utensils, okay?" The water runs on the other side of the door. "Would you rather I said nothing and gagged when you went to kiss me? I feel like that would have been more traumatizing for you." When I hear the slide of a drawer opening, I know she's using her finger and my toothpaste like she does when she stays over. I give myself a mental head smack when I remember I still haven't bought her a permanent toothbrush to keep here for occasions like this.

Chapter Twenty-Five

BRODY

Val's been so good about letting me in on her life, and all its messy parts. It's not until I'm picking her up to take her home to meet my family that I realize I haven't done the same for her. Taking her home to meet my family is going to be like pushing her into the deep end of a pool when she doesn't know how to swim yet.

She knows the state of my relationship with my father, but inviting her into the belly of the beast is different than warning her of what's to come.

I know she's not the type to judge me for things beyond my control, but there's still a nagging voice in the back of my head telling me she won't like what she learns about me. What if she suddenly forgets all the progress I've made because of something my father says?

Thankfully, Luke and his family will be there as a buffer for the bullshit.

When I pull up to her house, Val's already running out the door, weighed down by her bags. I shuffle out of the driver's seat to take them from her in the middle of the sidewalk.

"Hey," I say, the breathlessness more about nerves than the strain of carrying her bags. I try to hide it with a quick peck to her lips.

"Hi," she smiles at me, squinting at the afternoon sun.

I take her hand, stopping at the back hatch to toss her things in next to my own, then rounding to open the passenger door.

Finally remembering myself, I pull lightly at her hand as she steps in until her foot lands back in front of me. She catches herself with a hand to my chest. "How about a proper kiss this time?"

The wrinkle between her brows releases as she smiles, linking her hands behind my neck.

Mine finds her cheek, the other settling on her lower back to pull her close.

Her eyes sparkle as they close. The kiss starts off slowly, but as our hands roam, it quickly turns into something hotter and heavier than it should be in broad daylight, so I force myself to pull back.

Our gazes catch and Val's smile lights me up from the inside.

"Ready to head out?"

She plants another quick kiss on my lips. "Yep."

"How are you feeling about the weekend?" I ask once we're on the road.

She yawns, turning her attention to me. "I'm nervous and excited. Can't wait to see Hannah and meet your family. Although I'll admit, from what you've told me, I'm nervous about meeting your dad. I have a feeling our personalities might clash, and if they do, is that going to make things worse for you?"

I nod, knowing exactly what she means. It oddly makes me feel better to know she isn't going into the holiday with rose-colored glasses. "If that happens, just know, anything you do can't make our time here any worse than it already would have been, okay?"

I glance away from the road in time to watch her nod. "But Brody?"

Her no-nonsense tone has my hackles rising. "Yeah?"

"If he disrespects you in front of me," she bites her lip like she needs to think before saying her next words. "I won't sit there and look pretty. I hope you know that."

I nod, a knot coiling tighter in my belly. Those words make me as nervous as they make me feel cared for. As I have since asking her to come home with me, I spend several miles wondering if bringing her here so soon will make everything we've built together blow up in my face.

"The good news is my dad's out of town until tomorrow. So you'll only meet my mom tonight."

She blows out a breath, laughing as she turns to me. "Well, that takes a load off my shoulders for now, at least."

"My brother, his wife, and my niece will stay at the house for most of our time here, too. It never happens, so I'm excited."

"I'm excited to meet them."

We sit in a comfortable silence for a few miles when Val turns to me.

"You know, something about this drive has tricked my brain into believing I'm only hours away from seeing my parents. Like I'm on my way there for the holiday." She looks longingly out her window. "I wish it were true."

I set my hand on her knee and squeeze. She lifts it, twining my fingers with hers. "I wish it were true *for* you, Val. I wish I could have met them."

She sniffles as she nods. "I wish that too. They would have loved you."

Val goes rigid and quiet in the passenger's seat when we reach the house, staring at the house in the last bits of evening light.

"Well, this is it," I say, throwing it in park in the driveway. I have to hold back a laugh at her expression.

"This place is *huge*," she squeaks.

I swallow a groan. "My dad enjoys unnecessary things," I say, gathering my things and making for the door. "Let's go in."

I round the vehicle and grab our bags. Val meets me there, trying to take hers, but I swerve her waiting hands.

"If you have posters of naked supermodels hanging in your childhood bedroom, I'll try not to hold it against you," she says, following me to the front door.

I turn to her, somehow freeing my hand to grab the door handle. "Give me five minutes to destroy the evidence?"

She scoffs and I wink, but before we can say another word, an excited scream comes from somewhere in the back of the house. "That would be my mother," I say, setting our bags at the foot of the stairs that wind the grand entryway.

I kick off my shoes and turn to Val. But her eyes are on my mom's favorite piece in the house—the glittery, over-the-top chandelier.

I feel a jolt in my chest, reminded of my ex and how she dreamed of a house just like this someday. It's never been something I strived for. It was the beginning of the end for us, looking back.

Val isn't her.

I grab her hand, bringing her attention back to me. "I'll give you the tour in a minute, okay? For now, let's find my mom."

She steps toward me with a genuine smile that eases my loud thoughts. "Okay, lead the way."

As I turn to do so, the sound of my mom's house shoes padding across the tile floor announces her presence before she bounces through the doorway.

"Oh, you're home!" She says, laser-focused on Val and I standing as a united front in the entryway. Instead of greeting me with all that excitement like I'd expected, she beelines straight to Val. If I hadn't been there to keep her upright, my mother would have knocked her straight on her back on the designer rug.

"Well, hello to you too, Mom."

She finally pulls away from Val. "Oh, I'm sorry. Val, right? I'm a hugger. Sorry if I made you uncomfortable. I'm just so darn excited Brody brought home a friend."

"She's my girlfriend, Mom."

"Girlfriend?" she yells, "Oh!" And her arms are around Val again, who's smiling at me as she returns the gesture. "Brody, that makes me so happy."

"Mom, this is Valerie Boyd. Val, this is my mom, Elizabeth."

She pulls away. "Oh, please. Call me Liz."

"It's nice to meet you, Liz."

"So do I get a hug too, or——"

"Of course, my baby boy," she says, finally wrapping her arms around me, and I return it tenfold. I didn't realize how much I needed it until I'm enveloped in the warmth of it. Although my dad and I don't see eye to eye, my mom is one of my biggest supporters. "I love you, you know that, right?"

"If I didn't know better, I'd say you like my girlfriend a lot better than you like me." They both laugh and mom waves a hand through the air. "I love you too, Momma."

"You two get settled. I'm about finished with dinner. Make yourself at home, Val. Soup will be done when you're ready."

"Ooh, what kind?" I ask, already bending to grab our bags.

"Your favorite!" Mom yells back as she retreats to the kitchen.

"What kind is your favorite?" Val asks when we're out of earshot.

"Loaded baked potato soup. The one my mom makes is the best."

As I open my bedroom door, I realize Val isn't behind me. I toss the bags on the floor and return to the stairs to find her halfway down, her hand on the rail and jaw slack as she takes everything in.

"You good down there?"

She shakes her head as if to clear it, turning toward me. "Yeah, sorry. There's so much to look at, I keep getting side-tracked." She continues to stare at the chandelier as she makes her way up the steps.

I heave a long breath, dropping onto my bed. Val sits beside me.

"You good?"

"I'm great. Just tired from carrying your bags up a flight of stairs while you lagged behind, gawking at everything. What the heck did you pack in there?" I say, trying to make light of the dark turn my mind took.

She laughs. "You know, I said I could carry my own bags, Mr. Stubborn."

I snort, "I know you did. And I think you meant chivalrous."

"Nope, definitely meant stubborn," she says, standing to roam my old room. She takes in all the personal touches I left behind when I moved out for college, a bunch of awards and medals from high school, mostly. I watch as she continues to the bookshelf on the opposite side of the room. For our road trip, she wore a simple t-shirt and black leggings that hug every curve, the soft material stretching across her ass as she leans over.

"No books, Brody. I'm disappointed," she says, turning

toward me. Then, when she realizes I'd been checking her out, grabs a pillow and smacks me with it.

I wrestle it away from her and pull her onto my bed. She tries to wriggle away at first, but relents when I brush her hair behind her ear, leaning into my touch. "Thanks for coming back here with me."

"Thanks for inviting me," she says, planting a quick kiss on my lips before I have time to react.

She makes a show of getting up, but I hold on tighter. She laughs, settling back on top of me. "Fine," she says, then drops her mouth to mine in a slow and sensual kiss, but still pulls away before I'm ready. "Now get up and show me around."

I shake my head, letting her pull me to my feet.

We spend the next several minutes walking through the house. She fawns over every square inch of the place.

I end the tour in the kitchen, where mom is stirring a huge pot on the stove. It smells delicious.

"Perfect timing," she says, reaching into the cupboard for a stack of bowls, pouring one after the other as I pull a barstool out for Val at the oversized kitchen island.

"You have a beautiful home, Liz."

Mom waves a dismissive hand, always acting as if she doesn't work her ass off to make it so. "Oh, thanks, honey."

"She's being modest," I whisper to Val. "Knowing her, she spent the past week making sure each nook and cranny of this house is the cleanest it's ever been."

Mom sets a bowl in front of each of us, glaring at me. "Hush, you. Eat your soup."

"Hit the nail on the head, didn't I?"

She looks over her shoulder as she pulls a baking sheet of garlic bread out of the oven. "Your point?"

Val and I laugh.

After dinner, I show Val the one place I hadn't covered in my earlier tour. My sanctuary anytime I'm home—the basement.

I lead us down the extra wide stairs, Val's hand in mine. When we reach the bottom, I watch Val take in the movie area that holds a huge, plush sectional couch and a large screen for a projector. Then she moves onto the fully furnished bar, but what catches her eye is the pool table on the other end of the room.

She lets go of my hand to walk toward it, running her hand across the barn wood rails. "Holy shit, this is gorgeous," she looks to me, then back to the custom piece made with a deep red felt to match the details of the basement.

"It is. Have you played?"

She bites her lip and swings her nervous smile in my direction. "I haven't. Wanna teach me?"

I smile, coming up behind her, kissing her neck as I wrap my arms around her waist. "Absolutely."

Once I've explained all the basics, Val stands in front of me at the end of the table, bent over just right so she has a perfect sight of the cue ball. I'm awkwardly standing behind her, checking her lines and whatnot when she turns her head and asks, "So you gonna help me, or what?"

I line my limbs with hers, my hand behind hers on the grip, my front plastered against her backside, and my other arm around her to settle my hand on hers at the front of the stick. I help her adjust her hands as we practice, swinging our arms forward and back a few times.

"Practice this motion until it feels comfortable and we'll put some power behind it."

She does what I ask, and I try not to add any resistance.

I move my head to the other side of hers, where I'm forced to breathe against the side of her neck, her perfume wafting straight to my nose. I understand why they say teaching someone how to play pool is such an erotic experience. Damn.

"Okay," she says breathlessly. "I'm ready for some power."

"I'll help give you a little extra push."

We try it, and as always, she impresses me.

"Ready to hit the ball?" The words rumble into her neck.

"If you keep doing that, I'll drop this stick and tackle you to the ground."

I chuckle against her ear, satisfied when I see goosebumps spread across her skin.

In retaliation, she shoves her ass into my groin to lean further over her stick. I groan at the contact and shake my head, trying to remember myself. *Point taken.*

"On your count."

She takes a deep breath. "Three, two, one," we pull back in perfect unison and slam the tip into the cue ball with enough force for an impressive break.

I step back, giving her room to do the same as the balls scatter across the table.

"How was that?" She looks at me, fingers grasping that four-leaf clover at her throat.

"That was a great. You want to take the rest from here? Or do you still want my help?"

She smiles. "I'll try it on my own."

She follows her cue ball around the table as I stand near the return and tell her everything that fell. She chooses stripes.

I give her a quick rundown on aiming and pressure before she bends over to shoot. She sets up her shot perfectly without my help and surprises me by going for one of the hardest shots on the table.

"Wait—" I begin, but it's already too late. Her hand extends and slams forward toward the cue ball with perfect precision. One ball goes straight into the corner pocket, but before it fell, it hit another ball that slowly rolls to the other corner pocket.

I turn to Val, my jaw hanging wide open.

The smile on her face is magnificent. "Are you starting to figure out what's happening here yet?"

Before I can answer, she lines up her next shot, sinking

another ball. That's when I realize I've just been swindled by my girlfriend, a pool shark by the name of Valerie.

I'm still standing in the corner, awaiting my turn as she sinks the eight ball, winning the game.

"Okay, seriously. What just happened?"

She sets the pool cue down safely swishing, those hips toward me slowly. She wraps her arms around my neck and leans in.

"I haven't played in years, but my dad taught me everything I know, sorry."

Chapter Twenty-Six

VAL

The next evening, Brody drives us to Hannah's for dinner. It hits me on the way, even though I had a recent visit, I'm nervous to be back in town again.

"How are you feeling?" Brody asks, settling his hand on my knee that had been bouncing.

"My stomach always feels a little funky when I'm going back home," I swipe my hand along my torso as if it'll help. "Having you here by my side makes it better, though," I say, setting my hand over his.

He flips his hand, intertwining our fingers and bringing mine to his lips. "Have I mentioned how grateful I am that you've been so open to sharing this part of your life with me?"

I turn to look at him. No one has said anything like that to me before. "It's scary, but worth it."

"I'm sure it is. I've only recently realized I haven't given you the same transparency."

I squeeze his hand. "You will in time. I'm not holding it against you."

He lets go of a sigh. "I'm hoping you'll still feel that way over the next few days. I have a feeling you'll get a pretty good glimpse while we're here."

I shake his hand until he glances over. "You know it's not going to change the way I feel about you, though, right?"

His face turns hard. "That's what I'm hoping for, but wouldn't blame you if it does."

I lean across the center console, planting a kiss on his cheek. "It won't."

I watch the cornfields and acreages pass along the highway outside my window as we go silent. I take in the changes the land has gone through since the days I used to drive this road regularly. There are houses built in what used to be the middle of a cornfield, newly paved stretches of the highway. The old blinking stop sign outside of town is now a full-blown stoplight. While I was living two hours away, feeling like my life was at a standstill, this place moved on without me. I can only imagine what it'll be like, coming back after years of living wherever my future takes me after graduation. Will I even recognize this place anymore?

That thought makes me incredibly sad.

Brody navigates town without me having to give him directions, finding the Hawkins residence all on his own.

We look at each other for a beat as Brody unbuckles his seatbelt. He's wearing that smirk I never get sick of, and I lean across the center for a kiss. Pulling away, I see a flash of black against the white of the garage door we're parked in front of and turn to find Hannah dressed in a chunky black sweater as she throws open my door.

I try to step out and greet her, but she tackles me back against the center console.

"Stop kissing your boyfriend and get your cute little butt over here!"

Finally recovering, I wrap my arms around her. "Glad to see you too," I say, laughing.

She pulls back, tears swimming in her eyes. I smile, because if there's a perfect word to describe my Hannah, it is *emotional*. "You better dry those eyes up before you make me cry too."

She swipes at her eye with the sleeve of her sweater. "Shut up."

Hannah finally seems to remember Brody's with me and turns to throw her arms around his neck.

"Brody!" He removes his hands from his coat pockets to wrap them around her and pat her on the back like an awkward big brother. "Glad to see you again. Thanks for making my Val so happy."

He smiles over her shoulder at me. "She makes it pretty easy."

When we're in the house, I hear Hannah's parents call from the kitchen.

"Hey!" I call, pulling off my boots and dashing across the open living room to find them. They pull me into a group hug that feels like home. When we pull away, Jenn looks over my shoulder and smiles. "Glad to see things are going well."

I turn back to Brody, who's talking to Holt and Hannah across the room. He looks up like he can feel my gaze, both of us smiling at each other, faces glowing.

"Brody, great seeing you again!" Bobby says, clapping him on the shoulder as he makes his way to us. "I'd say I hope you've been treating our Val well, but judging by the smile on her face, I think you have."

Brody pulls me into his side, kissing me on the crown of my head. "She's the best, and putting that smile on her face is my favorite thing to do." He pokes the dimple in my cheek and I swat his hand away playfully.

"The real question is, has she hit you with one of her infamous glares, though? Those things are deadly."

I turn around at the sound of Holt's voice and give him one of those glares he was talking about. He laughs. Luckily for him, the jingle bells on the front door chime, and we all turn as it opens. Miles smiles from the doorway, "Hey everyone," he says and we all jump in with greetings. "Val, you're back in town. Glad to see you. Brody," he says, waving before he toes off his boots.

As far back as I can remember, Miles has been a brother figure, just like Holt. Since we were kids, it's been him and I that the Hawkins family has brought in as a part of their own. Vacations, beach days at the lake, pool parties—you name it, the four of us kids did it together. Jenn was best friends with Miles' mom throughout grade school, and their boys were born four months apart and became best friends too. My dad and Bobby remained friends after they dated two girls who were best friends back in high school. Neither of those relationships lasted, but their friendship lasted the ages—and they had girls in the same year, and Hannah became my built-in best friend. Remembering these small and significant details of my life, I don't know why I ever thought this place was going to feel like anything but home.

I forgot how much I enjoyed the holiday season in this house. Between Bobby and Jenn, there's a plethora of delicious food to go around. Baked goods and desserts from Jenn, and delicious smoked meats by Bobby. Tonight, he smoked a rack of ribs.

After Holt's girlfriend, Serena, arrives, we all make our way to the sprawling dining room. There's plenty of conversation going on and I bask in the moment, tuning into each different conversation, thinking about how happy I am to be here—especially since I don't know where I'll be for Christmas next year.

Brody's chuckle breaks me from my depressing reverie. He's holding his own in a conversation with Bobby and Holt about his hopes of becoming a strength and training coach after college. They pepper him with questions, and I think about saving him from it, but he seems to enjoy having someone take an interest in his future. It makes sense, since it's something he's passionate about, and from what he's told me, his father directly opposes it.

After dinner, Jenn enforces the Hawkins family Christmas tradition of watching *It's a Wonderful Life*, threatening to hold us hostage if we try leaving before watching. We all find our places around the large sectional couch in the basement. It's hard to recall the amount of times I've watched this movie, but it's a large number. I guess I can thank Jenn for that, since it was with this family I watched the movie for the first time. I've always called her my second mother, and I'd never want to replace the amazing woman who raised me, but as the main character is introduced on-screen, I realize just how true that name has become for Jenn in recent years. Especially after losing my mom in the middle of high school. They're some of the most important years of your life, and not having my mom there through half of it was really hard.

Back then, Dad was in a terrible place after losing his best friend, which I still believe became his demise. It's not what the doctors called it, but I lived with him after we lost my mom—he died of a broken heart. While he was still here, Jenn stepped up for me, making sure I was signed up for school, helping with my college applications and financial aid when my dad was MIA those last several months of his life.

After my dad passed, the Hawkins family took me in until I left for college. I was not myself for several months, but they loved me through it. I'm not sure I've ever truly thanked her for that.

A tear falls down my cheek, and before I can brush it away, Brody's knuckle is there to do the job.

I look at him, surprised he found me crying in the dark room, but I'm grateful. He's so in tune with my every need—has been since our friendship began. It's a foreign feeling after the walls I built in years past to keep people out. Walls he scaled with determination. Have I been taking that for granted?

Brody squeezes the hand he's holding, pulling my attention from my thoughts. *You okay?* He mouths.

I smile and nod, nestling into his chest before he has time to realize the lie. He pulls me in closer, kissing me on the top of my head.

I hardly pay attention to the rest of the movie. Instead, I spend the remainder glancing around the room at the people who welcomed me back into their lives with open arms after the brat I was those last few months before I left for college.

The same melancholy feeling I had as we pulled into town returns as I try to imagine giving this up. If I move halfway across the country as an event planner, I will most likely miss out on moments like this in exchange for hosting lavish parties for strangers. At least for the first handful of years, I'll be the newbie, assigned to work every holiday. In a year, I may not make it back for Christmas at all.

Sometime toward the end of the movie, Brody's phone goes off. He pulls it from his pocket and I feel him immediately go rigid.

I don't want to be nosy, so I keep my eyes trained on the television.

"Everything okay?" I ask once the light is back on, and everyone's stretching and removing blankets.

"Yeah," he says, but contradicts his answer with a shake of his head no. "My dad's home, and the last thing I want to do after a night like this is to have to deal with him."

I nod, as if I can understand. But as the daughter of two deceased parents I'd give anything to spend another holiday with, I just don't. With that, an idea forms. "If you don't want to go home yet, I might have an idea."

As soon as I realize I've piqued his interest, I brace myself for what's coming.

Chapter Twenty-Seven

BRODY

"So where, exactly, are we going?" We just said our goodbyes and are headed to my vehicle.

"I've got an idea, but I'm not sure how you'll feel about it."

"Tell me." I pull her to a stop against the passenger door.

She fists the sides of my jacket, staring a hole through my chest with an intense gaze that won't lift to mine. "I've been back here plenty of times in the past few years, and I still haven't visited the house." She looks at her feet as she says, "Technically, it's mine, but I haven't been back since I moved out."

My eyebrows jump at her words. "You're sure that's something you want to do tonight?"

She nods. "I wasn't sure when I'd have time, so this is actually kind of perfect. You can get your momentary reprieve, and I can get some closure."

I comb my hands through her hair, and she pulls me in

until our hips are aligned. "If it's what you want, we'll go." I watch tears pool in her eyes. "But only if you're sure."

She doesn't say anything, just nods.

I look around, trying to find the right words as I carry the conversation. "Are you sure you want *me* to be there with you? Or I can go get Hannah...or maybe you'd rather do it alone..."

"No, I want you there," she says as a tear slips down her cheek. I brush it away with my thumb as she adds, "Unless you don't want to—"

I don't even let her finish the thought. "Of course I want to be there for you. Please never question that."

She reaches up on her toes and I return the kiss she plants on my lips. "Let's go then, before I chicken out."

Val holds onto my hand for dear life the entire way across town, only opening her mouth to give directions. It's been so quiet in the car, neither of us bothered to reach for my phone to start the music, given the current mood in the vehicle.

When we're parked in the driveway of her childhood home, I turn to Val. "You okay?" I reach through the darkness to find her hand and pull it into my lap.

She called her late mother's best friend, who watches the house when she isn't around. Figured it was better to tell her we're here than to have her call the cops because of an unfamiliar vehicle in the driveway.

"So far, so good," she says, but her voice breaks. She digs through her purse, producing a silver key that glints in the light from the street behind us.

She's fidgety, looking anywhere but at me.

I squeeze her hand to settle her movements. "Valerie," Her full name feels foreign on my lips. Her gaze swings toward me and I ask, "Are you sure you want to do this? I don't want you to feel like I'm forcing you. Just say the word and we'll leave. We can come back whenever you want."

Her lips curl into a smile as she nods, but the rest of her

face contorts as the first sob racks her body. I reach across the cab and pull her over the center console until she's in my lap. Her head falls to my chest as the tears flow.

I wrap my arms tight around her, keeping her grounded as she falls apart, combing through her hair until her breaths even out. "You're the strongest person I've ever known, Val."

Sniffles are her only answer until her voice finally breaks the silence. "I don't feel very strong right now."

"Are you kidding me? Instead of telling me to suck it up and take you back to my parents' place, you take me to yours. You're sitting in the driveway of your childhood home for the first time in—"

"Over three years," she says.

"Exactly. When it comes to strength, you beat me every single day of the week."

"But you do have bigger muscles," she says with a weak smile, making me laugh as she wraps her small hands around my biceps, squeezing as if to prove her point. Then her hands slide up my body to curl behind my neck as she snuggles her face against it.

My chest opens with the oddest sensation as I settle my chin on the crown of her head.

Just over a month ago, she was pushing me away at every turn. Now we're sitting together in the driveway of her childhood home as she prepares to share one of the most emotional moments of her young adult life—past losing her parents—with me.

I kiss the crown of her head and she props herself back up on my lap, fiddling with her keys. "I think I'm ready."

I put my hands on either side of her face, staring straight into her eyes. That little twinge in my chest is back, and I know for certain I've never felt this way for another person in my twenty-two years on earth. If I could take the pain I know she's feeling away, I'd do it in a heartbeat. But since I can't, I'll do the next best thing: be here for her.

I stand behind Val with what little we have in tow, one hand on her hip as she reaches to unlock the front door.

The lock clicks, the midnight blue door creaking as she pushes it open. She flips on a light to the right of the door like it's muscle memory, flooding the porch and entryway in light. She stops just inside the door assessing the space, and I do the same, seeing the home Val spent most of her childhood with fresh eyes. There's a doorway and steps descending into the basement directly past the entryway. On one side is the kitchen, and the other is the living room.

The air is stale with lack of use; the molecules confused at being shifted by our presence.

She doesn't even kick off her shoes, just continues through the living room and I finally step into the house and close the door. I set everything down and remove my shoes, buying her some alone time. I can only imagine how loud her thoughts are.

Slowly, I make it across the room where she's standing in front of a bookshelf stuffed full of knickknacks and framed photos of Val at varying ages and her parents on their wedding day. I see a duplicate of the picture she has on her nightstand back at school.

I sidle up behind her and feel her lean into my presence.

"You know what I saw the first time I spotted this on your nightstand?" I say, pointing to the photo in question. "Your big brown eyes and beautiful smile are a replica of your mom's. From these pictures, I can imagine she's where you got that laugh I adore so much." I brush a hand through her hair, pulling a loose strand taut, then letting go to watch it bounce back. "You got these blonde curls from your dad." I wrap my arms around her and kiss her hair. "Have I ever told you my favorite hair days are when I can tell you were running a little late, and it has that crazy curl to it? Like you manipulated it in front of the mirror forever, but it wouldn't do what you wanted, so you flop it over this way or that."

She lets loose a laugh. "I hate it when it's like that."

"I love it." I say, burying my nose in its scent. "The fact your hair always smells like a cupcake might have something to do with it, though," I say, squeezing her a little tighter. "They're gone, but they live on through you and all the other lives they touched during their time here. I think that's pretty damn beautiful."

She turns around in my arms, and I don't miss the tear that trails down her cheek. I wipe it away with the pad of my thumb.

"How do you do that?" She asks.

I give her a sad smile. "Do what?"

"Make me smile, even while I'm crying."

I lean in to press a kiss to her forehead and say, "I'm here to point out the beauty in case your mind makes you believe it doesn't exist."

She smiles sadly, leaning in to kiss my neck before snuggling into my chest.

I rub her back, basking in the feel of her in my arms.

Later, she insists on showing me the rest of the house, taking my hand to drag me upstairs behind her. As we reach the top of the steps, she halts, staring at a closed door at the end of the hallway. I run into the back of her before I realize what's happening.

"That's my parents' room," she turns to look at me. "I'm not ready to go in yet, if that's okay," before I can answer, she's pointing at another door. "There's a bathroom, and here's my bedroom," she says, pointing at the door across from the bathroom as we walk in.

The walls are a light grey. Everything else is white or black, including the bed, dresser, and vanity.

The wall behind her bed is filled with a collage of photos that makes a wallpaper. Most of them have curled up at the edges, but I laugh when I notice the poster of a shirtless actor who played a superhero in movies back when we were in high school. "A pretty big fan, huh? To think you asked if I had naked chicks taped up on my walls, and here you are with naked men."

Her cheeks flush pink. "Shut up. I haven't lived in this house for almost four years. Besides, Hannah's the one who put that up. And he's shirtless, not naked."

"Sure," I tease, keeping my eyes on her as she walks around the space, relearning the version of herself that once lived inside these walls.

She opens the closet door and runs a hand past all the long-forgotten clothes still hanging inside, stopping on a dime to pull something off the rack. "Gosh, I missed this sweater," she says, pulling it from the hanger and holding it up to herself, walking in front of the mirror. I admire her every move and follow as she moves to her collage wall.

She snuggles into my side as we take in the photos in front of us. One in particular snags my attention. "Wait, what is that?" I ask, pointing to a picture of an ass in white baseball pants that looks oddly familiar, thanks to the orange jersey tucked into it.

Val jumps to attention as she sees what I'm pointing at. She gasps and throws a hand over the photo as if I didn't already have ample time to see it.

"Oh my god, it's nothing, I swear!"

Instead of trying to uncover it, I lean down close to her ear, where I know my breath tickles her skin. "Valerie, tell me that isn't my ass plastered to your bedroom wall."

"It's not!" She tries to add authority to the words, but fails. "It's—uh, Mal's!"

I pull away quickly; the mood ruined even though I know she's lying. "And you think that's better?"

She clicks her tongue and throws her arms out to her side. "Yep, you caught me. I had a huge crush on Mal back in high school. So glad to have that off my chest. It's been bugging me for a while."

A flicker of jealousy ignites in my chest, even though I know it's not true. "Has it, now?"

She wraps her arms around my waist, leaning in. "Yes, I didn't want that information to come between us—or between you and Mal when I finally meet him, you know?"

"Don't worry. I won't let it get to me. Especially since I know Mal was catcher back in high school, and the glove dangling from the hand near the ass in this picture is the one that *I* used for several years. That ass is mine."

"Shit," she says, giggling into my chest.

"But I guess the real question is, why is my girl so worried about me finding out there's a picture of my ass on her wall from high school? As if it isn't the highest compliment."

"You aren't wondering why it's there?" She asks, still talking into my chest.

I brush back her hair, pulling her closer. "Of course I'm curious. I figured you'd tell me when you were ready."

"Well, like the poster of the half-naked actor, Hannah put it up."

"Because…" I start.

"Because she took sports pictures for the yearbook every year, and she'd always drag me along to games with her. She took that picture and printed it out for me our junior year of high school because it was a long-running joke between us, that I had a crush on number 13 in the Falcons outfield." She covers her face, shaking her head. "Let's just say the baseball games against the Falcons were the easiest to get me to."

My grin grows wide. "A crush, huh?"

I watch in awe as her cheeks turn pink. "Yes, and I'm sorry if that makes everything between us weird, especially since I never let on that I knew who you were, but there it is."

She's standing about a foot away, so I take her by the hand

and kiss the back of it before I fall back onto her bed, pulling her on top of me.

Pride swells in my chest at the same time. I feel like an ass for being oblivious to her existence for far too long. "It doesn't make it weird, just makes me wish I could go back and find you sooner." It's odd, knowing we both grew up this close and never knew each other. "Do you ever think about what it would have been like?"

"You didn't even know I existed back then, Brody."

"I wish I had."

"Me too," she whispers, lying on my chest as our breathing syncs.

We lie there in silence for a few moments as I try to wrap my head around this new development. Val yawns, and I can only imagine how this night has exhausted her.

"Should we go to bed?" I ask.

"Yeah, just one more thing," she says, bringing her lips down on mine.

She leans her body into mine as her hand roams my hair, neck, and chest. I follow her lead, wrapping my arms in a vise grip around her as her hips rock back and forth against me. She pulls at my sweater, and for a moment I think about throwing caution to the wind. But as her tongue tangles with mine, the sight of her sobbing against my chest earlier enters my mind, and I pull back.

The embarrassment in her expression as she sits up almost kills me. "What's wrong?"

"Val, as much as I'd like to see where we're about to take this, you've had an emotional night. Can I please just hold you?"

Chapter Twenty-Eight

Val

Waking up in my childhood bedroom as the light of morning leaks in through the windows is such an odd sensation. Add the fact that I'm tight in Brody's embrace, it feels like two worlds colliding.

When I made the choice to come here last night, I tried to hide my nerves from Brody for fear he'd turn around and let me chicken out. But the thing is, I've been avoiding this house for too long and there's been a nagging voice in my head telling me I needed this. As much as I dreaded going through with it, I'm glad I did.

I run my finger in haphazard shapes across Brody's chest as his soft breaths become the background music to my morning.

Brody weaseling his way into my life has been a blessing I didn't expect, in more ways than one. Not only has he helped me break free from the shell I've kept myself contained in throughout my college experience, but he's part of the reason coming back here actually felt easier than I thought it would. I can feel myself falling, and instead of scaring the hell out of me, it feels…right.

I lean up on my elbow, taking in the beautiful features of his face. Strong, dark eyebrows, long lashes that are usually hidden behind his wide-rimmed glasses, a straight Grecian nose that crinkles when he laughs, and his perfect, kissable lips that I've become well-acquainted with.

My fingernails scrape lightly near the waistband of his boxer briefs, and he takes a deep breath through his nose as his body wakes from his slumber, making me giggle. I continue grazing my fingernails over the skin of his abs and up his chest.

"MMM," he moans, letting me know he's enjoying my perusal, the sound rumbling into a greeting. "Mmm-morning."

He pulls my head closer, kissing the top of it before his boa constrictor grip wraps around my body in a hug I lean fully into.

"Good morning," I say into his chest, but it doesn't take long to figure out his intentions for pulling me on top of him.

Not when his hands grip my hips and press me right into the proof that it's morning, and he is, in fact, a male.

As if men can't already pop a boner fast enough—they really needed another excuse with morning wood? When I make it to Heaven's gates, that's going to be my first question —*what is the reason?*

But when Brody pulls me in for a kiss, I forget the injustice, and decide instead to take advantage of it.

He doesn't complain one bit.

———

I stare at the closed door of my parents' room for a long moment as we prepare to leave. "Are you sure you don't want to go in there?" Brody asks, standing behind me with a hand on my hip.

"I don't think I'm quite ready," I say, knowing this is just another case of me putting off the inevitable. But at least I have an excuse—Brody's Christmas is this afternoon, and we've got to get moving if we plan on making it. "Let's go."

He looks between me and the door. "If you're sure. But we can come back anytime."

He takes my hand as we descend the stairs, letting me linger for a moment before we walk out the door.

When he pulls out of the driveway, I rubberneck until the house is out of view, imagining what it would look like right now if my parents were still here.

My mom always supervised as my dad put up the Christmas lights. Standing behind him and his ladder, making sure everything was straight. White lights—warm, not cool—strung along the eaves and gutters along the front of the house. Then, as a family, we went to the local tree farm to pick out our tree, and buy a garland Mom would wrap around the front porch railing of the house with another string of white lights.

It's the little details like these that hit me the hardest when I remember. All their little idiosyncrasies that made them who they were—and why I miss them so much.

"You okay?" Brody asks, picking up on my mood like he always does.

He stretches his hand out between us and I accept the connection, linking our fingers before answering. "I am, I just —" I fumble for the right words to describe the melancholy, "Now that we left, I'm eager to get back there. I'm not really sure why, but it's the same nagging feeling that talked me into stepping foot into the house in the first place."

"We can go back, I promise."

I nod, thinking it over. "Okay. It's like my brain's

reminding me that the thing I'd been most scared of wasn't as bad as I expected, so I should try harder next time."

Brody squeezes my hand. "There's nothing wrong with taking your time to heal."

"I know, but it's been so long, I feel like I'm supposed to be over it by now."

"But with each additional step of the healing process, you're opening old wounds, as well as creating new ones. That's why there's no perfect timeline for healing. Anyone who tells you differently is wrong. Besides, it's Christmas, a holiday typically spent with family. It makes sense to miss them more this time of year."

"Thanks for making me feel less crazy."

"You aren't crazy, you're normal."

"Well..." I screw up my face, letting the syllable drag.

"Okay, not normal. Normal's boring. You're my little weirdo."

We're sprinting into his parents' house when a tall, severe man with black hair, greying at the temples, stops us with a clipped tone. "Where have you been?"

My spine snaps straight at the sound of his voice. Not because he scares me, but because I instantly know who he is, and I've already decided I'm not a fan.

"Dad," Brody says, surprising me with how quickly his demeanor changes in his presence. Gone is the sunshine boy I've grown accustomed to the past several months and I miss him immediately. "This is Val, my girlfriend. We stayed in her hometown last night."

"Hi, Val," he says, giving me a curt nod. "Brody, I don't want to see your mom upset if you aren't ready and downstairs on time this afternoon. Go get cleaned up. There's plenty to be done before our guests arrive."

Brody nods, "We will."

His dad, who didn't even introduce himself to me, turns on his heel and walks away.

"Well, that was cold," I say, only paying half a mind to whether or not he's still within earshot.

"Told you," Brody says, taking my hand and hauling us both up the steps.

We shower, and Brody walks up behind me as I sit on the bathroom vanity to get ready.

"You're looking beautiful," he says, kissing me on the cheek as I finish putting product in my hair.

I turn to kiss him, "Thanks, you don't look too bad yourself."

I lean back into his chest as he sidles up behind me, holding me in place. "Finish up whatever you need to do here. My sister-in-law texted to say they'll be here in about fifteen minutes."

"Shit," I say, turning back to the mirror. I will not be the reason he walks downstairs late to the wrath of his father.

"Take all the time you need. I'll be lying on the bed watching—and staring at your ass. Did you know you poke it out about every five seconds when you're up there?"

I smack his chest. "Shut up!"

"You should only start to worry if I stop staring."

I laugh. "So I'm forgiven for all the times I checked out your ass in baseball pants back in the day?"

He turns around, checking out his backside in the mirror. "Can't say I blame you."

I reach back to squeeze a cheek. "Yep, and somehow they've gotten better with age."

He finally turns away from his ass's reflection to look at me. "If you wanted me to do more squats in the gym, Cupcake, it's all you had to say."

He kisses my cheek, then runs out of the bathroom like he's on a mission.

A few minutes later, he's back, leaning one hip on the door jamb wearing an old pair of white baseball pants.

I only have one eye fully done, but I drop what I'm doing and swing around on my butt to jump down and tackle him onto his bed.

"Merry Christmas to me."

We make it downstairs just as his brother's family arrives.

"Are you Valerie?" an older, lighter-haired version of Brody asks, stepping closer to me when I'm busy drooling over the sight of Brody picking up his niece.

I smile, holding out a hand. "Hello, yes. I'm Valerie Boyd, Brody's girlfriend. You can call me Val."

He smiles, placing his hand in mine and shaking it, "I'm Brody's brother, Luke, and that over there is my daughter, Mia, and my wife's around here somewhere." He turns to Brody, who's throwing him a warning look. "Nice to finally meet you. This guy has told me a lot about you," he says, slapping his younger brother on the shoulder.

I laugh as a muscle in Brody's jaw pops. "Luke."

Luke shrugs, looking around. When he doesn't find what he's looking for, he yells, "Babe, where you at? Brody's blushing, you can't miss it!" He's basking in his brother's embarrassment as a beautiful, curvy brunette walks in.

She's too busy taking in the gorgeous seasonal greenery Brody's mom has decorated the space with. "Wow, Lizzy. This place looks gorgeous," she says, stopping to hug all her in-laws along the way.

Then she settles next to Luke, tossing her arm around his waist as he mirrors the gesture, something they've clearly done at least a million times. She finally spots me, eyebrows popping as she turns to Brody. "Is this your girl?"

Brody smiles. "Yep, that's my girl. Kaitlyn, this is Val. Val, this is Kaitlyn, the best sister-in-law I could ever ask for."

Her smile bursts open wide. "Oh my gosh, it's so great to finally meet you—and to have another girl in the house. Liz and I have been praying to even out the testosterone levels in this family *forever*."

I laugh, holding my hand out awkwardly, but instead of shaking it, she uses it to pull me into a hug.

"Sorry, I'm a hugger," she says pulling away to hold me at arm's-length. "I can't wait to get to know you better."

"I'm a hugger!" A little voice whines next to me. I turn to see Brody's niece holding her arms out to me.

I smile and open my arms, welcoming her. He closes the distance between us to drop her in my arms, looking baffled. My heart melts when her arms and legs wrap around me like a little koala bear, as if she didn't meet me two seconds ago.

"Okay, she's got Mia's approval. Now we know she's a real one," Brody says, smiling at the two of us tenderly.

"Yeah, she doesn't normally warm up to people this fast," Luke admits with an astonished laugh.

Kaitlyn brushes her baby's hair back and kisses her forehead before returning to her husband's side.

Mia's head pops up from my shoulder and starts giggling when she looks at me, causing me to do the same.

"What on earth is so funny?"

She giggles more, flopping back onto my shoulder again. "Noffing, I'm just yaughing!"

"Is there something wrong with my face?"

She examines me as I cross my eyes and over-exaggerate my smile.

She busts a gut, splatting both hands on my cheeks and leaning her forehead against mine.

"How you do dat?" She asks, immediately trying it for herself, and failing miserably. The look on her face has me cracking up, though, along with the rest of the room. She basks in the attention she gains from her whole family, and I can feel all eyes drift to me. When I meet Brody's, the adoration I find there puts me at ease.

The day is a blur of meeting Liz's side of the family and trying to remember their names. I'm in the kitchen with Liz, Kaitlyn and some of Brody's aunts and cousins. It didn't take long to learn that Liz and Kaitlyn live for holiday baking and cooking. I asked Liz to keep me busy, and she kept her word. I'm wiping down the counter with a dishrag when Brody pops into the room to grab me, as he has each time a notable family member gets to the house.

"Come here. I have someone for you to meet."

I follow him into the living room, where an assortment of people are watching football and chatting.

Brody leads me to a man standing next to the couch, talking animatedly with Brody's grandpa. He looks to be a little older than us, with dirty blonde hair that's barely long enough to have a little wave to it. His skin is tan and peppered in freckles, weathered in the way of someone who spends plenty of time outside. He's a rugged type of handsome, wearing a dark blue henley and grey jeans.

Brody's grandpa, who I adored the moment we met a few hours ago, turns away from the conversation to smile and wave. The man standing turns, and I'm assaulted with the full attention of his bright blue gaze. Good lord, this family carries some damn good genes.

He claps Brody on the shoulder, then, turning to me, says, "You must be the Valerie I keep hearing about."

I snap my jaw shut and answer lamely, "Yep. That's me!" Holding my hand out to him.

"Val," Brody says, setting a grounding hand on my lower back, which I'm thankful for. "This is my cousin, Andrew."

"Oh, hi. It's nice to meet you," I say, and the words come out an octave too high.

"The pleasure's all mine, Val," his gruff voice answers, making me swoon. By the tightened grip on my hip, Brody must notice. "Brody here tells me about you all the time. Pretty smitten, this one. So glad you could make it to the big ol' Harvey family Christmas. No pressure, right?"

I chuckle, "Right. Yeah," I say with sarcastically wide eyes. "Everyone's been great, though."

"Where'd you two meet?"

"She tried to toss her coffee at me one morning at the coffee shop just off NIU's campus."

I poke him in the chest. "I did not! I accidentally spilled it. But I ran off before he could woo me that day. Little did I know, my efforts would be in vain, because three days later, I sat down next to him in class and we got paired together for a semester project—that we earned an A on, by the way. But I grew up just down the road."

"No shit?" He smiles, looking between Brody and I. "And you met in college?"

"Yes. I knew of Brody back in high school, but he had his head stuck too far up his ass to see me back then."

Andrew, Brody's grandpa, and a few other people within earshot laugh at that.

Huh, hadn't realized they were listening. Whoops.

Andrew turns to Brody, "I like her already. You better keep that head unstuck and keep her around," he says with a warning look.

Brody pulls me close and I lean into his embrace.

"I second that!" Brody's grandpa chimes in, pointing an arthritic finger at him. "It's about time you had someone who isn't afraid to put you in your place, Brody. Keep your head from getting too big."

Brody's thumb rubs across the back of my triceps. "Guess it's a good thing I don't plan on going anywhere, then." Then

209

he punctuates his declaration with a kiss to my hair. "Besides, I may have had my head too far up my ass to notice her when we were young, but she was the one who admired it in baseball pants. So I think she'll keep me."

I turn to him, shocked.

"It's okay to smack him," his grandpa jokes. "It's good for him every once in a while."

I smack his chest, but there's no force behind it because I'm too busy laughing.

Chapter Twenty-Nine

BRODY

The next morning, we gather for a quick brunch before Luke, Kait, and Mia have to head across town to spend the rest of Christmas with Kaitlyn's family.

Dad doesn't join us until we all finish passing food around the table. He's barely in his seat before taking a prolonged look in my direction. Between leaving Val's parents' and family arriving, I haven't talked to him besides a quick introduction to Val. But I know the tables are about to turn.

I'm shoveling leftover chili into my mouth when he says, "Brody, I trust you haven't forgotten that after this break, life goes back to normal. You have responsibilities, and in a few months, you'll have to stop screwing around," his eyes shoot to Val when he says it, making my blood boil. "Have you started researching jobs that align with your degree, or did you finally decide to further your education?"

I look at him, still chewing and preparing to answer, but Luke beats me to it. "Dad, not at the table, and definitely not on Christmas."

Dad levels him with a glare. "Holidays don't erase the fact that Brody isn't ready for the rest of his life to begin, come May. I'd say right now is as good of time as any. So tell me," he swivels his head to me. "What's your plan?"

"Charles, we're not doing this here," my mom says, touching my hand from her place next to me.

Dad throws daggers in her direction, and I turn to her. "No, Mom. It's okay. I've been wondering when this was coming. Why don't we get it over with?" Val links our fingers under the table—a silent show of support, but it doesn't make the furious heat inside me cool. If anything, knowing she's there in my corner fuels the fire of indifference I feel toward my father. "For your information, Dad, I know what my next step is, and I have known the whole time. You just don't like it."

He lifts his chin a little higher. "Don't be a smartass."

"Charles—" My mom starts, but I interrupt her.

"I'm sorry, but the last time we talked about this, you all but threw me out of the house. Then there was your outburst at Thanksgiving. You know, I'm seeing a trend here."

"You will not become a strength and conditioning coach, Brody. You won't have two dimes to rub together with a job like that. Not around here."

"If all money will do is turn me into someone like you, I don't want it, anyway."

"You will not speak to me like that in my own house!" Dad barks so loud, it causes Mia to start crying, sending Luke and Kaitlyn into a frenzy on the opposite side of the table.

Luke stares daggers at dad, nestling his baby girl into the crook of his shoulder. "That's enough. Let's not ruin yet another holiday meal with your opinions."

"I agree," Mom says, unable to even look up at dad.

"I just don't get why you can't be more like your brother and lock down a job that will actually support a family some-day," he gripes under his breath.

"You know, Dad, I actually admire Brody for not wanting to go down the same path I have. I—and Kaitlyn will vouch for this—wish every single day I sit in my big corner office with a city view that I'd refrained from listening to your advice about chasing money my whole life. I wish I would have followed my own interests. All that big job with a big paycheck does for me is take me away from my family, just like yours did while we were growing up. And the more I watch my daughter grow, the less I care for my career."

"Don't you dare try to say I didn't give up things to give you boys a good childhood. Besides, Brody still has no hope for a bright future, no matter what he does with that degree. With your atrocious grades and your inability to follow through with anything, you might not even graduate. Everything you've ever done fails. Let that be a warning to you, Valerie. Tread lightly from here on out."

"Leave her out of this," I say, my muscles in my neck and shoulder shaking with rage at my own flesh and blood. "And honestly, I can't wait to prove you wrong."

Seeing red, I stand from the table, not bothering with the formality of excusing myself, and leave the room.

Val

Forks are still poised halfway to mouths. Mouths that don't really know what to say.

"The kid needs to learn that life isn't all going out every night of the week and shirking responsibilities, hoping for someone else to figure it out for him," he mutters, and I can't believe he's still talking.

"Mr. Ryan," I say, before I've even made a conscious decision to react. "I normally respect people in their own homes, but I don't think I can stay quiet on this one."

His head rolls in my direction so casually, it only fuels my rage. "Excuse me?" His voice has raised, as if he's used to getting his way simply by controlling the volume of it.

"I—" I scratch my forehead in frustration, setting my fork down. "Do you even know your son?" Filter off, the words shoot right out of my mouth.

He stares at me with blank rage, as if he can't believe I have the audacity to question him. *Surprise, buddy!*

"The reason I ask is, every single descriptor you used to describe him was, for lack of a better word, bullshit."

I return his stare because I know he expects me to back down. Everyone else waits on bated breath, unsure if they should come to my rescue.

"I realize I've only known him a short time, but the way you talk about him—" I shake my head. "Do we know two separate people? Either that, or I know your son better than you do, and that's sad. Because he is a *great* person. Amazing, actually.

"You say he shirks his responsibilities, but we spent hours in the library together this semester. His studying skills were admittedly shit before he met me, but we worked on changing that. Did you know he earned nothing under a C-plus this semester? And even that grade came from a professor that's notoriously tough on campus. He goes out on weeknights, sure. But only because his roommate is a bartender. He takes his homework to the bar and drinks a beer, studying and keeping his friend company on slow nights.

"He's a social butterfly—the life of the party, but not because he's irresponsible. It's because his presence is enthralling. He's the brightest spot in any room he enters, and the fact that you don't see it—the fact that you're throwing rocks at his light, trying to cloak him in your darkness—it's a tragedy. I care so much for him, and it kills me to see him treated like this by his own father.

"Not sure you know this about me, but I lost both my

parents, and I'd give anything to get one more Christmas with them. Meanwhile, Brody walks on eggshells around here, waiting for your next comment, perfectly designed to knock him down a peg or two." Now that I know I've got his attention, I let my words sink in. "You'd be smart to change the way you look at your fucking *brilliant* son before you live out the rest of your days without him speaking to you."

The only sound in the room is my chair legs scraping the floor as I turn to the rest of the speechless family members at the table. My heart seizes in my chest when I see Liz's tear-stained cheeks.

"Excuse me," I say, removing myself to search for Brody.

I find him lying on his bed, his noise-canceling head-phones on, eyes closed. At least I know he didn't hear me telling off his father. I close the door, walking to his side, and drag my fingertips lightly over the back of his hand. His eyes pop open, likely expecting to see his father standing there in boxing gloves, ready for another round, but his expression softens when he sees it's me. He moves over, opening his arms for me to join him. So I do, resting my head in the crook of his shoulder and throwing an arm and a leg over his body.

We lie that way until we both fall asleep.

I only wake when he jostles me while removing his head-phones. He turns his body toward mine, keeping our limbs intertwined, and squeezes me hard as he whispers, "I'm sorry you had to see all that."

I chuckle. "You left too early. The real show began after you walked out of the room."

He pulls away to look at me. "Did he say something to you?"

My cheeks heat, "Quite the opposite."

His brow furrows, and I smooth it with my thumb. "Do you have a death wish? What did you say?"

"Just cleared up a few things. Told you I wouldn't be able to stay silent if he ran his mouth."

215

His eyes turn to slits, roaming my face. "Thanks for having my back."

I kiss his nose. "Always will, Brody."

His arms tighten around me and there's emotion in his voice when he says, "I'm not sure what I ever did to deserve you, either."

"It was the baseball pants," I say, both of us laughing before he kisses me.

Chapter Thirty

After BrunchGate, Dad makes himself scarce. He's at the office even though he promised Mom he'd take a break until the New Year. When they're in the same room, there's noticeable tension, which happens after our fights, but this is on another level. Mom won't even look at him, and he scurries in and out of the room like a scolded dog.

"Any idea what's up between mom and dad? They've been weird since yesterday." I ask Luke when we're in the basement watching *Moana*. Val is out to lunch with friends, so I'm cuddling Mia, spending time with my brother's family before they leave town.

"Val didn't tell you?"

"Tell me what?"

He turns to Kaitlyn, whose surprise matches his. "After you left the room yesterday, Val put dad in his place so hard, I'd be surprised if the rest of the neighborhood didn't feel the aftershocks."

"*What?*"

"She seriously didn't tell you anything?"

"All she said was that she *cleared up a few things.*"

He laughs at that. "She's modest then, Brod."

"Why? What did she say?"

He gives me one hard blink, shaking his head as if to clear it. "God, everything. Everything she's learned about you since you met, proving his assumptions wrong. If you aren't serious about her, I'll kick your ass right now."

I huff out a breath. "I'm serious about her. Like, scary serious. I've never felt this way for someone."

"Good," Kaitlyn cuts in. "Because I didn't want to have to kick you in the crotch."

"Damn, SIL. That's harsh."

"I mean it, Brody. You should have heard the way she talked about you. It's clear she feels the same."

"Not to scare the shit out of you," Luke says, "but if you don't marry her someday, you're an idiot. In the short time I've gotten to watch the two of you and your dynamic, it reminded me of Kait and I." He turns an adoring look on his wife, "She's the best thing to ever happen to me, Brody. This girl could be the same for you, don't f—screw it up," he amends, remembering his daughter is within earshot, although she's too enthralled with Moana to notice.

"I don't plan to," I say, trying not to dwell on the fact that she's leaving in four short months.

"What?" He asks—my fears must be written all over my face.

I take a deep breath. "When she gets a job post-college, she's not looking for anything near here. I've known since we met, and I'm trying to be supportive, but I'm scared of what the next several months will bring."

"Oh, crap," Kaitlyn says.

"Yeah. Part of me hopes rekindling relationships back home will help her change her mind, but I know better than to dwell on that idea. A part of me thinks she's only trying to outrun her past."

"If that's the case, maybe she'll see that before moving across the country," Kait says.

"And what's your plan if she doesn't?" Luke asks.

I shrug, already feeling the weight of future decisions sitting on my shoulders. "Things are still new, but I think I'd follow her just about anywhere." I palm the back of my neck. "Is it too presumptuous to put that option on the table this early in our relationship?"

"I guess it depends if you can see a lasting relationship. The feelings are obviously there." Kaitlyn says.

I nod. "But is that enough?"

Luke claps me on the shoulder. "The best way to find out is to talk to her."

"Shhhhhhh," comes from the little gremlin on my lap, telling us it's time to get back to listening to the movie.

But I sit in the dark, staring blankly at the screen without processing another scene. My mind's too busy trying to imagine how I can possibly make this work out in the end.

I'm tip-toeing through the house later that afternoon, afraid to stir the pot simply by existing. Luke's family left an hour ago, so it's just me here with my parents, though I haven't spotted either in hours.

I handed my keys to Val without a care earlier, but with this weird air to the house—and knowing it's because of me— I wish I wasn't trapped here without a vehicle.

I've almost made it to the door that leads to the basement when an all-too-familiar voice makes me jump a foot in the air.

"Brody," is all he says, the tone holding less authority than normal.

I stop mid-stride, pivoting my feet toward the sound of his voice at the end of the hallway. "Yeah?" I ask, heart in my throat. It's the first time we've faced each other since yesterday's showdown.

When I look up and really take him in, I notice the dark circles under his eyes. They're red-rimmed and instead of being held together by pomade like usual, his hair is in complete disarray, like he's been running his hands through it all day. He runs his palm over the bristly beard he's sporting—another difference from his usual self—and says, "What were your grades for the semester?" I'm bracing for a fight when he adds, "I only ask because the girl you brought with you said you had your best academic semester yet. Is that true?"

"Her name is Val, Dad," I say, hackles rising.

"Val, right."

"And she was right. My grades were one A, two B's, and a C-plus. A big change for someone who's used to only Cs and Ds."

"Why didn't you tell me?"

"Because I knew you'd find a way to make me feel like I still could have done better. I'm proud of myself, and I was just fine keeping it to myself."

He nods. "Okay, well. Good job." He rakes his fingers through his hair, disheveling it more than it already was. "I'm proud of you."

Then he turns away, and I'm left there wondering what the hell just happened.

That evening, when Val pulls into the driveway, my heart rate picks up. I run into the blistery evening without a coat to greet her.

She steps out, looking me up and down in my long sleeve

t-shirt and shorts. "What are you doing? It's freezing out here!"

"I don't care," I mutter, stepping into her space, wrapping her in my embrace. Our gazes meet for a moment before I'm lowering my lips to hers. Then I kiss her with everything I have locked up inside me.

Our lips should bruise with the way we connect, but I don't care. I've been waiting all day for this.

I bring my hand to the back of her neck, my short fingernails scratching against her scalp, and I catch her moan with my mouth.

My other hand finds her open coat and slides under her oversized sweater, stopping in the middle of her back to bring her impossibly closer. Her tongue flicks against my own in an invitation to deepen the kiss, which I accept before turning us, her back flush against the driver's door.

When I pull away, Val's eyes remain closed. "What was that for?" She asks breathlessly.

I lean my forehead against hers. *Because now that I've had you, I'm scared to lose you.* "Do I need a reason to kiss my girl?"

I don't miss the way her smile grows when I call her that. It's why I love saying it—other than it being the truth. She's my girl as long as she'll have me, and I already know she'll take my heart with her when she inevitably leaves.

"You can't kiss me like that and tell me there wasn't a reason behind it. I felt it, I'm just trying to decipher it."

The light breeze blows a stray curl into her face, and I carefully take it between my fingers to comb it behind her ear. Her eyes bounce between mine, and in the low light, I can still see how wide open they are. If my legs weren't about to freeze off, I'd gaze at her like this all night long.

"I just missed you."

She smiles. "I missed you too." Her arms tighten around my waist. "But I still know there's more to it than that."

She's fishing for details—fine, I'll bite. "Luke told me what happened with my dad yesterday."

All the blood drains from her rosy cheeks as her smile drops off her face. "Shit." She drops her gaze to her shoes. "I didn't tell you because I knew I overstepped—"

"Overstepped?" I ask, disbelief seeping into my tone as I put my chilly hands on either side of her face and tilt her gaze back to mine. "Val, you didn't overstep. You did the nicest thing anyone has ever done for me. You stood up for me when I wasn't there to defend myself. Do you have any idea what that means to me?"

She still looks worried as she awaits my answer.

"It means everything, Val. *You* mean everything to me."

Chapter Thirty One

VAL

A few days after Christmas, we head back to the house. I've spent the past several days hyping myself up for the return, but on the drive, my nerves get the best of me.

"I'll be right there with you," Brody squeezes my hand, telling me exactly what I needed to hear.

"Thanks again for coming with me."

I'm pretty sure I gave him mental whiplash back at his parents'. At first, I was going to tackle this on my own, but I changed my mind—then I changed my mind a few more times. He was perfect through the entire process, rather than pushing me to do things a certain way.

"Of course, Cupcake. I always want to be there for you."

That affirmation wiggles its way straight past the crumbling walls around my beard and imbeds itself.

"I enjoy being there for you too," I say, feeling another portion of that aforementioned wall crumbling. "I enjoy it a lot, actually."

His smile takes up his whole face. "Good."

He parks in the driveway like we've done this a million times, and I hope somewhere, in an alternate universe, we have. And in that separate reality, he's gotten to meet my parents, who love him, just as I think I'm starting to.

I let us in, still thinking that over—trying to allow myself to live in the here and now, rather than demand we figure things out and plan for the future.

I'm so drowned in my own thoughts, I don't think twice as I kick off my shoes and climb the stairs until I'm standing in front of my parents' room. I take a deep breath, grab the handle, then push the door open.

The tan walls, the gold frames that house their wedding photos, the red comforter—all of it has memories flooding back.

I used to sit on the bed and demand mom walk the floor to model clothes after every shopping spree we went on together. When I was in middle school, Hannah and I used to steal her makeup from the attached bathroom. We had no idea how to use it, and usually ended up with lip gloss on our eyelids and mascara as eyeliner or something similar, but it's a core memory for me. There are photos of it somewhere. Maybe I'll find them as I go through the house.

I turn back to the doorway, remembering I'm not alone. "Brody?"

"Yes?" He pops into the doorway like he'd been trying to give me privacy, but was ready to support me at a moment's notice. I do not deserve this cinnamon roll of a man.

Tears leak from my eyes as so many emotions overwhelm me at once. Brody's at my side in a second, swiping his thumbs under my eyes. "Let it out."

So I fall into his chest, grasping onto his sweatshirt as I let myself do just that.

Brody rubs my back until I regain control of my emotions. I plant an appreciative kiss on his neck before I back away, looking around the room as I try to decide where to go first.

The bathroom door is open just a crack, but it's calling out to me. I peek through, inching the door open.

When I walk into the space, my eyes snag on a clear bottle of yellowish liquid. I can practically smell the scent from memory, but I pick it up and spray it into the air. The vanilla notes bring back a thousand memories I lived through with Mom as she wore the perfume. I smile at the thought of her, spraying the perfume on my arm, and moving onto the next thing.

A few hours later, I've got many of their belongings in separate piles. Some of it will stay with me, but the rest will either be donated or sold. Brody's been a great help, and I've kept dry eyes for the most part, only tearing up when I find something that sparks an important memory.

By the time the sun goes down, I'm feeling rather proud of myself for finally going through the house. I think part of the reason I held off so long was because I thought going through their things would be disrespectful to their memory, but it turned out to be quite the opposite. I could practically feel them there in the room with me as I relived every flashback of our lives together. To find their belongings that I hadn't seen in years was cathartic.

"You seem lighter," Brody says when I'm locking up the house later that evening.

I smile. "I feel lighter."

His arms wrap around me as he plants a kiss on my forehead. And for the first time all day, I take a deep breath and feel...hopeful.

On New Year's Eve, Brody's friends that I have yet to meet, invite us to the bar in town. In true Midwest fashion, there's mildly shitty weather, just for the occasion. Seriously, I swear there's always snow and ice in the forecast to ring in the

New Year. I'd be willing to bet money on it every single year.

Brody holds my hand as I navigate the sidewalk in the heels I'm already regretting wearing.

"Did I tell you look beautiful?" He asks, one hand on the door to the bar, the other still in mine.

I smile at my feet. "Only like six times since I walked out of your bathroom earlier."

"'Kay, just making sure you're aware I'll be kissing the most gorgeous girl in this bar when the clock strikes twelve."

I boop his nose. "Only if you play your cards right," and since we've been lingering outside the door, I open it myself and walk through without him.

He catches me by the hips a moment later, pulling me back into him, nuzzling into my neck until my knees give out and I collapse into a fit of giggles.

"Brody, stop!"

"Promise me a New Year's kiss or no deal."

"Okay, fine. Fine! I'll kiss you, but only if you stop it right now."

He leaves his winter-cold nose against my neck, but stops the tickle assault. He turns me, planting a kiss on my mouth, and I forget we're in a crowded bar.

"Brody!" yells an unfamiliar voice.

We part like the Red Sea, turning to find the voices that yelled across the bar are Brody's friends who have probably been watching us since we walked in. Way to make a great first impression, Val.

Ugh.

Brody takes my hand, pulling me toward the bar where they're currently standing.

"Val?" A tall brunette I recognize from some of Brody's past Instagram posts as Lainey. I also talked to her on the phone forever one day when Brody was in the other room and asked me to answer.

"Lainey?" I ask, feeling Brody's hand on my back like an anchor, grounding me to the present moment.

"Yes! Ugh, it's so good to finally meet you! I've been hearing about you non-stop. I think you make our boy Brody here pretty damn happy. Thank you for that. He deserves it."

"Aw, Lainey. You're gonna make me cry," Brody chimes in from behind me.

Lainey and I both roll our eyes at him making light of an honest moment, and my sass feels immediately bonded to hers.

"Hey, Val," I turn to find another familiar face, this one I remember from baseball games back in high school. "I'm Mal, and our names are practically the same, so I think we're gonna get along great."

He holds a hand out to me, and I take it. "Mal, it's nice to meet you. This guy has told me plenty of stories," I say, patting Brody's chest.

Mal immediately swings his gaze to Brody. "What'd you tell her?"

"Nothing you need to worry about," Brody says with a smug smile.

"What'd he tell you?"

"Wouldn't you like to know?"

Mal's mouth falls open, but Lainey says, "Okay, I like her already!"

Mal scoffs, and she pats him on the arm.

"Sorry, but more girls need to put you in your place. Val, come get a drink and meet my sister."

I give Brody a quick kiss before I let her drag me away, across the bar where a woman who looks to be her sister is talking to the person in the bar stool next to her.. I say they're sisters because they look so alike in everything but their height. Where Lainey is tall and thin, her sister is several inches shorter with plenty of curves.

Jessica Costello

She turns when Lainey taps her on the shoulder. "This is my sister Ella. Ella, this is Brody's girlfriend, Val."

"No shit? Brody's got a girl, huh? Nice to meet you." She holds up her drink for a cheers, but I come up empty.

"Oh, honey, you need a drink. What's your poison?"

"How about a Moscow Mule?"

"Oh, Ricky!" Ella says, waving a twenty-dollar bill in the air to get his attention. He comes running.

"Ricky has a crush on Ella, can you tell?" Lainey whispers.

He's leaned halfway across the bar to hear Ella, which is normal. But his face lights up with a smile when he pulls himself back behind the bar. "Moscow Mule, coming right up."

"Thanks, babe!" She calls, then turns to me. "If you need a drink the rest of the night, just come to me."

I nod, still processing what I just witnessed. "That much is clear. You sure you're not a witch?"

She cracks the first smile I've seen from her. "You're not the first one to ask, I'll say that."

The three of us laugh, and I thank Ricky when he sets my drink in front of me.

We snag a free spot near the pool table, and as I'm sitting down, I spot Brody's cousin, Andrew, walking in the front door.

"Andrew!" I yell.

He turns at the sound of my voice, smiling when he spots the group.

"Holy hell, who is that?" Ella asks.

"Brody's cousin. Aren't the genes in his family ridiculous?"

"Wow," she says with heavy eyelids, looking him up and down as he approaches the table. She's still slack-jawed as he

228

stops in front of us, but snaps it shut when he looks her way, turning on the charm. It's amazing to witness.

The two of them immediately hit it off.

"So, are you and Ella both single?" I ask Lainey.

"Ella just got out of a shitty relationship, actually. I'm single."

She says it so fast, it's clear there's more to the story, but I choose to leave it alone.

"Andrew seems like he could do some damage. Do you think we should intervene?"

Lainey waves off my worry. "Nah, the sooner she gets over her asshole of an ex, the better. Helps that he's a hottie."

"Who's a hottie?" Mal asks, butting into our conversation.

She gives him a teasing smile. "Andrew," both guys groan, "but I think you two already knew how I felt about that."

Mal throws up his hands. "See?" He turns to Brody. "I told you inviting him was a bad idea. None of the girls in this place are gonna give the rest of us a chance with him around."

"Looks to me like he's all about Ella." Brody says, and we all turn to find them bent together, deep in conversation.

"Besides, I'm your girl tonight," Lainey says, elbowing Mal. "These other girls don't even matter, remember?"

Mal laughs, pulling her chair closer to his, leaning in close as he says, "None of them can hold a candle to you, anyway." Then he kisses her on the forehead.

I look at Brody, silently asking what's going on there.

He raises his eyebrows as if to say, *I know, right?*

Suddenly, I understand her evasiveness about her relationship status. Brody grabs my hand, pulling me to my feet in an instant. Before I know what's hit me, I'm headed toward an open pool table.

"Recovered enough to get your ass kicked again?" I ask, referring to our game in his basement the other night.

"More like trying to redeem myself."

I grab the triangle and start pulling the balls from their catch on the side of the table. "I'll rack if you go get us some drinks," I say.

He leans into my space until his eyes are all I can see. "You've got yourself a deal, my girl," he says before his lips find mine, then he's off to the bar.

"Do you two like coffee?" Lainey asks Hannah and I at the bar later that evening. Hannah had a family thing this evening and met us a little late. She's stone cold sober, so Lainey and I have taken it upon ourselves to get her caught up to the rest of us.

All our friends are meshing well together—and I couldn't be happier about it.

"Yes!" we answer in unison.

"Three Screaming Orgasms, please!"

I nearly choke on my spit, but Ricky just laughs and says, "Coming right up."

"So what's the deal with you and Mal?" Hannah asks while we wait for our shots to be poured.

Lainey turns to us with a deer-in-the-headlights look. "What do you mean? We've been best friends almost our entire lives."

Hannah furrows her brow. "You sure that's it? I had to ask Brody if you two were dating because it's the vibe you two give off."

Lainey bites her nails, looking between us both. "Oh yeah? What did Brody say?"

Hannah and I share a look, then Hannah says, "He said *they're just friends, but they're both in denial.*"

Lainey drops her face into her hands. "Shit. Yeah, that's a pretty accurate assessment. I've always felt something for him, but it was never the right time, you know? Now he lives in

Nashville for most of the year. It's safe to say that ship has sailed."

Hannah and I look at each other again. This time I say, "I don't know, Lainey. Maybe now isn't the right time for you two, but I think the ship is just sitting in the harbor waiting for its chance to head out to sea.

Ricky sets our shots on the bar and Lainey avoids our gaze while handing them out.

"On that note," Lainey says, holding her shot glass in the air between us. Hannah and I clink ours against it, then down the hatch they go.

On our way back to the table, Lainey tosses an arm around me and Hannah.

"I really like you two."

I tighten my grip on her waist. "Not sure if that's your Screaming Orgasm talking, but thanks, I like you too."

"Nah, the alcohol makes me honest. But since we're talking about boys, I just have to ask," she squeezes my shoulder. "Your intentions are good with Brody, right?"

I look up at her in surprise. "Of course."

"Okay, good. I—thought I heard you weren't sticking around here after college. Wasn't sure how that was supposed to work."

My gaze flicks to Hannah, and it hurts to see her face fall. "I mean, yeah, that's the plan," I say, not mentioning the fact that I've been having second thoughts lately. I haven't told anyone that yet.

"So where do you see things going with Brody after graduation?" Lainey turns from gal-pal to protective friend in the blink of an eye.

I don't answer immediately, because I don't have a perfect one yet.

Seeing my indecision, she adds, "I'll say this—I've watched a girl in the past play Brody, and I'd hate to see you turn into another one of those."

"I don't want to do anything to hurt him, Lainey."

"Good. He's a great guy, and we've been friends for years. I hope you're willing to prove that when push comes to shove." She claps, immediately fixing an excited look on her face. "Anyway, enough talking about real life. Let's have fun, shall we?"

I smile, although it feels forced. Even Hannah walks away without another word, which shouldn't surprise me. The other day when we went out to lunch with a bunch of friends, she brought up this exact topic all over again like she did at Thanksgiving. And being the defensive person I am, I stormed off back to Brody's instead of engaging in the conversation.

"Why do you look sad? You okay?" Brody asks when I land on his lap, giving up my seat for Hannah to sit.

I try to smile when I nod, but it doesn't feel real. He must notice, because his eyes roam my face for a long moment before he kisses my cheek.

Chapter Thirty-Two

VAL

The new semester takes some getting used to. It's my last before graduation and I always thought I'd be excited when it arrived, but I hate it. It serves as a reminder that things will soon come to a close—in more ways than one, if I'm not careful. I'm not ready to live apart from Bree, nor am I ready to face the decisions Brody and I will need to make sooner than later.

I didn't know how easily I had it at the time, but I'd give anything to go back to the ease of Christmas break, where we were essentially living together.

We also don't have class together this semester, and I never realized how much our built-in time together three days a week helped with our relationship until I no longer had it. The only time in a day we have for each other is forty-five minutes around lunchtime, where we're both between classes.

But it's finally midterms, spring break is a week away, and I'm gearing up to share some potentially hazardous (to our relationship) news with Brody.

I've been keeping one eye on job boards all semester, and something opened up at a company in San Francisco that I've always dreamed of working at. On a whim, I applied. I only told Hannah because she called me the night I applied and mentioned she has an elopement in San Francisco over my spring break. I filled her in on my own news, and she talked me into coming out there with her to explore the city and help her with her photoshoot while I'm there.

I promised to tell Brody as soon as we got off the phone—but things kept getting in the way.

I called him. He was at The Saloon with Wes and could hardly hear me over the phone.

Then I planned to tell him tonight, and he sprung a house party on me.

So my current plan is to tell him tomorrow morning when we're finally alone. It's been four days, and the stress it's causing feels like it's burning a hole through my stomach.

The worst part about it all is that Brody has spent the entire semester so far planning fun things to do during our spring break. So not only do I have to tell him I applied to somewhere nearly two thousand miles away, but now I have to tell him I'm going there over break and won't get to spend it with him. I was really looking forward to it too.

Nothing against Hannah, because I am excited to have a little quality time with her, but I'm actually dreading the trip already.

"What you thinkin' about over there?" Brody asks at a stoplight, shaking my hand to get my attention. We're on our way back from the liquor store because I volunteered to help the guys prepare for the house party they're throwing tonight. It's the first time I've been invited, which I finally understood when Wes admitted they've only had two this school year. It turns out Brody used to be the guy who planned these things, but he's been preoccupied.

"Just curious how rowdy this party will be later," I say vaguely.

He laughs, squeezing my hand. "No worries, my little homebody. Your extroverted boyfriend will save you from the scary partygoers."

I smile, knowing he's telling the truth. "You better."

———————

"Nooooo," I yell hours later. We'd been running the beer pong table for five games, but lost to two guys with old man names —Dave and Roger.

Who even invited these guys? And are we sure they're not two old men disguised as college students, trying to relive their glory days for the weekend?

Competitiveness aside, I'm kind of glad to get a break. Brody and I hug, then high five our opponents, leaving the table to them.

I'm following directly behind Brody, so when he stops on a dime to stand on a stray chair, I run right into his backside.

"Can I have your attention please?" He suddenly yells loud enough that almost everyone is looking his way.

Once Wes pauses the music from the other side of the party, he's got the attention of everyone in the basement.

"Thank you," he yells loud enough for the people in the back. "I wanted to take a moment to point out," he pauses, looking right at me and crooking his finger.

I'm a deer in the headlights, unable to move.

He smirks and holds his hand out. "Come here," his smile reels me in, and against my better judgment, I take his hand. He turns me toward the crowd, his hands on my shoulders. I smile awkwardly, searching out anyone I know, but they're all hidden in the crowd. "In case any of you didn't know, this is my girl, Val."

What is this?

"Her birthday is the twentieth of this month," and suddenly I see where this is going with embarrassing clarity. "Since we'll all be in different places for spring break, I wanted to ask everyone to sing Happy Birthday to her tonight. I'll start."

"Oh no," I say, holding up my hands and shaking my head no to the crowd, but the singing begins and I find out quickly that there's no pressing pause on a room full of drunk college kids.

Want to guess how long the birthday song lasts? To keep my brain from frying during the experience, I counted to one-hundred and twenty-three. I'm not sure how that compares to other versions, but Brody did some freestyling that drug it on.

When it's over, he jumps off the chair and wraps his arms around me, as happy as I've ever seen him. The parts of me who wanted to ring his neck instantly thaw, but I still smack his chest. "What the hell was that? And how'd you know it was my birthday? I don't remember telling you."

"The girl who's always writing in her planner and leaves it open in front of me is wondering how I know her birthday?" He gives me a teasing smile. "Come on. I paid attention, that's how I know. It was written plain as day in your planner in bright pink letters. I know you hated that, but I was by your side the whole time, *as promised*, so I'm hoping you won't disown me."

I smirk, shaking my head at his antics. "Thank you. Even though my anxiety was through the roof, you have a beautiful singing voice." I lift to my toes for a kiss. I only expect a quick peck in this room full of people, but Brody goes for gold, tipping me back and tangling his tongue with mine as people in the vicinity wolf whistle at us.

Instead of letting the attention pull me away from this man who has become a part of me in the past several months, I choose to enjoy the moment.

The further the night crawls on, the more nervous I get for my talk with Brody tomorrow, so here I am, trying to give myself a pep talk in the mirror of the upstairs bathroom. I've been in here forever, but a knock on the door forces me to go out and face the music.

Just go out there and have fun. Worry about the rest tomorrow, I silently tell myself, staring into the amber eyes I inherited from my mother. If only she were here, she'd know exactly how to handle this situation. She'd force me to come to my own conclusions, but she'd still be the perfect sounding board. Then again, if she was still alive, I'm not sure I'd be so against the thought of returning to my hometown after graduation. Ever since Hannah put that thought in my head over break, the more I believe she might be right.

I wipe the eyeliner that never seems to stay put from the creases of my eyes, take a breath, and head for the door.

"Holy shit—Val?" As soon as I open the door, I'm met with the familiar face of a girl from my internship last summer. We both major in Communications and take a lot of the same classes, but it's weird to see her standing in my boyfriend's home.

"Wow," I laugh, "Hey, Maurine. What brings you here?"

"Oh," she says waving a hand in the direction of the basement, "My boyfriend is friends with the guys who live here. How about you?"

I laugh at how small the world is sometimes. "My boyfriend *is* one of the guys who live here."

"No way! How have you been? Ready for graduation?"

Gosh, what a loaded question. I refer to my past self's sheet of predetermined answers to questions about school. "Yes, I can't wait to get out of here after graduation. What about you?"

She scrunches her nose. "Ugh, I don't know. I think I'm

gonna miss these days. I'm not ready for a big girl job, you know?"

Man, do I? "I know, it's so nerve-wracking. I actually just applied for a job out in San Francisco." I'm not even sure why I say it out loud. I've been waiting to tell Brody before anyone else, but add a little liquid courage and it slips right out of my mouth. If I'd known that trick, maybe he'd know by now and I wouldn't have this ball of stress in the pit of my stomach.

"Holy shit, that's so far away! I don't think I could ever do that. My mom would be so sad, and I think I would be too. But that's awesome for you! Nothing to lose, right?"

I chuckle at that because she couldn't be more wrong. One could say that between Brody and my friends, that are basically family back home, I have everything to lose. "Yeah, thanks. I'm excited about it." The lie feels sour on my tongue. "I'm even going out there over spring break with my best friend from high school to visit." I'm rambling at this point, and I need to stop before one of the three boys who live in this house overhears.

"That's so awesome. I'm just going back to my hometown for break. You'll have to let me know how it goes. I want to live vicariously through you!"

"Of course, I'll let you know. I better get back downstairs before my boyfriend starts wondering where I am. It was great running into you, though!"

With my heart racing even faster than it was before that conversation, I make my way back to the basement, thankful I didn't run into anyone in the main level on the way through.

Chapter Thirty-Three

BRODY

"Hey, man. I'll be right back. My girl's been gone for a while and I promised to keep her by my side. I'm gonna go check on her." I say, leaving behind one of Isaiah's high school friends that could talk my ear off all night if I let him.

I search the basement, but don't see my favorite blonde curls anywhere. She acted weird all afternoon, and it's had me on high alert. I'm trusting her enough to tell me if something's going on, so I didn't push. Besides, I didn't want to ruin tonight. We don't get as much time together during the week as we did last semester, and I'm desperate for every moment I can get in her presence.

Something you'll have to get used to if she leaves after graduation.

I ignore the words that have been echoing in my head lately. I've been trying not to taint any moments we get together with hard conversations about the future, but midterms are next week. If I don't ask soon, I'll run out of time to persuade her to include me in her future plans.

Giving up on finding Val downstairs, I head up to the

main level. It's deserted up here, since we make everyone stay downstairs unless they're using the bathroom.

She's nowhere to be found in the kitchen or living room, and I'm about to head for the stairs when I hear her voice coming from the bathroom hallway.

I nearly call out to her, but stop in my tracks when I hear what she's saying.

"I know, it's so nerve-wracking. I actually just applied for a job out in San Francisco." *Maybe it's not her,* my heart tries to reason with my head, but I know it's a reach.

"Holy shit, that's so far away! I don't think I could ever do that. My mom would be so sad, and I think I would be too. But that's awesome for you! Nothing to lose, right?"

She chuckles, "Yeah, thanks. I'm excited about it. I'm even going out there over spring break with my best friend from high school to visit." My blood turns to ice in my veins, the world as I knew it suddenly crumbling to pieces right there in the middle of my kitchen.

"That's so awesome. I'm just going back to my hometown for break. You'll have to let me know how it goes. I want to live vicariously through you!"

"Of course, I'll let you know. I better get back downstairs —" Those words put a fire under my ass. I'm not ready for this conversation, nor do I want my relationship to end in the middle of a party I threw for the girl I can no longer deny I've fallen for. Here I am, feeling like a lovesick puppy while she's making plans without me.

I grab the bottle of whiskey I keep above the fridge for special occasions and make for the stairs. I spin the lid off the bottle, not giving a fuck where it lands, because I won't be heading to bed until this thing is empty.

At the bottom of the steps, I stop and throw back a long pull, coughing at the taste. Damn, I've become a lightweight this year. And for what?

Wes pulls away from his current conversation to clap me

on the back, eyeing the bottle in my hands. "Breaking out the big guns. What's the occasion?"

I take a deep breath, glaring at the bottle like I have a personal vendetta against it. "Wes, just this once, can you join me and ask your intrusive questions later, please?"

He must see something in my expression because he overrides his need to know every little thing going on in my head and takes the bottle. "Of course," he says, ruffling my hair before taking the longest pull I've ever seen. Have I mentioned he's the type of guy who would kill himself to keep those he loves safe? I know that's exactly what he's doing—protecting me, even though he doesn't know what he's protecting me from. Damn it, I'm gonna miss him when he moves back home to Florida after graduation.

By the time I spot Val, I'm already drunk. She's surprised by my state of inebriation, if her lifted brow is any indication, but I can't find it within myself to feel bad. But when she gets close, I break down, pulling her into me, kissing the crown of her head, inhaling the scent of her hair as I wrap her in a tight embrace. She leans in and lets out a long sigh, like it's exactly what she needs too.

The next morning, I wake up to a heartbeat rhythm in my skull and a mouth as dry as the Sahara.

"Well, good morning, Sleeping Beauty," comes a voice from the foot of my bed.

I sit up too fast to look, and end up curled into a ball with my head in my hands.

"There's water and ibuprofen on the nightstand for you."

Moving slower this time, I lean toward Val, who's reading a book she left on my nightstand the last time she was over. I plant a quick kiss on her lips. "Thank you. Mind telling me what the hell happened last night?"

I move across the bed, reaching for the pills and water as she answers.

"You broke out a bottle of whiskey at the end of the night. I'm not sure who drank more—you or Wes. But I will say that getting you both up two flights of stairs was the highlight of my night." The sarcasm is hard to miss. The dots are connecting, and I suddenly remember my need for that blessed bottle.

"Nothing to lose, right?"

"Yeah."

I down the ibuprofen, then lie back on my pillow that smells like a fucking cupcake.

I hear the slap of a book closing before the bed sags near my feet and Val crawls her way up into my peripheral.

"Brody, should I be worried about that?"

"About what?" I ask, buying myself some time to think.

She sighs, then snaps her shoulders taut. A defensive move she hasn't needed to use on me in a while. She's wearing my t-shirt with no bra, but I keep my gaze focused on a respectable area, afraid to piss her off more. "I was in the bathroom for a few minutes, and when I found you again, you were chugging whiskey. What happened?"

Oh, so we're doing this now.

I pull in a large breath, preparing myself. "I could ask you the same question."

Her brows scrunch when she meets my gaze, immediately jumping on the defensive. "What the hell is that supposed to mean?"

I look at the ceiling, scrubbing a hand down my face. No sense in delaying the inevitable any longer. "Babe, I came to look for you. And when I did, I overheard your conversation outside the bathroom."

She only needs a moment to recall before her face drops, looking down at her hands.

When she doesn't immediately speak, I lean up on my elbow, grasping my forehead, trying to stop its pounding.

"Why didn't you just tell me, Val? Do you know how much it hurts to find out that way? Like I mean nothing at all to you— like telling me your future plans is an afterthought? I'll tell you —it fucking hurts, Val. I thought we were good, but apparently I was wrong."

When I look up, her hands are scrubbing her face. "No, Brody. I don't even remember exactly what I said, but I know it sounded bad," she says, crawling across the bed on her knees, touching my chest. "Fuck, I'm sorry. She was a girl I worked with at my internship last summer and I guess—" She bites her lip. "I guess she was my practice for telling you. That was my plan, I swear, to tell you everything today. I'm so sorry you found out that way."

I sit up, causing her hands to drop back onto her lap. "Oh, so you *didn't* apply to a job almost two thousand miles away? You aren't going there with Hannah over break when I thought we had plans?" We stare silently for a prolonged moment.

She takes my hand, but my skin crawls with unease at all the unanswered questions and I pull it back.

I don't miss the way tears pool in her eyes. This shit feels all too familiar. Except this time, it's another location, rather than another man.

"Brody, I swear it's not a sure thing. I don't even know if I have a burning chance in hell of getting the job."

"That's not really the point, though, is it? You still applied —which I would've supported, had you bothered to tell me, by the way. It's the fact that I thought we were strong enough to tell each other everything. Yet, here you are, keeping the big cards close to your chest. How long has it been?"

She picks at a loose thread on my comforter, avoiding my gaze. "It's only been four days. The plan to visit formed when Hannah told me she was going to San Francisco for a photo shoot. We'll only be gone a few days. We could still spend half the week doing whatever you want."

"Dammit," I drop my head in my hands. "You know that's not the point. You were waiting until the last minute to tell me."

"No, you've just been busy, and I knew you'd take this news hard. I was afraid to rock the boat with it, but every time I tried to tell you, something happened and I couldn't. I'm sorry."

"Is it because you don't trust me?"

"No, of course not. I fear what following my original plan means for you and me." She moves closer, taking my hand and unfurling the fist I'd had it in. "I'm going to visit with Hannah to decide whether I even like it there because I know there's a chance I won't."

"If I were even throwing around the idea of moving across the country, I'd tell you. Because if that was my plan, I'd want you there with me." She shakes her head, but I don't understand why. "Isn't that what you want for us?"

"I can't ask you to pick up and follow me, Brody. That's like relationship suicide."

"Maybe when the other party already has a life established, but my future can happen anywhere. I'd follow *you* anywhere."

"You'll end up resenting me."

I grip my head with both hands, trying to contain the throb, but it doesn't work. "That's a sorry excuse to give a man who already has you written into his future plans. Because I love you, Val. I think I have for a while."

She pulls my hands away to look me in the eye. "You what?" She asks on a breath.

I pull at her hips until she's lying on top of me. "I love you, and I'm not just saying it in a desperate ploy to keep you here with me. I'm saying it because I've never felt this way about another person. This burning in my chest has been there for longer than I'd like to admit. I was too naïve to see the signs. I love you, even if you're about to leave. I still want you to know because I think you've gone too long without hearing those words regularly, and you have to know you're not alone. So please stop pushing me away long enough to see it's true."

Her cheeks are drenched with tears by the time the words are out in the open.

I swipe both thumbs across her cheeks, holding her face in my hands. "I—" she starts, but a sob wracks her body, so she tries again. "Brody, I love you too."

Hearing those words makes my fears float away, at least for the moment. Because she loves me.

I pull her down to me, avoiding the throb inside my skull as she brings her lips to mine. The kiss progresses, and as I reaching my hands under her shirt to find her soft skin, she claps hers down on mine, pausing my progress.

"Wait," she says, kissing my nose before she sits up, still straddling my hips. "Let me say this before I can't. The fact that I've fallen for you is what has made this so hard for me. For months, things have been great between us and I guess I just wanted to escape reality with you a little longer." She rubs the backs of my hands with her thumbs. "I'm sorry I hurt you."

Her sincere apology hits me right in the chest. "Thank you. And I know we've got a lot to talk about still, but right now," I say, inching my fingers under the hem of my shirt she wore to bed last night. "I don't want to talk. I want to touch you," I trail my hand up her stomach, feeling it flex under my fingertips, "I want to hold you—love you."

Her answer comes in the form of a kiss that gains heat quickly.

I pull her t-shirt over her head so we're on even playing ground. She leans me back, straddling my hips. She leans over, kissing me again, this time slower. I slide my hand up the length of her back.

She sits up, ridding us both of the rest of our clothing, grabbing protection before settling herself over my hips.

Neither of us is in a rush, like we're both content in savoring each other, taking it slower than we ever have in the past.

Our hands roam stretches of skin we know by heart now. Each line my fingertips carve across her skin feels familiar now. Having my feelings for her out in the open—knowing she feels the same way makes each touch feel different. Each kiss has more connection than the last. Every nip of her skin, every thrust of her hips feels like another admission. Every brush of her fingertips on my skin seems to burn brighter somehow.

By the time she's rolled on the condom, I'm aroused from every touch.

Her eyes search mine as she lowers herself onto me, as if she can see every thought inside my head. We both inhale a shaky breath when she's fully seated, her mouth dropping to mine as she begins to move, finding what feels good to her. My headache is forgotten quickly watching my beautiful girl take what she wants. And when she bends to kiss me, I pour all the feelings I've felt bottled up inside me out into each brush of our lips, every swipe of my tongue. "I love you," I whisper as finds her rhythm. I grasp her hips tight, afraid if I let her go, she'll slip right through my fingers.

"I love you too," she gasps just before I feel her squeeze around me, sighing against my shoulder.

I flip her onto her back, and it isn't long before I'm right there with her, breathing heavily against her skin, my arms around her tight.

When I pull back to look at her, I'm alarmed to find her cheeks wet with tears.

"Did I hurt you?"

She shakes her head jerkily, covering her face with her hands. "No, of course not."

I scoop her up, lying her on my pillow and pulling her into me until she goes pliant in my arms. "Then what's wrong?"

She sniffles, a sob wracking her body. "I'm just scared. I love you so much, and I don't want to lose you."

"You won't," I say, pulling her into my chest, but even I can't say whether it's the truth.

Chapter Thirty-Four

BRODY

The weekend passed quickly, and it isn't until she leaves Sunday evening that I realize we'd been so lost in each other, we never truly talked about what happens next. I never got the chance to ask her to take me with her wherever she goes. But she has to know that after everything, right?

The good morning text I wake to Monday gives me all the reassurance I needed.

Val: I had the best weekend and I can't stop smiling. Have a good day, I love you!

Brody: I'm smiling like an idiot at my phone right now. I love you so much. Will you have time to get dinner with me tonight?

. . .

She doesn't text back immediately, but she has an early class on Monday mornings, so I don't sweat it.

When she still hasn't answered by noon, I don't think much of it since we'll be meeting for lunch soon. But when she doesn't show—or answer my phone call—I start to worry.

Brody: Did you have something come up today that I wasn't aware of? I missed you at lunch. Call me after class, love you!

She doesn't answer that either. Instead of waiting around for her to call me, I show up at her house that evening. I knock and knock to no answer, but as I turn away, ready to give up, I hear the lock clicking in the door. But it isn't Val who answers.

"Hey, what's up?" A disheveled Bree asks as she swings open the door, looking...guilty? Also, I wonder if she realizes her sweatshirt is inside out.

I shake my head, remembering what I'm here for. "Have you seen Val?"

She looks over her shoulder before meeting my eye. "Uh, not recently."

"Oh, okay," I say, backing away, trying to figure out my next move.

"Wait, Brody. Is everything okay?" She says, meeting me out on the front porch. "You're looking a little pale."

I nod my head. "I—I think so? Val hasn't texted me since this morning. She didn't show at lunch. It's been radio silence since then. Has she texted you at all today?"

She bites her lip as she thinks about it. "You know, I did text her earlier today, but she never texted me back." We share a worried look. "But you know her. She's probably drowning in homework or something. I wouldn't worry."

But even as she says it, I can tell she's just as worried.

"I'm gonna try to find her."

She moves for the door. "Let me take care of this," she says, pointing back at the house, "then I'll help."

"I'll scour the library. You take the coffee house, maybe?"

"Got it, I'll text you."

"Oh, come on!" I yell, smacking my steering wheel as I circle the parking lot closest to campus, trying to find a spot to no avail. I throw caution to the wind, parking in a tow zone just to get to the library faster.

I run across the street and onto campus, out of breath, before I even reach the front door of the library, but keep going. My feet pound the tiles as I get looks from every single worker behind the front counter, but I don't slow my pace. I look in all our hang out places, and then some. But she's not there.

Not in the stacks, or in our study room. Not even at the tables near the youth collection where we used to always meet last semester.

By the time I'm back out on the sidewalk, I've already caught her voicemail.

"Hi, you've reached Valerie Boyd. I'm sorry I missed your call. Leave me a message with your name, phone number, and a brief message and I'll get back to you shortly."

If I wasn't so worried, I'd laugh at the professionalism of her voicemail. When the beep sounds, I sigh and say, "Val, whatever is going on, please just send me a message to let me know you're okay. I've been trying to reach you all day, went to your house and the library looking for you, and I even have Bree looking for you. I'm worried sick. Please call me." My voice shakes when I add, "I love you."

I'm almost to my vehicle when my phone beeps with a new message. I nearly drop my phone as I fumble it on its way out of my pocket. My heart sinks when I see it's still not Val.

. . .

Bree: Leaving the coffee shop now, she wasn't there. How about the library?

Brody: Nothing there either. I don't know what else to do, Bree. I feel physically ill.

I drive home, my stomach roiling.

I'm pacing the living room and smacking my phone against my hand when Wes walks in the room.

"Hey, man. You find Val?"

I look up at him, a furrow to my brow. "How'd you know I was looking for her?"

He splutters. "Well, I—I was sitting in the living room earlier when my phone rang. It was Bree asking if I'd seen Val lurking around the house looking for you."

"How'd she get your number?" I ask, no recollection of giving it to her, although I would have, had she asked for it.

He shrugs. "Val, I assume. I guess I didn't think to ask."

Where the hell did she get it? From my phone? I think to myself, but stop when I realize none of that matters.

"No, I didn't find her. I'm freaking out. What if she's hurt? Or worse…" I trail off, trying not to let my thoughts go in that direction.

Thankfully, my phone beeps, keeping me from spiraling.

Bree: I just got home, and she's here. She's not talking, though. She's saying she's tired and had a terrible day. I told her to call you, but she asked me to let you know. I'm so sorry, I wish I had more to tell you. Let's let her sleep it off and try for answers tomorrow. Thanks for caring enough about her to come looking for her tonight, otherwise I never would have known anything was up. You're a great guy, Brody. She's lucky to have you.

"What is it?" Wes asks, stepping closer. I can't form words. I hand my phone over and wait. "What the fuck am I supposed to do with that?" I ask when he finally meets my gaze.

Chapter Thirty-Five

VAL

This weekend was everything I could have asked for. I finally got everything off my chest with Brody, and we spent the rest of the weekend together.

After the helplessness I was feeling Friday, I start the new week full of hope—for us and for my future.

After sending him a good morning text, I leave for my first class of the day without a care in the world. I smile at strangers on my way through campus. Most of them don't even acknowledge me because it's too early on a Monday morning to be this happy.

My class is in a smaller classroom, and when I walk in, I spot the girl I sit by every day. She's usually calm and collected, but today, she scrambling through papers, using the tiny stapler she keeps in her bag to attach a bunch of papers.

"Whatcha got there?" I ask, sitting in the chair next to hers.

"What do you mean? It's the ten-page paper."

I don't need further explanation, because when the words

are out of her mouth, dread pours over my body, starting at the top of my head, spread all the way to my toes.

"Shit," I say under my breath, which makes her snap her attention in my direction.

"Did you not finish it?"

I open my mouth to answer, but no words come out. I'd planned to work on it on Saturday, but stayed with Brody for the rest of the weekend, completely unaware of the fact that I was forgetting something.

My head snaps up as Professor Willingham walks in the door. On numb limbs, I make my way to her, sending a desperate plea into the universe that she'll give me what I need right now.

"Ms. Boyd. Good morning," she says with a serene smile. "I trust you had a good weekend?"

I've had a couple of classes with her over the past couple years, and she's easily become one of my favorites.

And I've been a good student, so we have a good rapport, which I'm hoping she'll remember once I say what I'm about to.

"Good morning. I actually had something important come up," Lie, "Unfortunately, I wasn't able to finish my paper." I watch in horror as the smile slides off her face. "I was wondering if I could get an extension?"

"You are the last person I would have expected to have to talk to about this," she says, shaking her head like she's disappointed in me. "I have office hours after class, we'll meet then."

"Wait, I actually—"

"If you want to salvage your grade on this assignment—which weighs heavily on your semester's grade, might I add—you'll visit during my office hours from ten to noon. Now if you'll find your seat, we need to get class started, please."

She turns away, pulling things from her bag and completely ignoring me.

I make the walk of shame back to my seat, looking around the room at all the people with their papers on their desks, ready to be turned in.

My stomach roils.

This is exactly what I'd been afraid of. Letting someone in, caring too much, and ruining my future.

———

After class, I head straight to Professor Willingham's office. She strolls down the hallway a half hour later, turning when she notices me in the chair across the hall from her door.

"I've got a few things to get done, then I'll be out to grab you. You'd be wise to use that time to come up with a good excuse, because this is very unlike you."

I check the time on my watch. I'm supposed to be meeting Brody for lunch in forty-five minutes.

I can't help but feel like if it weren't for our relationship, I wouldn't even be in this predicament right now. Then there's a searing pain in my chest, because he did nothing wrong. It was me. *I* forgot about my ten-page paper. *I* ruined my grade. But it happened because I let it. And now it feels like I have to choose. Him, or school and my future career.

I check my watch again. It's already been ten minutes. There's no way I'll be able to meet him for lunch.

I pull my phone from my bag, finding his name there on a waiting text message.

Brody: I'm smiling like an idiot at my phone right now. I love you so much. Will you have time to get dinner with me tonight?

His words take me back to this morning when everything felt perfect. How could everything change so quickly?

I start to type back when the door to Professor Willingham's office opens.

She looks pointedly at my phone and I throw it in my bag like a reflex. "You may come in now, Ms. Boyd."

I follow her in before she changes her mind. Maybe if I'm lucky, she'll see how punctual I've been in the past and decide to go easy on me.

"Okay, let's skip to the chase. What happened this weekend that you couldn't finish your paper, Valerie? And keep in mind that I did assign it two weeks ago, so you're already riding on a very sorry excuse."

I open my mouth, prepared to lie through my teeth, but I respect this woman in front of me too much to follow through. "I don't have a good excuse to give. I was simply busy living my life with people I care about, and completely spaced my responsibilities."

"Thank you for your honesty. Val, what is it you plan on doing with your degree after graduation?"

I take a deep breath. "My dream is to be an event planner."

She looks over her glasses at me. "And as an event planner, what do you think the repercussions would be if you forgot an important task for a huge event?"

I nod, already seeing where she's going with this. "I'd be in pretty big trouble, I'd imagine."

I can already feel the tears building, but I refuse to let them fall in front of her.

"So with it being my job to prepare your for such occasions—to teach you the right way to carry yourself in a professional setting, do you understand why I must hold on to my rules for this class and reprimand you for not getting your work done on time?"

"Yes, ma'am. I understand."

"Good. And just so we're clear, a late submission is an

automatic loss of fifty percent of your grade on the assignment."

My stomach bottoms out at this news. There's no way I'll get a passing grade, no matter how hard I try, all because I'm turning it in late. "Okay," I say, and my voice has never sounded so weak.

"If we're done here," she says, turning to her computer, "I've got a few things to finish before my next class begins."

I take that as my cue to leave, rising to my feet on wobbly knees. Just as I open the door, I remember one last thing, "And when does it need turned in by?"

She swivels in her desk chair, pinning me to the spot with her glare, which is answer enough for me.

"Right, I'll have it to you by the end of the day."

Chapter Thirty-Six

BRODY

Tuesday is three unanswered calls, and a half-assed excuse of why she can't come over. I try to surprise her at home, but the house is dark.

Wednesday feels hopeless, but I force myself to try again.

By Thursday afternoon, I'm pissed.

Unfortunately for her, it's the day we usually meet at the library, and I still plan to show.

When my feet cross the threshold of our study room that afternoon, my heart plummets in my chest at the sight of her.

I place the coffee I bought her next to her planner and turn to sit, going against my instinct to kiss her.

I sulked around the house long enough for Wes to demand answers this morning. He helped me make a game plan, and we both agreed that showing up with a peace offering might not be a terrible choice.

We both go straight to business without a word. Although it's driving me crazy to hold my tongue, I get satisfaction from the fact that she's just as antsy across the way.

I remove my notebook, select a pencil, then reach for the bakery bag I brought. I rejoice in every crinkle noise the paper makes because I know it's annoying her. If she's screaming at me, at least she's finally talking, right? At least that's the way I'm choosing to see it.

Once I've taken a huge bite of my scone, I roll the bag back up, tossing it across the table. It hits her hand as it lands —while she's writing in her planner.

Good. Fuck that perfect handwriting.

Out of my periphery, I see her pick it up and slap it to a different spot on the table with a *thwack*.

I feel the weight of her gaze as I answer one study question, then another, minding my own business. Do I realize I'm smacking my lips together as I eat? *Yes.* Do I know it's her biggest pet peeve? *Absolutely.* Do I care? *Nope.*

Out of nowhere, a pen flies across the table, skidding to a stop at my fingertips. I look up to find Val's face pink with rage.

"Dammit, Brody. Just leave if you're only here to annoy me."

Our glares are an old Western duel, daring the other to make the first move, ready to retaliate at a moment's notice.

"You truly think I'm here to annoy you?" My voice shakes with bottled up frustration. "Val, I'm here because you've been avoiding me for four days, and I want to know why."

Her jaw goes slack and her mouth opens like she has something to say, but I'm not finished.

"The only information I can get out of you is that *you're tired. You're busy*, so I ran across campus after my last class to grab us caffeine, and this is how you want to treat me? Fine." I shoot to my feet, flip my notebook closed and start shoving everything back in my bag. "I'm out."

I'm at the door in two angry footfalls. I pause, hand hovering above the doorknob, praying she'll say something to make me stay. But she doesn't utter a word.

Later that evening, I'm sitting on a squeaky barstool at The Saloon while Wes does his thing behind the bar. I usually pace myself while I'm here studying, but after the day—no, week— I've had, I'm drinking my feelings.

"Hey man," Wes slaps his bar towel down next to my notebook. "Sure you're good?"

I laugh, although there's not an ounce of humor in it. "I'm fucking *great*." I relayed the happenings of the afternoon to him as soon as I sat down, so he knows why I'm here.

Not wanting to repeat myself, I take a hefty chug of beer. A small bag of barbecue chips lands on my notebook.

"You need to eat something if you're gonna chug something that potent."

It wasn't lost on me that I chose the beer on tap that boasts an 8.5 alcohol percentage. I picked it on purpose.

"It's cool." I put my hands on my chest. "*I'm fine.* I'm not cut out for the relationship life, anyway. So if she's about to end things, it doesn't matter."

My heart clenches at the words, but my heart is the reason I'm in this mess, so he can go to hell.

Wes is standing there, looking suspicious with his arms crossed. "I'll let you have the evening, but tomorrow you're going to talk to her. I know you hate to hear it as much as I hate to say it, but you two either need to work it out or end it. This shit is ridiculous. I'm not gonna condone you drinking yourself into oblivion for long, either. That shit solves nothing."

"You're not a very good bartender, talking like that," I say, reducing my eyes to slits. I chug what's left in my glass, slamming the fancy snifter on the bar hard enough to make Wes reach for it with a glare. I wipe my mouth with the back of my hand.

"This feels a lot like history repeating itself," I admit out loud for the first time, although I've felt it for a while.

"For your sake, I hope that's not the case."

He'd know, Wes was there when my ex went radio silent my freshman year. A week later I found out she was dropping out of school at the end of the semester to be with her new boyfriend.

Wes' words are still swimming in my head as I walk back to our house in the dark. The wind tonight is bitterly cold. I'm regretting not wearing a hat and gloves for the short walk, but I've been numb all week, so what's the fucking difference?

As I cross the street in front of our house, a car door slams shut down the street. I turn toward the sound, but my body is moving slowly, like my limbs are underwater. Before I know what's happening, I'm a bag of bones lying in the middle of the street.

After the shock wears off, I lean up to find it was Val's body I saved from hitting the ground. She's lying on my chest, straddling my hips—the backdrop, a million stars behind her head. This wouldn't be a terrible way to die.

"Brody, where have you been? And why aren't you answering your phone? I've been so worried," she says, pulling me to my feet and up the driveway.

I loop my arm around her lazily, leaning most of my weight on her small stature. Ignoring her questions, I ask, "How long have you been here?"

She pulls away to look me in the eye. "About an hour? I went inside and sat on your bed for a while, but came to sit in my car because I didn't feel right being in the house without you."

A laugh escapes me. "My girlfriend doesn't feel right being

in my house without me. Let's add that to the pile of things I'll need to overthink about."

"Brody, I'm sorry about earlier. I was an asshole. I've had a terrible week and I realize I've been taking it out on you. I'm sorry. When you didn't answer your phone, I thought you were mad at me, so I came over to explain myself."

"I'm not mad, Cupcake," I say, feeling myself sway on my feet.

"You're not? It seemed like you were."

"No, I'm pissed. Pissed *drunk*, pissed *off*. And fucking confused. As for my phone," I reach into my back pocket. I click the side button, but the screen remains black. "Oh, it's dead."

"You're drunk?"

I look at her with one eye open, squinting the other. "Yup. But I'm good."

"Why'd Wes let you walk home in the cold while drunk?"

I shrug and look up at her so fast my head spins. "Wouldn't be the first time. Besides, I wasn't drunk when I left."

She takes a deep breath, pinching the bridge of her nose. It's cute, but I don't dare tell her because she seems to be in a mood. Plus, I'm still not that happy with her.

She loops her arm in mine, pulling me toward the front steps.

"This is the closest we've been since Sunday afternoon."

She looks up at that, but I stare at my shoes. They're muddy. Huh.

"I got drunk because you hate me. I thought I could handle this, but I can't." She halts her steps, turning to look at me. "Maybe it'd be easier if you'd just talk to me, but you're pulling away. You keep ignoring me—ignoring the conversations we need to have. I don't want to walk away from you, Val. I love you, you dummy."

I slap my hands to my face, scrubbing them up and down,

knocking my glasses askew, but it does nothing to clear my hazy mind. "Sorry I called you a dummy. Ignore that." Despite the morose mood I'm in, we look at each other and laugh. "Maybe I shouldn't have chugged that beer after all. But Val, I care too much to walk away, so if anyone does, it'll have to be you."

She pulls me in, squeezing tight. "I love you too, Brody. It's why I'm here," she says against my neck. I thread one hand into her hair as the other one wraps around her waist, pulling her in until our bodies are one seam. I bury my face in her hair and kiss the top of her head. My cheeks feel wet, so I wipe at them, realizing belatedly that the wetness is my own tears.

And as I lean back against it, the front door swings open. Isaiah does a half-assed job of catching us before we hit the floor of the entryway.

"Shit, Brody. Thank God you're here. Wes called to say you disappeared while he was pouring drinks across the bar. What the hell were you thinking, taking off like that when you're drunk? I thought I was gonna have to scour the town looking for you. Get in here and close the door before you two freeze to death."

Chapter Thirty-Seven

VAL

What I wouldn't give to have Brody sober. We need to talk, I'm vibrating with the need to do so, but we can't when he's in this state.

Despite everything, he's an adorable drunk and my heart surges as I set his glasses on the nightstand and watch him snuggle into his pillow.

Isaiah helped me get him upstairs. Technically, he did most of the work.

"You really did a number on him, Val." He says as we walk back downstairs and my heart jumps to my throat.

"What do you mean?"

He swivels around once we meet the kitchen. "I mean he's been down all week, and I haven't seen you around. I overheard him and Wes talking about what's going on between you this afternoon. It's easy to connect the dots."

I can't explain myself to Isaiah before I talk to Brody. Not after what happened Friday night when I was talking to

Maurine. So I give him a vague explanation, "School's kept me busy all week—"

Isaiah cuts me off. "Look, I'm not trying to make you feel bad. I'm just saying I've seen Brody date in the past, but I've never seen him as happy as he's been with you. Whatever's going on, I hope you two figure it out because he's been as miserable as I've ever seen him." He moves toward the living room then turns back to add, "And not that you're his caretaker, but you've changed him. I haven't seen him drink his feelings like this in a long time. He wears his feelings on his sleeve, I'm sure you've noticed. I've seen him like this in the aftermath of a relationship before, but I know his feelings for *you* are stronger. I'm worried for him, that's all."

He walks away, but I'm still staring at the place he left long after I hear the TV in the living room come to life. My ears ring with his words as I fill a glass of water, grab ibuprofen, and climb the stairs again to set it on his nightstand.

As I've done all afternoon, I obsess over every detail of the last week that I wish I could change.

If I could just go back and carve out some time to finish my paper on time, it would save me from every other mistake I made in the wake of it. But that's the problem, isn't it? I let my relationship get in the way of what matters most—school, my grades, my degree. Exactly what I was afraid would happen when I tried to push Brody away in the beginning has now happened, and I don't know where to go from here. I also don't know when he became more important than my studies. He snuck up on me.

A snore from Brody pulls me from my negative thoughts. I take in his features, his eyebrows and nose, watching his eyelids flitter under the weight of his slumber.

Does he dream of me? He's told me as much, but I want to know what he sees in these dreams. Do we make it out of this funk together?

When I lean in, I find his phone lying dead and useless next to his hip and I plug it into the charger that's always lying across his nightstand. I wait until it finally turns back on and his favorite picture of me—a candid of me laughing from Christmas break—lights up the screen. It's like a sucker punch to the solar plexus. What has happened to us?

You're pulling away, Brody's words echo in my mind. I can't even claim that he's wrong. It's exactly what I did.

I lean over to comb my fingers through his hair and plant a kiss on his forehead. He doesn't stir, no matter how much I wish he would.

Then I grab his phone one last time in search of his alarm clock. Even though it goes against my moral code, I toggle every single one from 6:45 to 7:15. I don't want him to miss his morning class because of my need to be right.

With his phone safely on the nightstand, I take him in for a long moment, watching his strong chest rise and fall.

"I love you," I whisper, feeling hopeless as I walk out of his room.

The next morning, Brody calls five minutes before we normally meet for lunch. I answer with a lame, "Hey."

He lets out a long breath. "Hey, Val. I'm sorry about last night."

"Me too."

"Uh," he pauses like he's not sure what to say. Why are we both so nervous? "If you aren't busy, would you, uh, want to get together over lunch?"

"Yeah, should we head to the Union?"

"Actually, I was thinking yours or mine. We need to talk. The U wouldn't be the best place for that."

"Oh," a lead ball drops and settles in my stomach. "Okay.

Bree's at work until close, so we can head to mine. I'm walking, but I'll be there in about five minutes."

"I'm at my car. I'll pick you up on the way."

"Okay."

I'm not even a half-block from campus when I hear a car slowing at the curb behind me and turn to see Brody's Range Rover.

My pulse beats overtime as I reach for the door handle and climb in.

"Hey," Brody says, leaning over to kiss me like it's muscle memory, but pulls back at the last second.

That lead ball in my stomach gains weight as I pull his head back to me, kissing him desperately. The kiss deepens quickly, as if we've both got something to prove, and when we pull away breathlessly, there's a terrible ache in my chest.

"I missed you," Brody says, then turns away to check for traffic before pulling back out into the road.

"I missed you too."

There's a white plastic bag on the center console between us, with a familiar scent wafting from it.

"Did you get Francesco's?"

Brody smirks, but it doesn't reach his eyes. "Yep. I got us our favorite."

I look inside. Sure enough, there are two to-go boxes. Too bad my stomach is in such knots, I'm not sure I can even eat it.

After Brody parks, walking to the front steps feels a lot like walking the plank. Hopefully, in an hour's time, I'll look back at this moment and laugh.

We're both quiet as we settle into the couch with our lunches. The silence is awkward, so I shove down a couple bites of a meatball until I can't stand it any longer.

"I'm sorry for how I treated you this week. I was so far in my own head, I never stopped to think about how my actions made you feel. It wasn't fair to you, and I'm sorry."

"What happened? I thought we were good after last weekend."

I nod. "We were," I say, "but I forgot about a paper that was due. Because—" the unspoken words taste bitter in my mouth.

"Because of me?"

I take a deep breath. "No, because I spent my weekend differently than planned and forgot about my responsibilities for the moment. And I'll admit, it was great while it lasted, but this is why I don't normally live my life like that. It's why I plan it out—so I don't forget important things like a paper that weighs heavily on the grade I'll have at the end of the semester. Instead of owning up to my own mistakes, I took it out on you all week as I put my head down and drowned in my studies. For that, I'm so sorry."

Brody sets down his fork and turns to me. "Thank you for apologizing. I just—" he scratches the back of his neck. "I need the reassurance that we're okay." He grabs his fork, picking at his food before adding, "We're okay, right?"

Tears prick at my eyes when they meet his hopeful gaze. "Are we?"

All the hope I'd seen disappears at my words.

"I mean, I want us to be. But I applied to a job nearly two-thousand miles away and we have yet to talk about what that means for us."

"I thought you said you weren't sure you'd get the job?"

"I'm not, but that doesn't mean the next job I find won't be just as far away."

His breath is exasperated. "So let me go where you go."

I clear my throat, but all my emotions remain lodged there. "It's too soon for that."

"Some would say it's too early to have feelings for each other. Yet, here I am, still loving you. And I don't want to stop."

Tears prick at my eyes. "I don't want that either. But I've

also worked so hard these past four years to make my future the best it can be. Our relationship has already gotten in the way of that. What happens when it's not just college anymore? When it's my career, my livelihood?"

"So let me be with you, Val. Wherever you'll go."

"No."

"Why?" His voice raises, but not with anger. It's something more like frustration.

"Because I know you'll eventually come to resent me, moving there for me and my dreams. What about yours? They deserve to come to fruition, too. We can plan all we want, but life still happens. My parents had plans. Now they're both dead. I planned on spending this year single, yet here you are. People make plans all the time, Brody. But a lot of those plans don't work out. I don't want that to be us."

He swallows thickly. "Yet you still meticulously try to plan every moment of your life. I'm sorry the weekend we spent together had such terrible repercussions for you, Val. I am. But would you listen to your own advice?" He takes my hand, squeezing it like it will help his argument. "Plan all you want, but life still happens. Your plans always included just one person, but guess what? Life happened and I'm standing here in front of you, asking you to make some revisions, but you won't even budge."

I wipe the tears that have just fallen, finally seeing his side of the argument. "I'm sorry. I just can't see how it will work long-term."

"So, what?" There's anger in his hazel eyes. "You just want to break up, then? To save us from the fallout that may not even happen later?"

The words are an electric shock to the heart. I rub at my chest before my fingers find the four-leafed clover at my throat. He just voiced my biggest fear, and with those words out in the open, we can no longer hide from them. Air releases from my lungs like a slow leak. "No," I say, but my wants don't change the fact that it might be what's best. "But…"

"But what?"

"If it's even a question in our minds, aren't we already halfway there?"

He looks at me incredulously. "So that's what you want?"

"No," I move to take his hand since he won't look at me.

"No," he repeats. "But," he takes a stuttered breath, "now that we've established this relationship has no future—no ground to stand on—it might be best if we parted ways now, rather than torture ourselves for the next few months. Right?"

His eyes are swimming with tears when his gaze meets mine. The sight knocks the breath right from me. I don't answer. Instead, I cry.

I cry for the relationship we had, if only for a little while.

I lean over, covering my eyes as I finally let the tears fall. Brody pulls me onto his lap, where I lean my head against his chest. He holds me tight in his embrace for who knows how long. When the sobs finally settle, I rise and wipe hastily at my tears, but it's no use. My cheeks remain soggy and swollen when I meet his gaze. He doesn't look any better than I feel.

So what the hell have we done—and why?

"I should go," he says in a voice thick with emotion.

"I don't want you to," I say, my voice breaking.

His hands move to my face, and for a moment, I think he'll find a way to salvage this. But he wipes my cheeks and says, "You don't want me to go, but you don't want me to stay. Don't you see how your words contradict each other?"

When his forehead bends to touch mine, my tears flow again. I fist my hand in his shirt, sure I'll never be ready to say goodbye to him.

"I'm sorry," I whisper.

He looks at the floor, nodding. "Me too," he says quickly, like if he talks too much, he'll lose his composure.

He drops one last kiss to my forehead and I inhale his

sandalwood scent, ingraining it in my memory forever. "Goodbye, Val," he says, and before I'm prepared, he pulls away, my fingers unraveling from his shirt one by one.

He tries to meet my gaze as he makes for the door, but his face contorts, making my last view of him, his strong fingers grasping the back of his neck.

Then the door shuts, and he's gone.

Chapter Thirty-Eight

BRODY

The next morning, I wake with crusty eyeballs from the mixture of last night's inevitable tears and a lack of sleep. I nearly throw my phone across the room when I tap the screen three times and still don't get the snooze button pressed. Finally, the shrill sound of my alarm shuts off.

I close my eyes, desperate for those nine more minutes of sleep, but as soon as they're closed, all I can see is her face. Her smile, the look she gives me when she finds me annoying, the ecstasy in her expression when we're tangled between sheets. Then it's all ruined by the look on her face as I walked away yesterday. Of all her expressions, that's the one that will be burned into my memory.

Since I walked out the door, I can't help but wonder if we made the right decision. I didn't want it, and neither did she. So why didn't I fight harder for us? Why didn't she?

Because you're not good enough, that voice she always helped silence in my head comes roaring back to life.

I open my eyes, giving up on the thought of sleep. If last night was any indication, it won't come easy, anyway. The guys threw a party downstairs without me, but I've been hiding out in my room since I got home from Val's. My head hurts, my stomach is yawning and empty, just like the cavity in my chest.

The rest of my day yesterday was spent in a fog. I was already late for my last class of the day by the time I left Val's, so I didn't go. Not that I would've been able to keep the facade in place for an hour and a half lecture.

Thankfully, no one was home when I walked through the door, then I pretended she was in here with me when Isaiah tried to invite me downstairs. They don't know what happened, and I plan to keep it that way.

"Bro, you moving in there?" Wes yells at the door, making me jump. I swear he can read my thoughts. "We going to the gym or what, man?"

"Uh, no," I yell, but my voice comes out weak.

I assume the thump against the door is his forehead, and it rattles on its hinges. "Are you fucking kidding me? You didn't even drink with us last night and you're still gonna dip?" When I don't answer, he asks, "Your girl in there?"

I look over at the pillow she used to always use, the one that still smells like cupcakes—the one I slept with under my arm last night like a lovesick idiot. "No."

He throws the door open wide and steps across the room to my bed. I bury my face in my pillows, but not quickly enough.

"Whoa, Brody," he shoves at my shoulder until my body turns enough for him to see my face. "What the hell's wrong with you?"

"I no longer have a girl," I mumble into my pillow. "Don't wanna talk about it, so save your million questions for someone else."

He flops on my bed so hard it makes me bounce. I hadn't

realized how sore my stagnant muscles were. Maybe it wouldn't hurt to at least stand up.

"Fuck, I'm sorry, buddy."

"I'm not gonna talk about it," I warn a second time, since it usually takes three with him.

"Good, because I didn't want to hear the sob story anyway." He smacks me on my ass. "Get those gluties up and drink this, because you've got an appointment with our boy blue." He says, shoving my pre-workout in my face. "You can talk with your hands, right?"

I groan, wanting nothing more than to stay under the covers. But I can't turn down a date with a punching bag.

"Come on, chug-a-lug!" Wes says, wiggling the shaker bottle in front of my face. I take it and shove him off my bed.

"Yeah, whatever. Now get the hell out."

He chuckles as he walks out my door.

I hate to say it, but an hour later, I realize Wes was right. Punching out my frustrations was what I needed this morning. Back in the day, I used to picture my dad's face on the bag. Today, I didn't picture a person, but my punches still had a purpose.

San Francisco, *punch.*

Never feeling good enough, *punch.*

Love—*kick, jab, punch combo.*

The list is long, and I rotate through it until my arms are numb and ringing with aftershocks. But when I'm chugging water on my way out the door, I feel better than I did when I woke up this morning. Not great, but better.

On the way to the car, I pull my phone from my pocket, swiping it open to my messages, but before I click her name, I catch myself.

It's so engrained in my daily routine to message Val, I

almost did it without even thinking. The severed action feels like a phantom pain left behind by a missing body part. Just like that, my improved mood is gone.

But imagine if I'd done that while still lying in my bed, wallowing.

"Hey," I say, turning to Wes as he pulls out of our parking space.

"Yeah?"

"Thanks for that. I needed it."

He claps a hand to my shoulder and nods, "I know, buddy. And even though you think my questions are intrusive and annoying, if you need to talk, I'm shit for advice, but I can listen."

My lips turn up at the corners. "Thanks."

That evening, when I step into the kitchen, Wes takes one look at me and hands me the beer he'd been unscrewing for himself.

"Hey," he says, heading back to the fridge to grab another one.

"Perks of a live-in bartender?"

"Only for you," he smirks and swigs his new beer. "Chug it and go get ready, it's time to have *one of those nights*."

"Nah, man. I'm not in the mood. Thanks though."

"Brody," he gives me a look. "What happened to the guy who was always down for a good time?"

"He changed." *Because of Val.* The words are unspoken, but the look on Wes' face tells me he can feel them under the surface, too. "You know what? Fuck it. Give me ten minutes."

An hour later, I'm stuffed full of tacos de carne asada and tequila. The combination just might have me on board for tonight's shenanigans.

When we make it to The Saloon, I beeline to the bar and buy the first round.

The place is packed even though I was sure most students would be off to some beach for break. My buzz quickly transitions into the kind of drunk my friends call "Fun Brody," where I talk people into too many shots, dance with random strangers, and belt out the lyrics to every song that plays over the speakers.

And when I'm dragged onto the dance floor by some random blonde I've never met?

I surprise her and all my friends by turning her down and sitting down in an open stool at the bar to order another round of shots.

That's one thing I can't do yet. I spent too many nights with Val in my arms on dance floors to be comfortable running my hands over someone else's curves.

When past relationships have ended, it was the first thing I'd do. Find a girl at a bar and lose myself in her. Point out all the differences between her and the girl before her. But Post-Val Brody is a different man, and I guess that's how I know she did a number on me—I'd rather be miserable and missing her than going home covered in some other girl's perfume.

The feelings I felt for her don't go away that fast.

Knowing what it was like to have her has wrecked me for all other women.

So when my roommates wave away the shots I brought them, I take a deep breath and down them myself before I slap the glasses back onto the bar.

"Let's go back to our table," Wes says, clapping me on the shoulder.

I oblige as he lifts me, but instead of making my way to the table, I get lost in the middle of a rowdy crowd on the dance floor and jump in on the steps to Cupid Shuffle. I don't even bother to turn my head when I hear the guys trying to get me to follow them.

When the song ends, I make my way to them, but I don't get far. Instead, I'm pummeled by a small body that nearly knocks me on my ass.

At first I don't realize who it is hugging me, but realize it's Bree when she pulls back to look at me. She wraps her arms around my waist like a vise and I pull her closer, realizing just how badly I needed it.

She finally pulls away to look me in the eye. "I'm so sorry about you and Val." I can smell the tequila on her breath, then again, she can probably smell it on mine.

"Thanks, Bree." When my brain chooses to join the party, I check my surroundings frantically for her companion.

"Don't worry, she isn't here. She leaves for San Francisco in the morning."

"Oh, okay."

"I think you're both stupid for ending things." She's nothing if not blunt. As if recognizing her mistake, she holds her hands up between us, palms out. "No offense."

"None taken. Honestly, I agree with you."

She moves to answer, but an especially bass-y song starts playing and I can't hear a thing no matter how close she yells to my ear. After an exasperated eye roll, she pulls me toward the back patio. As soon as the door is shut behind us, the static in my ears thanks me.

Bree leads us to an open picnic table, running her hands down her face and huffing out a long breath. "Did you say you agree with me?"

"Yes, I did."

Her hand lands on my forearm. "Then Brody," she shakes her head, looking off into the distance. "Why the hell did you let her go?"

I let out a breath I think I've been holding since last weekend when this all began. "Bree, have you ever been in love with someone who has one foot out the door?"

Her eyes are sad when I meet her gaze. "Can't say that I have."

"You know, I let myself believe that she'd stay. Or at the very least, she'd let me go with her." I pick at the label on my beer bottle. "But I'm realizing you can't follow someone who keeps covering their tracks."

She nods. "You deserve someone who doesn't just want you to follow them. You deserve someone who will stand by your side as you walk together through life." She shakes her head, smiling at me. "How'd you do it?"

"How'd I do what?"

"How'd you get me to empathize with you enough to say such sappy shit?"

That makes us both laugh.

Chapter Thirty-Nine

VAL

It's the night before our red-eye to San Francisco and I'm at the Hawkins' with Hannah. I'm sprawled on her floor with a notebook and pen while we double check she's got all her gear packed.

"This is my first time traveling for my dream job. Can you imagine if I got to do this more than once a year someday?"

She's said some version of this same phrase a million times since I got here. Needless to say, she's excited. I'm so freaking proud of her. "It's crazy. I can't wait to see all the beautiful places that camera takes you."

She smiles at me. "I know. And I'll get jobs wherever your dream job lands you! Then I won't have to miss you when you're gone."

My fleeting good mood is crushed under the weight of those words. "Yeah, maybe." I barely get the words out without my voice breaking and unfortunately, Hannah notices.

She gives me one look before her camera gear is forgotten and she's sitting cross-legged in front of me. "Okay, I wasn't going to say anything, because I figured if something was wrong, you'd eventually tell me. But Val, there are tears in your eyes. If you wanted to stay home and hang out with Brody—"

I shake my head, hoping she'll stop. When she does, I say, "We broke up."

"What? That—" she jumps to her feet and starts pacing the room. "That fucker! I thought he was in love with you."

"He was," I say, but she doesn't hear me over the sound of her own yelling. "Hannah!" She finally turns to look at me. "It wasn't him—it was me."

"What?" Her voice jumps an octave. "When did this happen? Why didn't you say anything?"

I swipe at my tears. "Two days ago, and I'm ashamed."

Without another word, she falls into me with a hug. "I'm so sorry. I thought you two were a forever kind of thing."

"What if we were?" I mutter more to myself than to her.

She rubs my back. "Shit, Val. I wish I would have known. I wouldn't have made you come with me."

"No, I'm glad I'm going. I need to know if this will all be worth the pain."

"Wait, is San Francisco the reason you broke up?"

I brush my hair out of my face. "It came up in the conversation, but it wasn't the only reason."

"You told him about the job you applied to, right?"

Her voice switches to mom mode so fast it gives me whiplash. Although tough love isn't what I need right now, I know I deserve it. The tears fall faster. "I kept trying to after we talked on the phone, but it was like the universe was against me. So I made a plan to tell him last Saturday. Then —" I stop when I remember what comes next, because it kills me every time I think about it. No wonder he didn't put up a fight. "Then I ran into a girl from class at his party Friday night. She asked if I was ready for graduation."

"Uh oh," Hannah says, covering her mouth.

"I'd been holding in the words for so long, desperate to let it out. And I was a little tipsy, so I practiced on her with the plan of telling Brody the next morning. He overheard it. That was the beginning of the end, and I knew it as soon as he confronted me about it."

"Val," she says, grabbing my hand. "You know I love you—"

I lift my gaze to hers. "But?"

"But you should have told him. Long before you clicked the button to send that application. He deserved to know."

I nod, staring down at my hands. "I know that now."

———

Later that evening, we're drinking wine in the kitchen with Jenn. We've filled her in on my relationship problems, and I think she shed more tears than I did.

That's one of the worst parts of losing him—my people loved him as much as I did. As much as I still do.

"I've gotta pee. Be right back," Hannah says, leaving the room.

I watch her go, and as soon as she disappears down the hallway, a soft, warm hand lands on mine. "Are you okay? Really?" Jenn asks.

I take a deep breath and try to smile, but I think it comes out as more of a grimace behind wobbly lips. "I will be. No matter what happens next."

She squeezes my hand. "You know, you don't always have to be the strong one." Her eyes penetrate the walls around my heart despite my best efforts to resist the power of her motherly gaze. "Even back when you lost your father and started living under my roof, those are the words I wanted to say to you, but I didn't. And watching you now, I wonder if I should have said something, but at the time, I underestimated how strong you are."

I let loose a watery laugh as twin tears fall down my cheeks. "I don't feel all that strong."

"I don't think a weak person would even consider moving halfway across the country to start over, Valerie, dear."

I lean my elbows on the table and hold my head in my hands. I hear the scrape of her chair legs against the floor as she scoots her barstool closer to mine, then her arms are around my shoulders.

"I tell you what, Val. I knew your momma for a long time. I'm going to say a couple things I think she'd tell you if she could. Okay?" The mention of Mom takes away my ability to speak, so I nod. She rubs my back, and I hear her sniffle before the words come. "You're an adult now, and have the right to make your own decisions. Your heart has been put through more hell than anyone your age should have to go through. Which is why I hope all these decisions you're making aren't you trying to punish yourself. Because we love you, Val."

She continues rubbing my back while we sit in silence.

"You've always been our headstrong girl with a soft gooey center. And for a minute there, I thought we might have lost her. But she's back. I'm not sure what did it—your experiences at school, that boy you were bringing around, or just being back in this place more often. Maybe it was a mixture of all those things. Anyway, I know whatever you decide to do, you will succeed because you're the most determined woman I've ever met. There's a fire that burns in that blood of yours—if you want it, no one will stop you from having it. I know you'll be okay, thousands of miles away from here, if you decide that's the life for you." She releases a shaky breath. "But damn it, Valerie, if you're doing this because you don't think you've got a family here, you're dead wrong. We love you as our own, and you always have a place here with us. I can't stand thinking you might not have known that."

"Thank you," I say through my tears, squeezing her hand.

"I'm not just thanking you for this, but for stepping up for me when Mom passed, and taking me in after Dad. I know I sucked to be around back then, so you deserve the world for giving me so much grace while I was grieving and loving me through it. I'm not sure if I ever thanked you for it, but even if I did, I know I didn't do it often enough."

She throws an arm over my shoulder, pulling me in for a hug. "You don't need to thank me, but I appreciate it. I love you—and Miles, for that matter—like you're my own flesh and blood."

San Francisco is beautiful. Yesterday we traveled all along the coast, finding gorgeous places for Hannah's shoot. Cliffs overlooking the Pacific Ocean, iconic bridges, cityscapes like Lombard street, and beautiful rows of houses on the city's famously slanted streets.

The whole time we explored, I tried to picture myself existing here. Living in a tiny, overpriced apartment in the city. Exploring the art scene, or the Fisherman's Wharf on the weekends. As cool as it all sounded, the thought of moving there full-time made my skin feel like it didn't fit on my body quite right. No matter how hard I tried, I couldn't picture myself staying longer than a few days.

After I follow Hannah around all day as she shoots in some of the most beautiful spots in the city, she asks what I'm thinking about the place.

I look around the adorable bistro we're eating dinner at. "It's beautiful here. We've seen so much of what it has to offer."

"Sounds like there's a but in there somewhere," she sounds far too hopeful.

I shrug. "But," I say pointedly, making her laugh. "I just don't get the feeling that this could ever become my home."

She tries to tamp down her smile, but I see it before she can hide it behind her wine glass. "Really? So what does that mean?"

I shrug. "I think it means I need to keep looking for what gives me that feeling."

"Any idea what it could be?"

I smile. "I might have an idea or two."

Chapter Forty

BRODY

I'm not sure what possesses me to do so, but I make the hour and a half drive home on Tuesday afternoon. I'd planned to stay at our off-campus rental, enjoying having the house to myself all week, but I grew restless by day two of that plan.

I thought about calling up Luke, or Lainey to see if I could spend the rest of the week bothering them, but neither idea quite worked out in my head. I even tossed around the idea of hopping on a plane and surprising either Malakai or my cousin Andrew, but decided against that too.

Instead, I did what any twenty-something guy who had his heart broken would do—I run home to my momma.

I'm still questioning the decision as I pull into the drive-way. It's been months since the big blow up that happened with dad, and I'm still wary of being around him. His texts have taken on a different tone, lighter somehow, but that doesn't mean he'll be different in person. I just hope I'm not making a mistake here.

So when I walk into a dark house, I'm not disappointed to find that no one's home for the moment.

I pull the small bag I packed from my shoulder and toss it to the foot of my bed, but stop in my tracks when I see what's sitting on the nightstand.

Most people wouldn't even think twice at the sight of a black hair tie, but it's a glaring reminder of Val's lingering presence in this room. I peek into the bathroom and can still see Val sitting on the counter with a makeup brush in her hand.

Fuck, this was a bad idea.

I grab my bag and leave the room as quickly as I enter it.

After raiding the fridge, I settle in front of the projector downstairs and switch over to Netflix. This is better. As long as I don't look in the direction of the pool table, I won't have to think about her.

Oh, who am I kidding? She's been the only constant on my brain lately.

At some point, I must fall asleep watching one of my favorite feel-good comedies, because I wake up to a kiss being planted on my head. I'd be startled if my mom's rose-scented perfume didn't waft into my nose.

I find her over my shoulder with a smirk on her face and her hands planted on her hips. "To what do I owe the pleasure? Last I knew, you weren't coming home."

"Yeah, well, plans change," I say, not realizing how deep the statement is until it's out of my mouth.

"Val with you?"

I look back at the sprawling screen in front of me. "Nope."

"Where is she?"

"San Francisco, last I heard."

"Oh, what's she doing there?"

I take a deep breath and let it out, wishing I wasn't having this conversation. "She's finding a new life that doesn't involve me."

She rounds the couch and sits down gingerly, like I might lash out at any second. Smart woman. "Brody, what do you mean?"

I rub my nose back and forth before turning to her. "We broke up, Mom."

She immediately scoots closer, brushing a hand through my hair. "Aw, Brody. I'm sorry. Are you okay?"

I shrug. "Will be. Don't really feel like talking about it, if that's okay."

"Of course it is. But if you change your mind, you know where I'll be. You hungry?"

We both look around at all the dishes and wrappers I left on the coffee table. "Not quite yet, but thanks, Momma. I promise I'll clean up my mess when I go upstairs."

"Oh, I know you will."

"Hey, Mom?"

"Yes?"

I scratch the back of my head, suddenly nervous. "Are things better between you and dad?"

She chews at the inside of her lip. "Yes, and no. We're working on it, but Brody, the way he ruined all recent holidays —I just hope you know I wasn't going to let him get away with that."

I nod, looking away. "Thanks."

"Are things better between the two of you?"

"We've still a ways to go, but at least he's trying."

"Good," she slaps my knee. "He'll be home late tonight, but I'm sure he'd be happy to see you."

Later that evening, I get a phone call from Lainey, who's in town for break.

"Brody! I'm going to look past the fact that you failed to inform me you were coming home for break, only because I'm picking you up in ten minutes, and you can't say no. We're gonna go have a drink."

"Lainey—"

"Ah, ah, ah! What did I say? You're already on friendship probation. Don't make me come up with worse consequences."

I blow out a breath. If there's anything Lainey knows how to do, it's bending me to her will—she puts on a sweet act, but she's a tyrant when you get to know her. "Fine, I'll be ready."

Twenty minutes later, we're sitting at the local bar—the one we spent New Year's Eve at, so it's yet another reminder of Val. What was I thinking, coming back home to all of this?

"So, Mal gave me some news," she baits once we're seated at the bar with drinks. She talked my ear off about her life on the way here, so I'd thought that maybe, just this once, I'd be in the clear. I should have known better, and looking back, I realize she was just trying to fill the silence in her own awkward way. "What happened?"

"You're gonna have to spell it out for me. What news are we talking about?"

She meets my glare before her eyes dart away. The only chance I have to get her to drop this is to make her uncomfortable. "Don't be a smart ass, Brody. What happened with Val?"

"You know I don't want to talk about this, right? Let's go back to talking about the manicures you and your sister got. Or the puppy you saw at the park the other day. Hell, let's talk about the weather."

She taps her newly manicured nails on the bar top, her jaw working back and forth. "You know I'm just trying to be there for one of my best friends after he got his heart broken, right? I've known you long enough to realize how hard it is for you to talk about your feelings, Brody, but damn. Do you think I'm going to judge you? Because I won't. I'm one of the most emotional people you know. It's okay to be sad, or mad, or whatever it is you're feeling right now. You don't have to lock it all up in a box and hide the key. You're the happiest guy on the block most days, but I know you've been through some shit. I consider you to be one of my best friends, and I hope you feel the same way about me. So…" She trails off, and when I look up, she's got one eyebrow raised in challenge.

"Dammit, Lainey," I mutter, lifting my beer to my lips. "I thought it was the real deal, but I wasn't enough for her and her big dreams. It sucks, but I'm fine."

"You're fine," she deadpans.

I nod, looking across the bar. Anything to avoid eye contact with this girl to my right that knows me far too well. "Yup." I pop the p for good measure.

"So Val was just another Melinda for you then? Nothing special."

She was so much more. "Exactly," I lie, and the answer feels bitter on my tongue.

"Oh, thank God you said that because I could hardly stand her," she blows out a breath, "Feels good to get that off my chest."

My head swivels in her direction, liquid fire running through my veins. "What the hell are you talking about? Don't talk about her like that. She was the best thing that ever happened to me."

When I'm done with my rant, she breaks into a grin. As soon as I see it, I know I've been played. "Aw, see? Now we're getting somewhere." She hides her smile behind her drink.

"Now I see why Mal's always in a tizzy when it comes to you. You know how to drive a man crazy."

She smiles as if it was a compliment, then ignores the comment completely. "Did you love her?"

The question is like a blast to the chest. "Yes."

"Did she know that?"

I nod. "She knew."

She pats my shoulder before going on. "What happened then?"

"Things had been building up for a while. Like, we were both happy, but it was almost this false happiness, and we were both waiting for the other shoe to drop." I tell her about what I overheard at the party.

"You really do love her, don't you?"

"Yeah, I did."

"No, I mean now. You still love her. Despite the breakup, those feelings don't just evaporate."

"You're right, they haven't gone anywhere."

"So if you love her, and she loves you too, where do you go from here?"

"No offense, but if I knew the answer to that, I wouldn't be sitting here with you right now."

Chapter Forty One

VAL

After we got back from San Francisco, I talked Hannah into staying with me at my parents' place for the remainder of my break. She's working, so I'm sitting alone, staring at the mess I've made.

I finished up what I started over Christmas with Brody. At first, I started rifling through things for nostalgia's sake. Then when I realized how careful I was being with belongings, they'd never return for, it's like a switch flipped inside me. I've been cleaning and tossing things ever since.

For sentimental reasons, I can't get rid of everything, but even those items will need a place. I no longer feel the need to preserve their belongings because I know they're never coming back for it.

I take another trip to the garbage with a sack of old papers. Just as I swing it in the air to toss it, a thick envelope falls out, landing on the pavement with a thwack.

I set the bag on the ground, crouching to overturn the

envelope. And through blurry vision, I find my name on it—in my mother's handwriting.

I try for a deep breath, but it comes out shallow. I bring the envelope to my chest, protecting it from the drizzly, spitting rain that started up this afternoon. I leave the bag near the trash, forgotten as I run into the house.

I find the junk drawer in the kitchen that has always housed my mother's vintage letter opener and slide the pointed end under the edge of the envelope flap, careful to preserve her letters on the front.

When it's open, I set it down on the kitchen counter and back up against the island. I've lived the past several years without her, afraid to lose her voice in my head, or to forget the way her half-cursive, half-printed letters curl from one to the next.

I may not get to listen to her voice one last time, but there's a letter I've never read sitting in front of me with my name on it, and it feels a lot like a second chance at closure.

All last week, I'd wished I could talk to her one last time, to get her opinion on where I'm going in life. Could this envelope contain everything I've ever wanted to hear?

My curiosity finally wins out and I cross the space to grab hold of it. When I slip my fingers inside, they're not only met with folded papers, but something thicker, the material smooth against my fingertips.

I pull, the items come loose as I'm met with my mother's smiling face, just the way I remember it—only I've never seen this picture before.

That fact hits me like a ton of bricks.

It's an odd feeling, losing someone you love and thinking that the day they're buried in the ground, you've seen everything you're ever going to have the pleasure of seeing about their life. Every tidbit of information, every memory they ever shared with you, left behind to be recycled over and over each time you think of them. Then something like this happens—

something new after years of missing them. And if you're lucky, the face they're making, or their hairstyle, is different from the person you have in your mind. It's like another piece of the puzzle of their life clicking into place, just for you. And you've got the proof in a picture that you can add to the rotation of memories in your mind.

I don't realize I'm crying until a tear falls onto my thumb, missing the photo by mere inches.

I set down the stack, using the collar of my shirt to wipe at my eyes, starting again after a deep breath. Thumbing through, I find a photo of both my parents. It has to be from when they first met. They look so young and in love, smiling at each other instead of the camera. Another memory.

The rest are pictures I vaguely remember, but had yet to find copies of, some of the three of us, some of mom and I. I put them in the envelope for safekeeping, then unfold the paper.

My Sweet Valerie,

It hurts me to write this because I know what's coming. Although I've made peace with God's plan for me, I worry every day what it means for you and your father. We still had so much left to do together, and I can only hope when you're reading this, you can look back and say that you've lived. And if you're looking back, ashamed because you haven't, I ask, What are you waiting for? Go before it's too late!

I could use this time to reflect on all I haven't done, but I choose to do the opposite. I'm sitting in my hospital bed at Melcher Wilson Hospital dying, thinking about how grateful I am for the life I've lived.

After years of trying, your father and I finally received a miracle child, and that was you. I always felt sorry that I couldn't give you another brother or sister, but it wasn't for lack of trying. Either way, I want you to know you were an amazing child. Sometimes after you go to your room for the night, your dad and I look at each other in awe and say,

We made that! Like neither of us can believe that something so beautiful could come from our love for each other.

Speaking of love, I hope you find it. Sure, I dated before your father. Some turned out to be terrible, others were great, but not for me. Your dad though, wow. We both know he's not perfect, but things between us were effortless, and that's the kind of love I hope you find someday, too.

If you fall in love with your best friend, do me a favor and marry him, because a love like that will give you something to smile about, even on your last days.

And I know you've always been my little bookworm, but promise me you won't get stuck in your studies—in your future occupation and forget to enjoy everything life has to offer. After fifteen years in the hustle and bustle of a corporate job, the best thing I ever did was slow down and enjoy a life with you and your dad.

They say this all the time, but I'm living (just barely) proof that it's true: on your deathbed, you won't sit here thinking about that meeting you got to on time, or the client you helped your company acquire. You'll remember the morning your boss reamed your ass for being twenty minutes late because you couldn't possibly get out of bed on time when your sleepy toddler wanted five more minutes to cuddle. You'll remember that paid vacation time you spent at the ocean with the two people you loved the most, watching your baby girl experience the vastness of the 'big huge lake' for the first time.

And I'm not saying your dreams shouldn't consist of personal goals and glass ceilings I know you can shatter if you put your mind to it. I'm just saying don't wear those blinders the whole way. Take them off, look around—and most of all, love, baby girl.

Because it hurts like hell when you lose it, but the beauty you'll find between finding it and losing it makes that pain worthwhile.

I love you more than I could ever put into words. Thanks for making me the proudest momma. And in case your father forgot, there's a four-leaf clover pendant in my jewelry box that I want you to have when the time is right. Anytime you're missing me, wear it and know that I'm out here on the other side, cheering you on every step of the way. There's a story behind it—it was the first thing your father ever gifted me. Called me his lucky charm for a number of reasons. I wore it on many of the most important days of my life, including the day you were born. I hope it brings you the best of luck, and can serve as a token that reminds you that even when I'm gone, I'm right there with you.

I can't wait to watch you grow and learn and love wherever I go next. I love you so.

Love,
Your Momma

I fold the page back up nice and carefully through blurry vision. Once it's safely in its envelope, I drop to the floor and cry.

Chapter Forty-Two

BRODY

The worst part about sleeping on the couch in my parents' basement is that it's so dark down here, I think I could sleep all day. Either way, it's a better option than the alternative, because I haven't been able to step foot into my bedroom since the day I got here.

But on my last day here, I don't have to worry about that. At six am, I get a wake up call in the form of a pillow hitting me square in the forehead.

"What the f—" I pop up and it takes me a moment to register my surroundings. Then I see my dad standing behind the couch and it all comes back to me. "What was that for?" I ask, more than a little annoyed at being woken up after only four hours of sleep.

He chuckles. "Sorry, I tried waking you up nicely, but you sleep like the dead, just like your mother."

"Oh."

"I know it's early, but I was hoping I could talk to you

before I leave for work. I don't feel like I've gotten to see you since you've been home."

"Oh, yeah, that's fine. Let me go to the bathroom and I'll meet you upstairs."

"Okay, I'll have some coffee ready. Meet me in the living room."

Five minutes later, I walk to his office on autopilot. It isn't until I reach the dark doorway that I remember he asked me to meet him in the living room. Years of confrontations in his office are a hard habit to break, but at least it means there's a chance he might be as hopeful for a change as I am.

When I finally get to the living room, I find him reclined in his chair, holding a newspaper up in front of his face. He folds it, setting it down on the coffee table.

I walk toward the mug he points to, sitting on the end closest to him. Part of me still mourns for the relationship we could have had my whole life, the other is hopeful we can actually have a decent relationship someday.

"So, what's up?" I ask after taking a giant sip of my coffee. I try not to notice the power shift between us where he's wearing his suit pants and a light blue button-down shirt with the collar unbuttoned—he usually waits until the last possible moment to throw on his tie and suit jacket each morning. Then there's me in my athletic shorts and baggy sweatshirt. I usually wouldn't care about the difference, but since I have no idea where this conversation will go, I hate any little advantage he has on me, purely out of habit.

"Well, first, I wanted to apologize to you. You deserved my apology long ago, and I'm sorry you're only getting it now. I've been working on myself since Christmas, and I know I don't deserve your forgiveness. But I hope one day I can prove I'm trying, and be worthy of a second chance."

My brow furrows. Nothing that just came out of his mouth was expected.

"I also wanted to see how you're doing. Your mom informed me about Val."

"Oh," I stare into my coffee cup. "I'm doing fine."

"You don't have to hide your feelings from me, Brody. I know you cared about her. That much was clear at Christmas, so I can only imagine how the feelings grew in the months since then."

Christ, what's with everyone trying to dredge my emotions out of me?

"I don't know what to tell you. I was in love with her, Dad. I was willing to follow her anywhere, but she didn't want me to. So what good was our relationship if it already had an expiration date?"

He nods. "I'm sorry you're going through that, son. I hope you two can work it out."

I swirl the coffee in my cup, unsure how to reply to that.

"I ran into your old baseball coach a couple weeks ago."

That puts a genuine smile on my face. "Really? How was he?"

"As good as he's ever been. We got to talking, and I told him about your interest in strength and training after graduation. He gave me his number and wants you to call him—one of his old baseball acquaintances at the local community college is planning to retire after this summer season. Might have an opportunity for you to get in the door and train with him in his last season. The point may be moot, with your post-graduation plans up in the air, but I think you should call him either way. He had nothing but great things to say about you."

He hands me a white business card, and I run my finger over the name Buster McKinley, Head Coach, and smile. That man was one of my biggest role models throughout high school, and always will be. "Thank you. I'll be sure to call him."

"Good deal," he says, getting to his feet. "Well, I've gotta head out, but I'm glad I got to see you before you head back. Drive safe, and hopefully we'll see you soon."

I stand too, and we look at each other awkwardly for a moment before I pull him into a hug. We hang onto each other all loose and awkward at first, but as he pulls me closer, my arms tighten around him, too. I take a deep breath and we let go. Things aren't perfect between us, and they may never be, but I'm grateful for the work he's putting into trying.

"Brody!" my mom calls from the kitchen after my dad walks out the door.

I was about to go back to sleep, but I peek my head in the room, anyway. "Yes, Momma?"

"Come here."

I walk in further to see she's doing some sort of food preparation at the island. "What's this?"

She smiles. "I know you're leaving later, so I made cupcakes. Figured you could take them back for you and your roommates."

"Oh," I say, mustering up the strength to pretend this doesn't phase me. But as soon as she said cupcake, my stomach dropped. My smile shakes, so I drop it and say, "Thanks, Momma, you're the best."

Chapter Forty-Three

VAL

I spend one of my last days of break on the couch with my laptop searching for jobs in the area while Gilmore Girls plays in the background. Ever since we got back from San Francisco, I've been wracking my brain for what my next step should be. Should I stay in Cedar Falls? Go somewhere else entirely? Or I could come back home and live here...

I look around the room, trying to picture it. Could this house be a home again? I'm technically the owner, but I still refer to it as my parents' place. Could I ever consider it my own? I look at the olive green paint on the accent wall and smile, thinking about the time I helped Mom paint it back in high school. We finished one wall and stepped back to admire it only to realize she loathed the color.

We spent too long painting it. We're not gonna change it now, she'd said.

Instead, she spent too much money on decor to cover the color and make it less noticeable.

But I could paint over it, right? She'd probably love that.

300

When I was taking decor off the walls in my parents' bedroom, I uncovered so many scuff marks in the paint. Maybe I could give that fresh paint too. Suddenly, my head is swirling with so many ideas for the house, I can barely sit still.

I'm about to close my laptop and get to work, but before I snap it shut, I get an idea. I've been looking at different cities around the country all week. This time when I go to the search bar, I type in Wellford. I've been avoiding my hometown and the surrounding area so far, but a quick search won't hurt. Nothing will pop up anyway.

But when I press enter, the first thing that pops up actually sounds promising.

I stare at it long enough for my eyes to water before I finally click.

Assistant Event Planner: Assistant with a chance to advance.

We're growing at Bright Side Events, and we want you to join our amazing team!

Please email your resume or drop off at our office.

I type out the address to realize it's only eleven miles away.

If this isn't a sign that I'm finally on the right track, I don't know what is.

Then, I turn back to my laptop and spend the next twenty minutes making changes to the resume I've been perfecting the past few months and print it out. After typing the address into my phone, I bring the four-leaf clover pendant to my lips, silently sending out a request for help from up above.

I'm pulling a lasagna out of the oven later that evening when Hannah walks through the door. I set down the dish and turn to look at her, excitement clear in my expression.

I'm grateful she's been staying here with me, not only for the quality time it allows us, but I don't want to be here alone.

"Hey!" I say with more spring in my step than she's seen in me since Christmas. "I've got news!"

She wears a dubious expression. "Did you talk to Brody today or something?"

I immediately feel my shoulders droop, and the smile drops off my face. "No."

"Oh, shit. Sorry. What's going on?"

I link my fingers together in front of my chest and give her an exaggerated smile. "Okay, well, I'm trying not to get my hopes up, but I might've found an even dreamier job than the dream job I thought I always wanted."

She kicks off her shoes, tosses her purse on a hook by the front door, and walks into the kitchen to lean over the still-steaming lasagna and taking a big ol' sniff. "Holy shit, tell me more!"

The buzzer for the garlic bread goes off, so I turn to grab it from the oven. Once it's on the stove, I throw a smile over my shoulder. "For starters, it's a twenty-minute drive from here."

I hear her gasp as I'm digging through the drawers looking for a knife and spatula.

"It's a fairly new event planning business, women-owned, and there are only a few employees, so I'd be getting my foot in the door pretty early."

"Did you apply?" She asks.

I look up at her, unable to hide my smile—one that I don't even have to fake. "I took it straight to the office this afternoon. They gave me an interview on the spot." I set my utensils down on the counter, placing both hands on the island between us and leaning across so our faces are close. "I felt good about it, Hannah."

"That's great news, Val! It was the last thing I expected to hear you say, but I'm so happy for you."

I smile. "Thanks," I say, sobering my expression. "I'm going to leave my options open and not get my hopes up about any particular job," but even as I say it, I know which job I'm pulling for—and all the possibilities that could come with the opportunity. All my friends, new and old, would be in close proximity. I may have lost what was left of my family four years ago, but I've still got amazing people in my corner, and now that I have them, I don't want to lose them.

And then there's Brody. I try not to think of how close I'd be to him, now that I screwed things up between us. But that fact doesn't stop me from typing out a message about the news that isn't even news yet, then deleting it, then reading our messages well into the middle of the night until I'm blurry-eyed with tears and lack of sleep.

Our feelings for each other were so obvious, it hurt to read. But I did, until I was so tired, my body gave out on me and I dropped my phone on my face.

Despite the late night, I wake up before the sun, full of purpose. Yesterday I did small things, like making the bedroom feel more homey. The dusty bedding that sat in the stagnant house has been washed and put in the linen closet. I bought new sheets for all three beds in the house. I've been sleeping in my childhood room and Hannah's been staying in the guest bedroom.

I whip up pancakes, slathering them in peanut butter so I can walk around the kitchen and start organizing things while I eat.

When Hannah finally comes into the kitchen, I'm sitting

on the rug in front of the sink, thumbing through my mom's recipe cards. I wasn't going to go through them, but when I lifted the lid to her recipe basket on the counter, her handwriting gave me pause. I started with tears in my eyes, missing her with a throbbing ache in my chest, but by the time Hannah finds me, I've got a stack of recipes I'll be trying soon.

"What on earth are you doing down there?" She asks me, taking in the mess all around me.

"There are pancakes on that covered plate over there. They need warmed up, but help yourself. Toppings are still on the counter."

She laughs, waving her hand in a small circle, gesturing at the mess I've made. "No, I meant what's all this?"

I shrug, looking back down at the pile of cards I have yet to go through.

"It's been four years. It's time I go through things, right?"

My parents were pretty organized, but in the twenty-plus years they lived here together, they collected plenty of junk that hasn't seen the light of day in a decade.

She shrugs, nods, then busies herself with pancakes.

After she's off to another shoot, I have a stack of stuff to be thrown away, one to sell and donate, then the stuff I want to keep, I put in their respective places.

I move on to another room, then another, until half the house has been cleaned and organized.

Later that morning, I'm standing at the paint card wall at our local hardware store trying to choose a color I like. So far I have a greige and an eggshell white—original, I know. But what I'm trying to decide is if I want color on the walls, or to integrate color with accents.

After more time spent in my parents' room, I got to thinking. I've finally cleaned out their things, the closets are empty, the adjoining bathroom is clean, there are new sheets and a comforter ready to be put on the bed. As much as it sucks to admit to myself, they aren't coming back. So why not make the bedroom—the house, my own? Like, really my own? I know I'm only here for a few more days, but maybe a positive mindset will bring me what I want in life—that job, and the possibility of a life within the walls of the home I grew up in. Hope.

I decide on neutral colors in four different shades, and one pastel bluish-green color called sea glass. I order a sample size of each, along with new paint brushes and liners for the paint tray.

Twenty minutes later, I have a large square of each color on the wall and I plop down onto the bed to take in the different colors. After much deliberation, I decide the greige is my favorite. I return to the hardware store for enough to finish the entire room.

When I'm back in the room that's starting to become my own, I move the furniture anywhere it will fit. The nightstands get shoved into the hallway along with an empty dresser. The mattresses are the hardest part to do alone, but once they're removed, the bed frame comes apart easily.

I dump a small amount of the paint in my tray, prepare my painter's blanket and stepladder, start some music over my bluetooth speaker, and get to work.

The repetition of paint strokes soothes my overactive thoughts. So much so, I don't notice as the afternoon rolls into evening. With the music blaring over my speaker, I don't even hear Hannah return until she walks in the room and startles me so badly, I nearly lose my balance on the second rung of the stepladder I've been standing on.

"Holy shit, Hannah! Warn a girl next time."

She stands in the doorway with wide eyes and her hand to

her chest. "Crap, I'm so sorry! Walking in to find you on a ladder painting was the *last* thing I expected."

I set my paint roller in the tray, turn down the music, and turn to her, "I guess I can't say I blame you. I've gotten a lot done today. Thank goodness tomorrow is trash day, because the bin outside is full of things I got rid of."

"You've sure been making a lot of changes to the place the past few days."

I smile at her, with the paint on my face and my hair a rabid mess. I'm sure I look insane, but it doesn't stop me from asking, "How would you feel about being full-time roomies?"

Chapter Forty-Four

VAL

I feel a new sense of purpose after returning to school. I still haven't heard from Julia about the job, but I've also put some feelers out in the area surrounding my hometown. After playing house there all last week, I made my mind up about what comes next.

The next order of business will be finding a way to run into Brody organically so we can talk. I brainstorm ideas, and even frequent the places we used to go to together. But after too many days of no sightings, I realize he must be avoiding the same places. I don't want to knock his front door down, guns blazing, unless I get desperate enough to do so.

The answer I've been looking for kind of falls into my lap the second week after we're back at school. I'd let Bree know it would be a late night of studying at the coffee shop—yes, I went there after hours—I'm desperate for a run-in, remember? But I'd over-estimated the time it would take to finish my workload and walk through the front door two hours earlier than expected.

I hear Bree's giggle coming from her room, and make for the hallway to say hello. But as I do, I'm assaulted with a naked, full-frontal view of Wes on his way to our bathroom.

I can only imagine that my shock and horror match the hilarious look on his face. He lets out the highest-pitched scream I've ever heard from such a burly man before he covers himself and sprints into the bathroom, slamming the door behind him.

Bree hears him and comes barreling around the corner, still tying her robe, "What's wro——" but the question falls off her lips when she sees me still standing there in shock.

I haven't moved from the place my feet were planted, but I can't hold back my laugh bubbling up the back of my throat. "What the hell did I just walk in on?"

"Shit," she says under her breath. "You weren't supposed to see that for *so many reasons*——" she yells the last three words. "But mostly because I'm hooking up with your ex's best friend."

I try to get control of my laughter before saying. "It's fine. I knew this would happen. Although I'm pissed you waited until after the chances of a double date were gone." I lift a finger in the air in the universal sign for I have an idea! "Actually, no. This might work."

"What do you mean?" Bree asks, looking at me like I asked her to eat dog shit.

"I'll be in my room. Come get me when you're both decent. I have a favor to ask."

A hysterical laugh comes from the other side of the bathroom door. "If you think I'll be able to look you in the eyes after you just saw me naked, you're insane. All I've been thinking about since closing the door is, 'oh my god, how am I going to tell Brody I flashed his ex-girlfriend?'"

"Um, idea!" Bree interjects. "You *don't* tell him. Not sure if you remember, Wes, but before *my roommate so rudely came home early*," she says, glaring in my direction, "we'd decided no one was going to find out about this."

I hold my hands up, a grimace on my face, claiming my innocence. "I won't tell anyone if you promise to help me."

"What do you need help with?"

I take a deep breath and smile at my best friend. "I'm going to get Brody back."

The bathroom door rattles, then opens, and a still-naked Wes peeks out just enough to see me. "Are you fucking serious?"

I bite my lip, suddenly aware of the fact that this guy standing in front of me might know inside information about Brody that I didn't want to know.

I haven't talked to him in weeks. What if he's already hooked up with someone else? What if he's over the thought of us? Maybe I don't want to know.

"Do you think he'd go for it?"

He forces a laugh. "Val, he's still in love with you. Of course he'd go for it." He smiles at me, then turns to Bree. "Babe, will you grab my clothes? It's time to talk business so I can help my boy get his girl back."

"First of all, you don't get to call me babe."

"Bree," I cut in, "Please save the lectures for later and grab his clothes? For me?"

She bounces her glare between us both, but slowly backpedals toward her room.

Chapter Forty-Five

BRODY

Val is standing right in front of me. I'd been walking through campus between classes, watching my feet step one in front of the other, feeling a little glum for no other reason than my life has turned into a monotonous series of days as of late. Then I looked up, and the first thing that caught my eye was her unmanageable curls. I felt a pang in my chest when I realized enough time had passed between us she was no longer wearing her bright red hat over them to cover the cold.

She's in the middle of the sidewalk about fifty feet in front of me, looking down at her phone. Instead of continuing on my way and crossing paths, I stop on a dime at the sight of her, causing someone to slam into the back of me.

"Damn, watch where you're going, man," a guy built like a linebacker glares as he passes by.

I whip my head back in her direction to find her still standing there. My feet are moving toward her before I make the conscious decision to do so. But as I do, I see her smile down at her phone and take off in the opposite direction without noticing my presence.

My heart plummets and I stop pursuing her, imagining who could make her smile at her phone like that—and did she used to do that when it was me?

I haven't even been able to so much as look at another girl since we broke up, so it hadn't even occurred to me that there's a possibility she's moved on so quickly.

The surprise of seeing such a private moment that was never meant for me sticks in my brain for the rest of the day. That fact doesn't get past Wes when I show up at the bar that afternoon, either.

His smile drops as soon as I belly up to the bar.

"What's wrong with you?"

I shake my head because there's no time to get into it. "Nothing. Just don't feel like being here tonight."

"Gee, thanks."

"Not because of you. I have a classmate coming here to get a head start on our paper that's due next week. It's the last thing I want to do."

Wes shakes his head. "Wait, you made a study date at my bar? What happened to the coffee shop—or the library, perhaps?"

After this afternoon, I've decided to boycott both places I'd been frequenting for weeks, desperate to run into Val, but I can't tell him that. "I needed a change of scenery. And it's not a date." Funny how the words I used to annoy Val last semester are the words that annoy me now.

"Shit," Wes says under his breath as he paces behind the bar. He pours my beer and sets it on the bar for me as I hand over my card.

"What's with you?" I ask as he bites his lip—something he does when he's nervous—as he types furiously on his phone.

"Um," he returns it to his back pocket, "You sure you can't reschedule this thing with your classmate?"

"Why?"

"Because—" he looks at the door, then back to me. "I need you up here with me tonight."

I'm about to ask for more information, but the front door squeaks open, slamming shut behind my classmate, Grace. I wave as she smiles from the entrance.

I turn back to Wes, who's pulling at his hair and avoiding my gaze. "Sorry, man. She's here, but I'll hang out for a bit before I go, okay?"

Without giving him a chance to reply, I meet Grace halfway and point us to a table in a secluded corner.

She's shorter than me, her head barely reaching my chest as she shucks her light jacket. "Hey, I got here as soon as I could after class." She rakes her hand through her black, chin-length hair and smiles up at me. "I'm gonna use the restroom."

We've sat near each other all semester, and she's always been friendly, but not in an over-the-top way. In fact, I talked to her about Val on more than one occasion when we were still together.

While she's gone, I prepare for our study session, pulling my laptop and notebook from my backpack.

I grab a pencil I stole from Val months ago from my bag, and there's someone standing at my table when I sit up. Expecting Grace, I plaster on a pleasant smile. It drops off my face when I turn and find the last person I expected to see.

I shoot to my feet. "Val. What are you doing here?" The words sound defensive, and I wish I could take them back as soon as they're out of my mouth. Especially when the hopeful light goes out of her eyes.

"Hi, Brody. I'm sorry for coming in here like this." Her amber eyes are framed by two pinched brows. "I was hoping we could talk."

I want to embrace her, but knowing it's no longer my place to do so holds me back.

"Brody," she says, and I realize I still haven't said anything. I'm too stunned by her sudden presence. My brain is still trying to catch up. "Please say something. It used to be hard to get you to stop talking, so you're scaring me."

I blow out a nervous laugh. "Sorry, I didn't expect to see you. I'm still trying to figure out if you're a figment of my imagination."

She readjusts her purse on her shoulder. "I'm really here—"

Val's attention gets snagged as Grace returns to the table. With Val's presence, I'd almost forgotten why I was here.

By the look on her face, Grace can tell she walked up at the worst time, but it's too late now. She smiles at Val as I can practically hear Val's brain whizzing a million miles a minute with every worst-case scenario, none of them true.

"Uh, Val, this is Grace. Grace, this is Val," I say, rubbing the back of my neck, trying to figure out the best way to go about this.

"Oh," Val says, looking at Grace and avoiding my gaze. "Nice to meet you, Grace," she says with a smile that doesn't reach her eyes. "I came over to say hello, but I was just leaving. Brody, see you around." She doesn't look back once before heading for the door. But I find my best friend glaring at me from behind the bar, and that's snaps me back to reality.

"Wait, Val—" I say, just as she pulls the door open. I'd settle for a glance back, but it doesn't come.

I move to chase after her, then remember myself, stuffing everything in my bag and turn to Grace. "I know our grade depends on finishing this damn paper, but by chance, could we reschedule?"

She smiles. "I may be small, but if you don't chase after that girl and tell her I'm no one compared to her, I'll kick you in the junk with my boots."

I look down at the clunky combat boots she's wearing and grimace.

She shoves at my chest. "Brody, go! We'll figure something out tomorrow in class."

Without another distraction, I fly out the door, hoping I'm not too late. I almost slam into a pedestrian on the sidewalk and apologize profusely, but it doesn't sound sincere with the way I'm searching the area for Val's vehicle.

I scour the parking spaces on both sides of the street, but find nothing. This area is notorious for no parking spots.

So that's it. I missed her.

I walk back through the door of the bar to find Wes looking at me with pity.

"She's gone."

"What are you going to do about it?"

"Find her, obviously."

Wes looks away from me, shaking his head. "Bree and I helped her come up with that plan, Brody. It's why I tried to get you to cancel your plans."

My hackles rise. "You knew and didn't tell me? If you knew she wanted to talk, why not just tell me so I can find a private place for us to do so instead of in a damn bar? Whatever, I've got to go."

I move to step away, but Wes tosses something, and it hits me in the chest.

With a metallic thump, his keys land on the floor at my feet.

"Take my car. It's parked out back."

"Thanks," I say, plucking the keys from the floor before I sprint toward through the back door.

Chapter Forty-Six

VAL

I ran away. Just like I always do. I tried to be strong, and at the first sign of trouble, I fucking ran. I'm still sitting in my car a block away from the bar, my skin crawling with unease.

Who was that girl? Now that I've had some space from the moment, I really don't think they were on a date or anything. The girl—Grace—was too genuinely nice for that to be the case. She's gorgeous in all her pop-punk glory. There's no denying it, and seeing her with him triggered my fight or flight.

But when Brody introduced us, she almost seemed... happy? So why didn't I stay and fight?

I pour all my nervous energy into doing a drum roll on the steering roll, trying to gear up for what I'm about to do.

"Fuck it," I say, throwing the car door open. After one deep breath, I take off in a sprint—and realize quickly I'm not cut out for this kind of exercise. But I push through for Brody.

For Brody.

That thought gets me across the block faster than I could

have imagined. Although I'm huffing and puffing when I finally reach the door, I throw it open, stepping through with purpose, as my feet carry me to his table—

The table is vacant.

"Val?"

I swivel, finding Wes behind the bar. I'd almost forgotten about his involvement in all this. He'd assured me that this would be the place to find him tonight, but he forgot to mention another girl. "Where is he?"

He looks at the back door, then at me again. "He went to find you in my car."

"He went to find me? Are you sure?"

"Yes, he's trying to find you. I didn't know he was bringing someone with him tonight."

My hand moves to my chest, rubbing the sudden ache there. "Do you know where he went?"

Wes grimaces. "He didn't say, but I'd assume he went to your place."

"Wish me luck!" I pivot, running back out the door, my sore lungs screaming their displeasure as I cover the block in record time.

I fumble my keys, trying to slide them into the ignition, they drop to the floor. "Oh, come on!"

I yell, folding in half to try to reach them. My fingertips barely brush metal and I somehow pinch them between my middle and ring finger and hit my head on the steering wheel on the way back up. But I don't drop the keys, so that's a plus.

Could this be going any worse?

Just kidding, universe. Please don't answer that question.

I drive past his place, since it's near The Saloon. My heart beats overtime when I find his vehicle in the street. Then I remember Wes said he borrowed his car, which is nowhere to be found.

The next logical place is my house, so I head across town, cursing every stop sign and slow driver along the way.

There's no sign of Wes' car, but Bree sprints out the door a second later and I slow to a stop on the curb, rolling my window down.

"What the hell happened? Brody was just here."

"What?" My voice raises an octave, looking around as if I could find him.

"Yes, maybe ten or fifteen minutes ago? I've been trying to call you."

"Shit. Did he say where he was going?"

She shrugs. "I told him you weren't here and his whole body slumped. He ran right back to his car and took off. Where are *your* places? I bet he was checking everywhere."

Beans.

"I think I know where he is. Thanks, Bree," I roll up the window and I'm on my way. The parking situation here is about the same as it is at The Saloon, so I round the block looking for him, but it's hard telling where he would have parked. Instead of wasting time, I park in the first spot I can find and take off toward the door.

There's a customer leaving as I approach, and the older gentleman holds the door open for me. My eyes swivel toward the table I always sit at, and when I see brown hair, I walk straight toward it.

When I'm about to lean in and start my speech, the guy turns, and is definitely *not* Brody. He's not even wearing glasses.

"Shoot, I'm sorry," I say in response to the dirty look I receive and hightail it away from the table. I search the space for Brody, but he's not here.

"Val, right?" I hear to my left.

And when I turn, it's the hipster-bearded barista who was working the day I met Brody—the day I spilled my coffee in the middle of the crowded coffee shop.

"Otis, right?" I say, mirroring his unsure greeting.

"Yes. Not to make assumptions, but I just saw you running

around the place. Were you looking for Brody, by chance?" He asks while wiping down his station.

"Yes, I was! Have you seen him?" I ask, champagne bubbles rising and popping in my stomach.

"He left maybe fifteen minutes ago. Asked me if I'd seen you. Seems you two might have something to say to each other."

I nod, putting an insane amount of trust in this guy who makes a mean cup of coffee. "I need to tell him I still love him."

Otis' brown beard shifts, a sliver of white peeking out it as he smiles. "He didn't tell me all the details, but it seemed like he might have had the same intentions. You better go find him. I see plenty of people come through here, and I see you two in here plenty. Don't see chemistry like that every day, so don't waste it."

I take a deep breath, then smile. "Thank you, Otis. I'll let you know how it ends."

"Ah, but it's not the end," he says with a smirk, his blue eyes sparkling with so much wisdom. "No, I have a feeling that it's just the beginning for you two."

My smile grows wider, then I turn on my heel to rush out the door to—where? Where else could he possibly be?"

I've been to The Saloon, his house, my house, Beans. But Otis did just say he'd been looking for me. One more place comes to mind, and the urgency that rushes through my body in that moment carries me back to the car.

———————

I pull open the door of the library, and a sense of calm settles over me. I just *know* he's here. He has to be. I get dirty looks from the library personnel as I take off in a light jog toward the stairs. I pass the table we usually meet at, then loop through the hallway that passes the study rooms, getting plenty of raised eyebrows from the students inside as I peek through each window, looking for him. But I get to the end of the hallway and there's still no sign of him.

I look every direction, and then I spot it. The stacks I pick all my books from. If he was looking for me here, this would be one of the most likely places for him to find me. I make a beeline for the aisle the takes me there, side-stepping slow walkers the entire way.

There are a surprising amount of people in the section, so it takes a minute to figure it out, but he's not here either.

I move back out to the aisle, turning this way and that until it finally clicks into place. The room. We went there handfuls of times to study after he found it, but I haven't been back since. It was too painful to be there without him.

The ground thunders under every footfall as I sprint the short distance. I turn the corner, and there he is. His back is to me, but he's dressed in the same green shirt that brings out his eyes. It was always my favorite, and when I saw him wearing it at the bar earlier, I took it as a good sign.

I can't stop the corners of my mouth from turning up at the edges as my feet carry me toward him.

Just before I reach him, he lets go of a long breath, turning on his heel like he was about to walk away. But he stutters to a stop when he finds me standing in front of him.

"Val."

"I've been looking for you—" we both say at the same time.

Brody's mouth hangs open like he hadn't been expecting me to say that. Not surprising, given how fast I ran off earlier.

"Look," I say, taking a hesitant step forward. His eyes rove my face like they're looking for answers, "I'm sorry I ran away earlier I—" I shake my head, getting ridding it of all the excuses I was about to start listing. "I love you," I say, and although it's what I came here to tell him, I'd been meaning to lead up to it. I drop my head in my hands. "I'm sorry, what I meant was—"

His hands land on my wrists, pulling my hands from my face.

He drags his teeth over his bottom lip, meeting my gaze. "I love you too, Val. I never stopped. Now tell me why you made some grand scheme with my best friend to talk to me. I've been dying to know the answer since you showed up."

Hearing him say he still loves me spurs me on. "I've done a lot of thinking these past few weeks, and I came to one conclusion: I made a huge mistake in letting you go."

His arms wrap around my waist, pulling me closer. I bring my hands to his shoulders—touching him feels like something nostalgic and brand new all at the same time after the weeks we've spent apart.

"How'd things go in San Francisco?"

I start shaking my head, lips spreading into a smile. "I can't live there."

"They didn't hire you?"

I roll my lips, "No, they actually reached out to me last week for a video interview."

"I'm sure you did great."

"I turned it down, Brody."

His eyebrows threaten to migrate into his hair. "Why?"

"Because I've realized a lot of things since the day we—" I meet his gaze, unable to say the words aloud. "I don't think San Francisco was ever the dream. It was a crutch I'd been using to avoid a lot of buried feelings I didn't want to face. Moving across the country wouldn't have been a thought in my head if my parents were still here.

It became my dream when I started drowning myself in my studies the second semester of my freshman year. I wanted to escape, to run away. But I started to see I've been doing that a lot lately. But facing the buried feelings in other aspects of my life proved my fears of working through it were blocking me from enjoying my life. I was scared that having you meant putting my own dreams on the back burner. But a job really isn't the only part of the dream, is it?"

"What are you trying to say?"

"I'm saying that when someone amazing drops into your life, you make accommodations to ensure it works out. I'm saying that even if we make plans, there's no guarantee that life will go according to that plan. But you wake up every morning with a choice of what matters the most. And if you let me, I'm going to wake up every single day choosing you."

He wets his lips, and the world slows down as they spread into a smile before he leans into me. Just before they land on mine, he pauses, "I choose you too. Did a long time ago, so I'm glad you finally decided to catch on."

Then his lips are on mine, the sounds of the library fading out around us until it's just the two of us who exist in this moment. His hands clutch onto me like he's afraid I'll slip through his fingers. I grasp the back of his shirt, lifting my other hand to the back of his head as I hold him close.

I'm wrapped in his familiar sandalwood scent when he pulls back to look at me, his hand outstretched between us. "What do you say we get out of here?"

I take it and ask, "Where should we go?"

We start walking through the library. "Your place? Bree's home right now."

"My place works. Isaiah's barely ever around anymore. And obviously Wes is at work."

"Speaking of our roommates, you know Wes and Bree are hooking up now, right?"

He pulls me to a stop. "Are you serious?"

I pull him along, desperate to get out of the library for this conversation. "Ah, so he didn't tell you."

"Tell me what?"

I lift my eyebrows. "I walked into my house the other night when Bree thought I was going to be gone for a while. Turns out she invited Wes over, and I was greeted by a naked Wes on his way to the bathroom."

"No wonder why he's been acting so weird all week. I was beginning to think I was crazy. I swear, he can barely look me in the eye."

"For the record, he can't look me in the eye either. But I think he also felt a little weird keeping all of this from you. You know, it was mostly him that helped me with all of this."

He holds the door for me when we finally get to the exit. The night air is cool, although today was pretty warm for spring, and it sends a shiver right through me. Brody puts his arm around me like he always used to when I was cold, and the thought of having that back brings a tear to my eye.

I lean on his shoulder as he finally answers. "It makes more sense now that you told me about him and Bree. He told me right before I ran out the door to go find you that he had a hand in whatever that was back there at The Saloon."

I find his hand dangling over my shoulder and squeeze it. "I'm sorry I ran away."

"You already apologized."

"I know, but I'm going to work on that. I'm done running away when things get hard." I look up to find him already looking at me.

"Good," he says, dipping to kiss my forehead.

"I heard back from my dream job yesterday, and I already accepted it."

I feel him stutter step, but he does a good job of hiding his reaction to that statement. "Really? Where?"

"A fifteen minute drive from Wellford."

He stops us, swinging me until we're facing each other on the sidewalk. "Wait, are you serious?"

My face breaks into a grin as I start to nod. "I stumbled upon the perfect job while sitting on the couch in my parents' house—I mean, my house. I finished clearing it out, like we started around Christmas, and painted a few of the main rooms to spruce it up. I'm going to make it my own, rather than treating it like a museum to my parents, who aren't coming back." That statement hurts my heart, no matter how true it may be. "Hannah spent the rest of spring break with me in the house, and she's going to be my roommate. But I'm hoping that someday, when she and I both move onto the next stage of our lives," I run my hand down his chest, right over his heart that beats wildly underneath. "That you'll be the one who's there with me. Or, who knows, maybe we'll decide to move across the country by then. I don't care. As long as I've got your hand to hold through it all, I'll be happy no matter where I am."

His fingertips find my own, linking our fingers before he lifts our hands between us, smiling the whole way. The corners of my mouth lift too. He does the same with my other hand, kissing my knuckles before he leans his forehead against my own and says, "Valerie Boyd, you can hold these hands of mine whenever and wherever you want, because they're yours. I'm yours. This," he rests our hands over his chest. "Is yours too. I was just waiting for you to realize it." He kisses my nose. "I haven't gotten to tell you, but I found a job too. Or, oddly enough, my dad is the reason it landed in my lap."

"Tell me about it."

His fingers trace lines and shapes on the back of my hand as he stares at the connection. "My old baseball coach has an acquaintance who's planning to retire after this season." He turns to me. "They're giving me some bullshit position on the team this year so I can learn from him and take over his position after his retirement."

I squeeze my arms around him, and he comes to me willingly.

"I'm so proud of you. I wish I'd been there for all of it. I'm sorry I wasn't."

"You'll be there for all of it from here on out. That's all that matters. I love you so much."

"I love you, too," I whisper against his lips, every nerve ending in my body hyper aware of each small touch, every brush of my lips against his.

I'm not even sure which of us moves first. All I know is that when his lips meet my own, the kiss contains everything I've missed over the past several weeks. Instead of urgency, it's a confirmation that we made the right decision.

Chapter Forty-Seven

BRODY

"Looks like everything worked out," Otis says, smiling at Val and me when we show up at Give 'er the Beans for one last visit before graduation. I peek at her, cuddled under my arm as we wait for him to make our drinks.

She wraps her arms around me. "Yep, couldn't have done it without you pointing me in the right direction that night. Thank you for that."

He shakes his head. "Don't mention it. I recently learned the importance of going after what you want. I figured it was only right to forward on the message."

"Thank you, Otis."

"You know, if I weren't such a humble man, I might take full credit for the fact you two are even together."

I laugh, because there's still a tidbit that Val doesn't know. "Yeah, did you know Otis was the one who talked me into buying you that replacement latte the day we met?"

She looks between the two of us, mouth hanging open. "No, I had no idea. Thanks, Otis, and thanks for not permanently banning me from the place after my behavior that day."

His beard shifts as he smiles. "Don't mention it."

"You know, we're gonna miss you when we move. Nobody makes a white chocolate mocha quite the way you do." she tells him.

He nods. "Yep, I've managed this place for years, and it's always sad to see my regulars go, but you two have so much greatness ahead of you. Don't be too sad. Besides, I'll still be here, if you ever want to visit." He sets our cups on the counter. "Best of luck to you both."

"Wait, so you two have been together since before Christmas?" I ask, squeezing Val's hand under the table as we sit across from Wes and Bree. We're all at Beans, because Val somehow talked them into joining us.

Looking across the table, it appears one of them looks far more excited to be here.

"Yes," Wes says at the same time Bree says, "No, we're not together."

I toss my hands in the air. "Alright, I'm officially confused."

"We're just having fun before the semester is over," Bree says, unaware of the puppy dog eyes my best friend is giving her. "We're both heading in separate directions after graduation, but there was an attraction, and we decided to act on it —no strings attached. Has it lasted longer than any real relationship I've ever had? Maybe, but that doesn't mean we're *together* together."

My gaze flicks to Wes. Anyone with a current prescription can see that he's completely gone for her.

"They sound like us," Val whispers.

"Yeah, you two are in denial," I say, reaching for my

nearly empty coffee cup. "Wait, if you two were sneaking around for that long, how the hell did you hide it from us?"

Bree looks at Wes. "Well, for starters, you two were so hung up on each other that it really wasn't that hard to hide."

"Until you two broke up," Wes finally speaks up. "Then you two weren't together in one place anymore. So we had to cut back on our—" he turns to Bree, then looks back at me. "*Meetings* a bit after that."

"Yeah, let's not forget that the only reason you two found out about this is because Val lied about how long she'd be gone one night, and Wes overstayed his welcome."

"Didn't hear you complaining about that fact until we got caught," Wes says under his breath.

"Not to get sentimental, but you two better still come to visit us," I say, hoping to cut the tension across the table.

"Yes, we're gonna miss you both," Val agrees, getting that same glassy look in her eye I've seen too often lately. I toss my arm over her shoulders, kissing her hair.

"You know I'll be there whenever I have a chance," Wes says, reclining in the booth. He's heading back to Florida right after we graduate.

Bree's looking down at her hands as she picks at the napkin rolled around her silverware. She's uncharacteristically quiet, and I realize why as soon as she meets Val's gaze. She's crying too. "Same," she tries to smile, but her wine red lips quiver.

Wes comes to the rescue with an extra napkin for her to wipe her eyes, and to my surprise, Bree leans into him when he wraps an arm around her shoulders.

"I love you all," Val says. "I don't know how I would have made it through without any of you."

Wes blows out a breath. "Unless you want to see a grown man cry, we need to change the subject pronto."

"True, but it's hard to think of anything else with graduation tomorrow. Wes, you know you've made a friend for life out of me. And Bree, I don't know if this girl would have even given me the time of day without your persuasive arguments, so thank you."

The whole table laughs, and even though I'm feeling a bit melancholy myself, I laugh too.

Epilogue

Six Months Later

Brody kisses my bare shoulder, smirking at me in the mirror. We're in the bathroom connected to my room—the one I repainted and redecorated—the one Brody and I just christened for what must be the thousandth time since I moved in after graduation. I'm trying my best to finish getting ready for the night, but Brody busted down the door with other plans after sending Hannah out for one last (and pointless) errand before our guests arrive.

His hands roam my body until they settle on my hips. "You need to give me some space, sir. Or I'll never be ready for this damn party you and Hannah talked me into."

With help from Brody, Bobby, Miles, Holt and a few of their friends, we've spent the past several months making necessary updates to the house, making it feel more like it's actually mine. Brody and Hannah insisted we needed to have a housewarming party now that all the work is done. I attend enough parties to last a lifetime with my new job (that I'm loving), but I saw the point they were trying to make, so here we are.

The funny thing is that I swear I can feel my parents' presence here more now with all the changes than I did when it was exactly as they left it, another sign from above serving as a confirmation that I did the right thing. I've been getting a lot of those lately.

"Yes, ma'am," he says, planting a kiss on my forehead and posting up on the bed to watch, a ritual he's continued since that first time at his parents' house last Christmas.

Speaking of Christmas, Brody's relationship with his father is still far from perfect, but I cry every time I witness the progress they've made in such a short time. It gives me hope for the future, since I plan to be there in order to witness it all.

"Is Mal going to make it?" I ask as I work my eye pencil across my eyelid.

Brody lifts his phone from where it'd been settled on his stomach. "He's an hour away."

"Good. I'm sure Lainey will be happy to see him, too."

Brody laughs. "I think that changes from day to day."

I laugh too, because he's right.

"It's about damn time you two resurfaced," Hannah says. Pressing a hand to her forehead in distress before turning to us. "Miles texted to let me know he's on his way. I didn't even invite him—and I did so for a reason!"

There have been many recent developments in the Hannah and Miles saga, and she has yet to take my advice to make the next move. She actually did the opposite, making herself scarce when the guys were here to help with the house. The solemn look on Miles' face each time he walked in to realize she wasn't here hurt my heart.

His heart is Hannah's, but she refuses to see it.

"Good, he got my invitation, then."

"What?" She practically screams the words at me as the first ring of the doorbell sounds.

Saved by the bell is a popular expression for a reason. Hannah goes to answer it, if only to get away from me for the moment, but I see the regret in her posture as soon as she opens it to Miles standing on our front step.

"Hannah," he says, holding a bottle of wine. "Brought your favorite."

I can see every thought in that head of hers move across her face. She tries so hard to hold back her emotions, but it's just not who she is.

Then she surprises me—and Miles, by the look of shock on his face—when she pulls him in for a hug. Once he finally registers what's happening, his arms go around her, too.

I turn to Brody, pulling him toward the door that leads to the deck overlooking the backyard, where we're holding the party tonight.

"That felt like a really private moment, did it not?" Brody asks, voicing my exact thoughts as I make my way to the food table that is practically full already, even though everyone's bringing something to add to it.

"Yes, it did."

"Those two are gonna end up together if I have anything to say about it."

"One of the many reasons I love you—we find importance in so many of the same things."

He pulls me into his arms, stealing a quick kiss. "Oh yeah? What else do you love about me?"

I take a deep breath, looking around the backyard. "That when I've got my tunnel vision, you remind me it's okay to take off the blinders for a moment and enjoy life. Kinda like right now," I look around the backyard, which we touched up with some light landscaping. "I'm glad you and Hannah talked me into doing this. I can't wait to see everyone."

331

He wraps his arms around me, hugging me from behind as he kisses my cheek. We stare out into the rolling hills and cornfields in the distance as the sun gets lower in the sky, burnishing everything in a golden light. Out of all the landscapes I could have found a home in, I'm glad it was this one —even better in Brody's arms.

"There are two things you can always count on," he whispers against my temple. "One, I love you. And two, I'll always make sure you take a break to enjoy the view."

Acknowledgments

Typing this right now is such a surreal feeling, maybe it's the fact that it's the middle of the night, but wow, I'm emotional. I still don't think it's hit me that my very first book baby is about to make its way out into the world.

When I was seventeen years old, sitting in my childhood bedroom, I was writing down quotes in a leather-bound journal. On a whim, I flipped to the back page of the journal and started a bucket list. The second item on that list says *Get Published.* To say this day has been a long time coming would be an understatement.

Kelly — You've showed me what it feels like to be truly loved, and I hope you see bits and pieces of our story in all the stories I write. I always joke that if it weren't for you tearing me away from my writing and making me get out of the house, I would have been published a long time ago. And while that may be true, I also wouldn't have many stories to tell either. Thanks for always pushing me to see my potential, especially on the hardest days. I'm so glad I've got a love like ours to serve as inspiration for my novels. Thanks for daring me to finally get published, it was the push I needed. I love you so much.

Rachael—You've been my number one cheerleader ever since I started writing. Even before I started sharing my words with the world, you were always right there to tell me I could. Thanks for always checking in on me during the writing process to make sure I reached my word count, and for being my sounding board anytime I came up with an idea that deviated from the plan. And for keeping me grounded anytime I swore my new idea was better than the one I was currently working on. We finally made it! I love you.

Mom—Thanks for all the books you've bought me throughout life, my author career would not exist without my love of books. Thanks for reading all my favorite series with me growing up so we could obsess over them together. I love you.

Dad—You're no longer with us, but one thing I always think about is how much you loved reading books. I know romance wasn't your genre of choice, but I hope you're still proud. I miss you.

Winston—You are the best pup, thanks for always keeping my feet warm while I write. You're my unofficial co-author. Thanks for always keeping me company at my desk, even in the middle of the night. I love you.

Sam—Thanks for welcoming me into the #SamFam. Your Ink and Laurel creations are so beautiful. Thanks for making me love my first book cover. Do you remember the hand-drawn inspiration I sent you in that first questionnaire? Yikes. Thanks for giving me grace each time I changed my mind. You're the best.

Paige—Thanks for being my #1 Beta Reader. I truly couldn't have done this without your help. Your feedback was so helpful for this stressed out, first-time author, and I'm forever grateful for your help. Thanks for taking a chance on me. You're the best.

To my Bookstagram Friends, Authors and Readers, Alike — I'm not sure I'd have much of a readership without you. There's so much negativity out there surrounding social media, but I've truly found my people here. Whether you've been around since my poetry days, or if you're a new friend, thank you for your support. I can't wait until I get to meet each and every one of you in real life.

About the Author

Jessica Costello is a creator and adventure enthusiast living her own rom-com with her husband and Miniature Australian Shepherd in Iowa, where they love chasing sunsets and spending time at the lake. Her favorite genre of music changes by the day, but one thing that will never change is her adoration for love stories.